Rebecca Dominick

Cover photo taken by my mom,
Laura Dominick

Cover model: Genevieve Berman

Still That Girl
Rivershore Books

ISBN: 978-0692347416
ISBN-10: 0692347410

Dedication

To the memory of my grandpa.

Chapter One

Katarina sat, holding open her worn volume of *Little Women*; she had gotten it on her tenth birthday three years before. Her knees were tucked underneath her on the plush couch. She stared into the roaring and crackling fire, tired of reading. Outside, the ground was thickly covered in snow with more falling gently down. She was waiting patiently for her fifteen-year-old sister, Therese, and her seventeen-year-old brother, Benedict, who had gone to the library this morning. Her other two sisters, eighteen-year-old Antoinette and sixteen-year-old Emiliana, were spending the night at their cousin's house. They had left earlier this morning as well.

Katarina got up from the couch, laid her book down, and stretched; her tunic shirt shifted down around her. She left the family room and tiptoed down the hallway, the soft, thick carpet muffling all sounds. She tripped a bit and her chocolate-brown braid flopped over her shoulder. The house had an almost unearthly silence to it. Katarina didn't really like it. It was as if she was the only one home.

"Mum, where are you?" She called out, sort of to herself; there was no response. She checked the kitchen and her parents' bedroom before concluding that she must have had to run out and get something. The front door creaked open and she heard Therese and Benedict hustling out of their boots and coats. She pulled open the door to the front hall.

"Hey, guys!" she said excitedly.

Benedict's brown eyes lit up excitedly and he grinned at her as he shook the snow out of his shaggy brown hair.

"It's snowing good and hard out there." His comment ushered the girls into the living room and out of the cold, front hall. "Did you find any books for us to read?" Katarina asked cheerfully. Benedict groaned; his face twisted up to stop from laughing out loud. Therese punched him playfully in the arm.

"Yes, we did," Therese replied. Benedict settled himself onto a couch.

"I had to drag her out and narrow her down to ten instead of fifty or so."

Therese giggled while Katarina tossed a pillow at him.

"So, what books did you get?"

Therese picked up her bag from the floor before answering her younger sister. "Well," she said, pulling a book out, "the library got a new series! *The Fairy Tale Novels*! I read most of this one already." She held up a good-sized book; on the front, gray letters spelled out *The Shadow of the Bear*. "It's the first one in the series."

Katarina took the book in her hands and looked at the cover. Half of a young man's face stared back at her. He had shaggy black hair and dark eyes. His hair looked on the long side as well.

"He looks kind of cute," Katarina mused, staring thoughtfully at him. Therese looked up at her.

"Bear?"

"Who?

"Bear. It's a nickname he got in Juvenile Detention."

"Oh."

The three of them sitting there, with Benedict dozing, Therese drawing on a slip of paper, and Katarina reading, in the cozy room with the firelight sending a beautiful, warm glow on them made a wonderful picture.

Katarina glanced up from her book and let her gaze wander around the room resting occasionally on her siblings. She had a pretty great family; of course they all had their faults. Katarina liked how all their personalities were like puzzle pieces and they fit together perfectly. Antoinette, sweet and kind. Benedict, funny but polite with his jokes. Therese, soft and silently sweet. Emiliana was the troublemaker in their family. It was hard to get her to dress up or look presentable in the way the other girls thought she should be. She would not admit she was pretty at all and went to great pains to act like Benedict in as many ways as she could. Her mother had tried in vain to stop her from doing it, but she couldn't–until her husband mentioned that she should try curbing Benedict, making him the perfect gentleman, without going as far as turning him into a princess. Mother hoped with all her heart that one day Emiliana would decide to live with being a girl, but she did not push the subject. Katarina sighed softly. *Oh well, Emiliana was Emiliana and that's all there was to it.*

"Where's Mum?" Benedict asked, stretching. He tapped Katarina on the head with his foot.

She brushed him away and replied, "I'm not sure where she went. Tonight's Mum and Dad's date, right?"

"Yeah, but they wouldn't leave this early. Besides, we have to help Mom get ready," Therese spoke up, glancing up at the clock: 5:02 p.m. They heard the door open and then their mother was standing in the doorway in front of them. Mrs. Anderson's eyes sparkled so much she looked like a child on Christmas morning. They all knew that look well, for their mother always looked like that whenever their parents went on their dates. Mother held a shopping bag in her hand.

"Girls!" She smiled excitedly.

Her youngest daughters, knowing the cue, jumped up to follow her into the bedroom and help her get dressed.

"What did you get, Mum?" Katarina asked her mother gleefully. Mrs. Anderson pulled out a dress from the bag. She held up a nice but casual purple dress. It had ruffles on the bodice.

"This." She fished a small bag out of her purse. "And these." In her hands she held a simple necklace with an amethyst in a heart shape, a simple beaded bracelet, and silver tear drop earrings.

"Those are so pretty," Therese breathed out. Mother sighed and set it on the dresser. Turning to her daughters, she asked them, "You don't think I'll be too dressed up, do you?"

Katarina flopped backwards onto the bed with a groan and replied, "Mum! You ask that every time! Dad is always just as dressed up as you! This date is a reminder of how much you both love each other. Besides, you look beautiful all dressed up," she added happily.

Her mother smiled at her. "All right." Mrs. Anderson got dressed and then let Therese fix her hair. She decided on a French twist while leaving a few strands of hair to curl later.

Katarina lay on her mother's bed, thinking. She spoke up thoughtfully, "Where are you and Dad going for dinner?"

"Ristorante de Francesca."

"Ooh! The new place! Down on Pargaini Avenue?"

"Yes, my dear."

A couple minutes went by in silence while Therese finished her mother's hair. There was a knock on the closed door. Katarina jumped.

"Are you ready, Mum?"

"One moment." Mrs. Anderson slipped on a pair of low silver heels. She looked at her two youngest daughters. "How do I look?"

Therese smiled and nodded as Katarina burst out with an excited: "Beautiful, Mum! Now, quick–Dad's waiting!" Katarina ran to open the bedroom door while Therese, being the eldest daughter at home, escorted their mother down the stairs. Katarina followed close behind.

Benedict stood below in the hall with Mr. Anderson. He grinned when he saw them; he tapped Father on the arm. Mr. Anderson looked up from fixing his tie nervously. His eyes lit up and he a smiled a slightly cheesy grin. Katarina never lost that little thrill of happiness when she saw her parents like that. After ushering their parents out, Benedict, Therese, and Katarina went into the kitchen to make pizza and watch movies as they always did.

"What movie should we watch this time?" Katarina asked, pulling out the dough from the bowls it had been rising in. She tossed some to Benedict and both of them began to spread it into the two greased pans in front of them. Therese began to get the cheese, spaghetti sauce, pepperoni, and sausage out of the fridge.

"Let's watch a Disney movie!" Therese suggested, her face breaking into a wide grin.

Benedict groaned loudly. "Nights like this, I wish I had a brother to hang out with and fight the never-surprising Disney movies!" Benedict gave a fake scream of pain that made the girls jump.

Therese burst out laughing her thoughtful, blue eyes reflecting the laughter, but Katarina became quiet and when she spoke it was in a soft tone of voice. "Benny?"

"Yeah?"

"Do you ever wish Aiden had lived instead of dying?"

"Ye-yes," he responded slowly, "but I know what happened was what God wanted to happen, so I guess I'm okay with it."

"Sometimes I wish I could have met him," Katarina said quietly. She methodically spread the dough out. Therese handed the spaghetti sauce jar to her with a small smile.

"I did meet him, but I don't really remember too much about it. I mean, I had only just turned one," Therese said.

"Hey, at least Mom and Dad always took pictures of us right after we were all born so we have pictures of him."

"Yeah. Don't tell anyone, but I took one of the pictures from the photo album of him. It's in my room," Katarina admitted, grinning suddenly. Therese looked at her, open mouthed.

Benedict chuckled and rubbed her head cheerfully. "Good thing mum doesn't look at that photo album very often," he joked.

"Let's not talk of such sad things. Let's put these pizzas in the oven and pick out our Disney movie!" Therese grinned teasingly at Benedict, who stuck out his tongue at her.

Antoinette, Emiliana, and their cousin Marial Turner were in the Turner's kitchen popping popcorn for the evening. Marial and Antoinette had–just moments before–dragged Emiliana away from the boys to have a girl's night with Aunt Marina and the twins Anna and Grace. They were going to watch *Sleeping Beauty* for the twins' sake.

"Are you ready, girls?" Anna asked as she came bouncing in. Grace ran in after her sister and grabbed Marial's hands and pulled.

"Hurry up!! Pweathe!" she insisted.

"Be nice, Grace," Marial gently admonished her little sister.

Grace's face fell and her lip quivered. "I'm sorry."

"Don't worry," Marial said kindly. "You just have to remember to be polite."

"Yes, Marial."

"All right, girls, are you ready? We need to start soon so the girls can go to bed on time," Aunt Marina said as she walked into the kitchen. Antoinette poured some melted butter over the freshly-popped popcorn and Emiliana liberally sprinkled salt all over the heaping bowls of it.

"We're ready, Mom," Marial said. Marial and Antoinette each picked up a bowl and they all trooped into the living room and sat down on the couches and chairs.

Chapter Two

The next morning, Katarina hopped out of bed. She wanted to know what her parents had done on their date, other than going to dinner. She had gone to bed at nine-thirty and they had come home at eleven. Katarina pulled on a knee-length, green skirt with a dark pink, long-sleeved shirt. After brushing her hair out and putting it into a ponytail, she hurried downstairs and into the kitchen and was greeted by the smell of crepes. It was Saturday. Katarina grinned cheerfully.

"Good morning!" she sang out joyfully and planted a kiss on her mother's head–showing once again that she was taller than her mother–and gave her dad a big hug.

Her mother smiled. "Someone's cheerful today."

"Why shouldn't I be? It's a beautiful, snowy,

Saturday morning." She took a drink of the orange juice she had just poured and added, "Plus I have no chores today..."

Mr. Anderson looked up to say something when she added with a wink and a smile, directed at him, "...for I did them all yesterday." He chuckled and shook his head. Mrs. Anderson handed her a plate of homemade, strawberry crepes. After fetching a fork from the drawer, Katarina settled into a chair at the kitchen table.

"Where's Therese and Benedict?" She took a bite of her crepe. Dad glanced up from his cell phone; he had one hand in his pocket and was leaning against the counter. He was also wearing his blue, Knights of Columbus sweatshirt.

"Prayers, Kat." He looked down at his phone again.

"Oh, right." Katarina dropped her fork, made a quick Sign of the Cross, and mumbled her prayers. "So, where are they?"

"Therese is still in bed, and Benedict is out cleaning the garage."

"He's out early."

"I sent him out after he had his breakfast, ten minutes before you came down," Dad replied. Katarina looked out the window over the kitchen sink at all the glorious, white snow.

"It looks cold out. It must be cold in the garage."

"Oh, he's got his stuff on."

Katarina turned back to her plate and continued eating the delicious food before her. Mother turned off the stove and brought the plate of hot crepes to the table and put a lid on them to keep them warm for Therese. Katarina quickly finished her breakfast while Dad headed out to the garage to help Benedict.

After she had washed her breakfast dishes, Katarina headed upstairs to pull her sister out of bed. Katarina noted that Emiliana's usually messy bed was very nicely made up. Therese lay bundled up in her bed sheets. Katarina pulled the sheets off of her and began to gently tickle her sister's feet. She knew what would happen, but she couldn't help doing it. Therese flew up into a sitting position and shrieked loudly. Her reddish brown hair was all messed up from sleeping.

"Katarina Rebecca Anderson!"

Katarina began to giggle uncontrollably, so hard she rolled off the bed and slammed onto the floor.

"I'm sorry! I really couldn't help it!" She gasped breathlessly. Therese couldn't help it; she broke into a playful grin. Katarina lay on the floor with her eyes closed, switching from breaking into giggles to catching her breath. Therese lobbed a pillow at Katarina and then another. Katarina threw her hands up to ward off any other flying objects.

"Truce! I call a truce!"

"Is everything all right?"

The girls looked up at their mother standing in the doorway. She looked pretty there; her shoulder-length, brown hair settled around her shoulders and her brown eyes twinkled merrily.

"Of course, Mummy." Therese beckoned her to come in. Mrs. Anderson walked in and sat on the bed opposite of her youngest daughters. Katarina sat up and leaned against Therese's bed, looking up at her mother. She tilted her head to one side.

"You look pretty today, Mummy."

"Thank you, my dear." Mother smiled down at Katarina. Therese picked up her hairbrush and began to brush her hair out.

"When are Nettie and Em expected back?"

"About dinner time." Mother got up and headed to the door. "Well, Therese, you should get dressed; I left you some crepes on a plate on the table."

"All right; thanks." Therese climbed out of bed and shooed Katarina out of her room, shutting the door behind her.

Later that morning, Katarina sat in the library. It was really just a sitting room, but the girls liked to call it their library because they kept almost all their books in it. She was engrossed in her book, the one that Therese had brought home yesterday.

"Hey, Kat? Could you help me out with my students this morning?" Mrs. Anderson asked.

Katarina reluctantly tore herself from the book and looked up. Every Saturday morning, Mrs. Anderson held music lessons. She usually asked Therese or Antoinette to help her out. Katarina looked from her book to her mother. Was this book worth disappointing her mother? Katarina mentally shook her head then she closed the book and placed it on the table without a sigh. Mother smiled softly at her daughter. Katarina stood up and walked to her.

"I'll help you, Mum." She smiled sweetly and truly at her mother.

"Thank you, darling."

Katarina reached out her hand and Mother took it in her own and squeezed it gently. The two walked down the hall to the office room where Mrs. Anderson taught her music lessons.

Katarina looked to her mother. "So, what needs to be done first?" She clapped her hands together and rose up on her toes.

"Just tidy up a bit, real quick," was the reply. Once started, Katarina could work as hard as anyone, but having to actually get up and do it was where it was really hard. She would complain often of having to do her chores, but then she would tell herself to shut up and do them and she would be done in a matter of minutes.

"Lions or Vikings?" Emiliana spoke, twirling the football in her hands. She stared at her five cousins. Her poker straight blonde hair was blowing gently in the breeze.

"Lions!" Jimmy Turner said excitedly; the seven year old jumped up and down.

Eighteen-year-old Patrick just shrugged. "Well, I guess that makes us the Vikings, Em."

"Splendid!" Her eyes sparkled merrily. Her cousin, Alex Farden, took the ball from Emiliana and they all tramped through the snow to the backyard.

"How do you play football in the snow?" Antoinette asked her nineteen-year-old cousin Marial Turner. She brushed her dark brown hair behind her ear. Subconsciously thinking about needing a new hair cut soon since her hair was past her chin.

"I ask that all the time, Nettie." She chuckled and shook her head at the group outside. At the girls' feet, Anna and Grace sat, playing. The two girls were four-year-old twins and were quite mischievous. Antoinette and Marial were both sewing doll clothes, much to the gratitude of the twins, whose pleas had gone quite unanswered the day before.

"Today her name is Isabelle," proclaimed Anna happily.

"Mine is Kateri, wike the Indian girl saint in the story you read me, Mariaw," Grace said, blissfully holding her doll in her arms. "Hewwo, Isabelle," Grace said, making her blonde-haired doll walk over to Anna's doll. Isabelle swooped to Kateri.

"Kateri! I missed you! Me is so gwad to see you!"

"How are you?"

"Me is good, Isabelle."

"Wet's go to the park!" Kateri yelled excitedly.

"Yay! Me wants to swide!"

The dolls, held by their wild "mothers," ran to the "park" on the other side of the living room. Kateri and Isabelle clambered up onto the "jungle gym"–the couch.

"Ooof! It's swippery!" Isabelle slid down a bit on the leather couch.

An hour swiftly passed and before they knew it, it was time for lunch.

"Anna, Grace, it's time for lunch." Marial tapped them on the shoulders, drawing them out of their brilliant, colorful, little play-world.

"Okay," Grace said. "Wet's go eat, Anna." They tucked their dolls under their arms and trooped out of the room, followed by Antoinette and Marial, into the kitchen to eat.

"City lights flicker, cars rush by. I can't believe this is happening to me. I left home just the other day....." Katarina sang softly to herself as she tidied up the room before the first student arrived.

"Mum?" She looked up at Mother as she spoke, pausing in her work. "Who's scheduled first?"

"Um..." Mother glanced at her music lessons planner. "Abigail is." She smiled at Katarina. Abigail Dunham had been Katarina's best friend since they were two years old. Abigail had the very same pale complexion as Katarina had always wished for, but you could hardly tell with all her freckles crowding her face and arms. You could always tell when the two were together; they always left a "trail of destruction" behind them.

"Can she stay after class?"

"You can ask Mrs. Dunham when she gets here."

Katarina felt a thrill of excitement go through her body. She had not seen Abigail for over two months, for at the beginning of November she had left with her family to go to Ireland to spend the months of November and December there. Abigail had only come home last week.

Oh, I hope she can stay for the whole day! Katarina thought joyfully. She cheerfully went back to cleaning up the office.

"Kat?!"

Katarina was going to the kitchen to get a drink of water when a voice made her stop in her tracks and turn around quickly.

"Abi?!" Katarina's face broke into the biggest grin ever. She ran to her best friend. The two hugged as if they had been apart for years instead of two months; two months is still too long of a time for best friends.

"I missed you!!" Abigail cried out excitedly.

"Me too!!" Katarina squealed happily. "I'm so ecstatic that you are home!"

"I'm so ecstatic that I'm home, too!" Abigail replied, squealing just as much as Katarina. "Two months is way too long!"

"Sorry to break up this happy reunion, but Abigail, you have to go in for class." Mrs. Dunham smiled at the two girls. Katarina suddenly remembered.

"Oh!" She gasped. "Can Abi stay after class for the day?"

Abigail's face lit up. "May I, Mom?!" Abigail asked.

Mrs. Dunham thought for a moment. "Is it all right with your mom?" she asked, turning to look at Katarina.

"Yes, it is; she already asked." The girls

looked up and saw Mother walking to them.

"Then it's fine with me. What time should I pick her up?"

They screamed excitedly. Mother chuckled at them,

"How about 4:30?"

"Wonderful. I'll be by then. G'bye, dear."

"Bye, Mom. Thanks!" Abigail waved as her mother left.

"All right, Abigail; it's time for your lesson," Mother said, turning back to the girls.

"Can I sit in, Mum?"

"Yes, you may" was the reply. Katarina and Abigail grinned at each other and followed mother into the room.

Chapter Three

Katarina turned up the volume of the speakers. The first strains of the girls' favorite song came on. Abigail shut the door of the bedroom.

"I watch from the sidelines and I whisper softly, quietly 'Don't forget me.' They don't hear anything at all and I'm still standing here." Katarina sang sweetly; she had inherited her beautiful singing voice from her mother.

"Oh-I catch my breath, how many times have I seen this happen to me." Abigail had a stunning voice as well.

"Slow down, let me catch my breath."

The girls decided to have a dance party. Abigail had pushed Katarina's rug against the wall so they could dance on the wood floor. Katarina was turning off the lights and setting up their "disco ball" that Benedict and Emiliana had helped them make a year ago. Abigail propped up flashlights around the area, all pointing at the disco ball. Katarina closed the curtains over the windows and headed to her balcony door. As she was about to close the curtain, she glanced out the door and saw their neighbor, Peter Marchen. The two girls were good friends with him, even though he was twenty. They begged all sorts of things from him from money for treats to having him play a game with them; he was really nice. Abigail and Katarina dearly loved to tease him. He took it all good naturedly.

"Abi!" She threw open the doors and stepped out into the snow that covered the balcony. "Come here; it's Peter!" Abigail ran forward, giggling. Katarina whispered to her and Abigail laughed out loud. They burst out, singing at the top of their lungs.

They began to shriek loudly as the snow became unbearably cold on their bare feet. Peter came over, laughing.

He winked, "Having fun?"

"It's cold!" Katarina hopped up and down.

"How is everyone?" Peter asked, still grinning up at them merrily.

"Everyone is doing great," Abigail answered.

Katarina slyly added with a wink at Abigail, "Antoinette will be home tonight."

"Oh." He blushed. "Where is she?" He glanced at his boots.

"She went to their cousins' with Em yesterday," Abigail replied.

"Oh, right; Benedict told me that. Well, I gotta run; see you later!" He turned and ran off, waving. The girls began to giggle at their victory.

"He blushed!!"

A while ago the two girls had discovered that Peter might be sweet on Antoinette They had gone to great lengths to figure out if he really was.

"Katarina Anderson and Abigail Dunham! Get in here right this minute and dry off your feet!" They turned sheepishly around to see Mother standing in the doorway. Katarina stepped back into the room, followed by Abigail. Mother shut the doors; she looked at them. Her face was blank.

"Stay here while I get towels."

"Yes, ma'am," they replied meekly. Katarina and Abigail looked at each other; they were ashamed. They should have known better. Mother came in with the towels.

"Dry off and come downstairs with socks and sweaters on; I'll be in the kitchen." She left quickly.

"I'm afraid she'll punish us, Abi. I mean, we deserve it." Katarina always got scared when anyone mentioned a punishment. She rarely needed them, though, mainly because after she did something bad she was always ashamed and very upset with herself. Most of the time her parents thought that was enough.

Abigail smiled sympathetically. "If we do, I'll be with you."

After drying off their feet and putting socks and sweaters on, they headed down to the kitchen. Mother was placing mugs of steaming hot chocolate with whipped cream on the table. Katarina glanced at Abigail, who shrugged.

"Sit and warm up," she ordered calmly. The two sat down quickly. Mother placed a plate of warm, chocolate chip cookies in front of them. Katarina and Abigail each took one as Mother left the room.

They ate and drank in silence for a couple of minutes. Therese sauntered in; she paused and raised a questioning eyebrow.

"Why so glum, chums? In trouble?"

Katarina shrugged; Abigail spoke up, "We don't know." She finished chewing. "Normally a punishment doesn't involve cookies and hot chocolate with whipped cream."

"I would have to agree." Therese smiled. She walked over and took a cookie. Mother walked in and Therese scurried out–they all knew the consequences of talking to someone in trouble.

"Done yet?" They gulped their last drink down and nodded quickly. Mother beckoned, "Come with me."

Katarina and Abigail stood up and followed

her down the hall to the library; Mother shut the door behind them. She turned to them and told them to sit down. Katarina leaned forward, looking upset.

"Mummy, I am *really* sorry; honest. I should have known better."

Abigail fiddled with her hands. "I should have, too; I'm sorry, Mrs. Anderson."

"It's all right; it's just, girls, you really should have used your heads and dressed warmly," Mother scolded, firmly, but gently.

"We would have, honest, we just saw Peter Marchen and I-I..." Katarina faltered.

"You what?" Mother questioned gently.

Katarina looked down at her lap and blushed. "I wanted to tease him about Nettie."

"Why?"

"We think he likes her, Mrs. Anderson," put in Abigail.

"Well, let me say this." She sounded grave.

"What?" They were instantly alert.

"Leave that idea to your father and me. But I will say that I agree, although I would like to watch Nettie."

Katarina giggled. "You sound as profound as Mrs. March when Jo told her about Mr. Brooke and Meg's glove."

Abigail groaned and rolled her eyes jokingly as Mother chuckled. "I do believe you know that story by heart, Kat."

Katarina giggled with Abigail.

"Well," Mother stood up, "why don't you go find Therese and see if she wants to watch a movie or something with you two, to keep you out of trouble." She winked and left the library. The two hurried out and skipped to the living room.

"Therese! Mum said to ask you if you want to watch a movie."

"So we stay out of trouble for a while," Abigail added, grinning.

"All right; what movie shall it be?" They headed to the movie shelf to decide. Therese held up one.

"What about *Mulan*?"

"Yes! That one's awesome!" Abigail cried out.

"Sweet! I love Mushu!" Katarina turned on the TV and popped in the movie.

Quite a few hours later, after *Mulan* and *The Lion, the Witch, and the Wardrobe*, they heard the door open.

"We're home!" Emiliana called out. Antoinette stepped into the room with Emiliana as the credits finished.

"What were you watching?" Emiliana spoke as she flopped down on the armchair.

"Oh just *Mulan* and *Narnia*," Katarina said

offhandedly.

"You guys were watching a *movie*?" Antoinette asked, pretending to look shocked. Usually they were doing something that turned out destructive. Abigail and Katarina laughed sarcastically.

"Yeah; we sort of got in trouble, so we were told to watch a movie," Abigail answered as Katarina rolled her eyes, grinning.

Father and Benedict came in from the garage.

"Hey, Dad!" Antoinette smiled at him.

"Welcome home!" Father hugged her hello.

"Did you have fun?" Abigail asked them excitedly. Katarina gestured to Abigail as Emiliana began to explain how their visit went. They sidled out of the room and ran up to Katarina's room.

They sat silently on Katarina's bed for a bit. Katarina fingered the pattern on the comforter.

"Abi?" she spoke softly.

"Hmm?" Abigail lay back on the bed.

"I wanna change the world." Katarina spoke this confidently.

"How?"

"That's the problem; I'm not sure how." She lay down next to Abigail and propped her head up with her arms.

"Well, let's think then," Abigail spoke thoughtfully. They were interrupted two minutes later by Emiliana.

"Hey, Abigail, your mom is here." The two shot up together.

"Rats!" Katarina and Abigail slid off the bed and followed Emiliana downstairs.

"Hello, sweetie." Mrs. Dunham turned and smiled at her.

"Hey, Mom."

"Are you ready to go?"

Abigail picked up her music binder. "Yup." She hugged Katarina good bye. "Bye, Kat!"

Katarina hugged her back. "Bye, Abi!"

Katarina changing the world was forgotten for a time.

Seven Years Later

Abigail was sorting through her stuff. It was a fine summer day; she had just finished her second year of college. As she shifted through a large pile of photos, she came across one of a girl with brown hair and bright brown eyes.

"Oh, my!" Abigail breathed out; the memory of that day came back to her. *That was the day she talked about changing the world. I know she believed she could; I believed she could, too! I still do!* As Abigail stared longer at the photo, it all came back to her. She had remembered that they had felt so young and free that day. They had schemed how Katarina could change the world. They were staying at Katarina's grandparents' house that month. Then their visit was cut short by... Abigail shook herself.

"No!" she spoke firmly to herself. She placed

the photo on her bulletin board–in the center–
and continued to clean.

Chapter Four

August

"Katarina, your grandmother just called and wanted to know if you and Abigail would like to go spend this month with her and Gramps." Mother was lovingly brushing her daughter's hair before bed. Katarina smiled; she loved her grandparents.

"Oh! By ourselves? I would love to!" Katarina's face lit up with excitement.

"Yes, by yourselves, though I am flying out there with you two."

"Does Abigail know?"

"Yes, she does. I called Mrs. Dunham and she said it was all right and that she would tell Abigail."

"Cool! When do we leave?" she asked while braiding her hair.

Mother smiled. "Tomorrow evening, so get a good night's rest."

"Okay; goodnight, Mummy!" Katerina hugged her mother goodnight.

"Goodnight, dearest." Mother kissed her on the forehead and left the room.

Katarina crawled happily into bed and fell asleep dreaming about the visit.

The plane slowly landed on the runway and soon came to a halt. The girls and Mrs. Anderson got up and Katarina grabbed her backpack. They left the plane and headed to the long line to collect the girls' baggage. Katarina shifted her backpack, almost regretting her decision to bring so many books. She wiped the sweat from her forehead. Abigail stood, tapping her foot impatiently, while pulling her hair into a ponytail.

"Finally." Katarina sighed as they stepped forward, grabbed their bags, and headed to the doors.

"Sarah! Katarina! Abigail!" a deep, kind voice caught their attention.

"Gramps!" Katarina hurtled towards him and was enveloped into a huge bear hug.

"Hello, my Kitty-Kat." Gramps grinned, his eyes twinkling.

"Hello, Mr. Jones!" Abigail said excitedly.

He smiled. "Call me Gramps." He hugged her warmly. "Sarah, my girl, how're you?" He hugged his daughter.

"I'm doing great, Dad!"

"That's fine! Well, your grandmother is waiting for us at home, so we best be on our way." They headed into the hot, summer night. Gramps loaded their luggage into the bed of his red, Chevy pickup truck.

"Hello! Hello! C'mon in! How are my girls? Abigail! How are you?" Granny bustled them all into the large, ornate kitchen. Abigail looked around. She saw many shiny, granite countertops. A large freezer/refrigerator stood to the left. Two large ovens stood on the other side of the island and the counter that stuck out from the wall. Granny had them sit down on stools at the counter.

"We're doing great, Granny!" Katarina said, grinning happily.

"Splendid. Here; have some lemonade." She handed them all large glasses.

"Do I get one?" Gramps said jokingly as he walked in from bringing the girls' bags upstairs. Granny handed him one and sat down next to him.

"So, Sarah, how long can you stay?" she asked her daughter.

Mother took a sip of her lemonade before

answering. "I have to be back at the airport by 11:15 tonight."

"All right," Granny said.

"Can't you stay longer?" Katarina looked at her mother, begging. Her eyes told her mother *I'm going to miss you.* Mother looked at her youngest daughter.

"I wish I could, dearest."

Abigail saw the love in Mrs. Anderson's eyes for Katarina. She knew that if she didn't have the wonderful mom she did she would want to be an Anderson child. Mrs. Anderson was so very sweet, kind, understanding, and ever-so-lovable. Mr. Anderson was nice, sweet, and funny, but he could be serious and stern. *I'm gonna miss her too*, she thought, smiling.

"Well, that's that. Sarah, you must rest till you leave," Granny said, smiling tenderly.

"Yes, Mom." They all stood up and washed their lemonade glasses.

Granny led them upstairs to show them their bedrooms. She gave Mother the room at the top of the stairs. Abigail and Katarina were given the room at the end of the hall.

"Granny?" Katarina stopped her grandmother outside the girls' room.

Granny smiled. "Yes, dear?"

"Thanks for letting us visit you."

"Oh, Katarina, you are our granddaughter! We do get to steal you from your mom and dad sometimes." Granny chuckled merrily. Katarina giggled; she said goodnight and closed the bedroom door behind her. She turned to Abigail and squealed.

"We're going to have a ton of fun!"

Abigail giggled, "Yes, we will!"

They got into their pajamas and Abigail climbed into her bed. Katarina sat across from her on her own bed, brushing her hair.

"Abi, I'm going to go talk to Mum, okay?"

Abigail mumbled back, "All right." Katarina left the room and hurried down the hall to her mother's room. She knocked softly on the door and waited.

"Come in."

She opened the door and stepped inside.

"Yes, dear?" Mother smiled, looking up from her cellphone.

"I was wondering if we could talk before you leave."

"Certainly." She placed her cellphone on the bedside table and patted the spot next to her. "Come sit with me." Katarina went over and hopped onto the bed next to her.

"Was there anything in particular you wanted to talk about, precious?"

"Can you talk to me like you talk to Nettie before she leaves for school or whenever they leave for a while?"

"Why, of course, dear! Let me think," Mother

said, thinking while holding Katarina's hand in her own. "All right; listening, precious?"

"What are your words of wisdom, Mummy dearest?" Katarina giggled. She lay down and placed her head in her mother's lap. "Talk, please."

"Precious," Mother began stroking Katarina's hair lovingly, "while you are here at Gramps and Granny's, watch your tongue; don't talk too sharply and watch your temper as well. I know you and Abigail don't argue you much, but you're like sisters so be careful." She sat silently. "Oh, also, as a warning, Gramps, when he gets angry, will accidentally let a word or two slip out without realizing it, so please, if you hear him yelling or talking angrily about something, please don't go near him and try not to listen."

"I will try, Mummy," Katarina promised.

Mother looked deep into Katarina's eyes and said, "My dear, just be yourself, have fun, and enjoy this month here. Granny told me she has a lot planned." Mother's eyes twinkled. "You have your phone, right? If you need anything, like advice or something, just call or text me; you can text me whenever."

"Yes." Katarina smiled. "Want me to text you about what we do?"

"Yes, please, precious dear." Mother leaned down and kissed Katarina's forehead.

Eleven o'clock came sooner than expected. They all were down in the front hall, saying goodbye to Mother. Granny hugged her daughter.

"Goodbye, Sarah. Don't worry; we'll take care of them." She chuckled.

"Thanks, Mom; love you!" Mother said, smiling. She turned and hugged Abigail goodbye. "Goodbye, Abigail" She lowered her voice and whispered, "Don't forget what your mother told you, and take care of Katarina."

Abigail smiled and promised to; not knowing then that her promise would last longer than a month.

"Goodbye, Mummy." Katarina hugged her mother really tight; there were tears in her eyes. "I'll miss you, and I love you!"

"I'll miss you, and I love you too, precious." Mother kissed Katarina goodbye.

"Tell Daddy I'll miss him."

"I will."

Mother grabbed her purse and followed Gramps out the door. They called after them.

"Goodbye! Goodbye!"

"Tell David and the kids we say hi!" Granny called.

"I will!" They drove off.

Granny ushered them back inside and shut

the door. She turned to them and clapped her hands.

"All right; off to bed–it's late!"

"Goodnight, Granny," Katarina said.

"Goodnight, Mrs. Jones."

Granny tsked, "I'm sure Gramps already corrected you, but please call me Granny." She smiled and hugged them. They hurried upstairs and climbed into bed.

"Goodnight, Kat."

"Goodnight, Abi."

Chapter Five

"Rise and shine, sleeping beauties! The French toast is gettin' cold, and we have a lot to do today!"

Katarina sat up and sleepily rubbed her eyes. She saw Granny standing between the beds. The sunlight shone brightly through the window. Abigail woke up and took a moment to adjust to the light. She covered her eyes, rubbed them, and blinked rapidly.

"Good morning, Granny!" Katarina spoke cheerfully.

"Good morning, girls! Let me leave you to get dressed before breakfast." Granny left the room.

Katarina flopped backwards and sighed loudly. "What time is it, Abi?"

"8:15," Abigail mumbled, glancing at the clock.

"Ugh; we should get dressed, then," Katarina

said, pushing herself up again, and swung her legs off the bed. Abigail followed suit. They sat staring at each other until Katarina burst out giggling. Abigail grinned.

"What?"

Katarina tried to control her giggles, "Sorry; I don't know why I'm laughing." Abigail giggled. They both sighed together.

"We should get moving," they told each other and then laughed. Abigail got up and rifled through her suitcase for some clothes. While she commandeered the bathroom, Katarina picked up her cell phone to text her parents.

"Good morning, Daddy and Mommy!"

After typing out the message, she hit send and placed it back on the nightstand. She stood up to start putting some clothes away in the closet and the dresser.

"Okay." She looked at her suitcase and assessed the situation. Katarina pulled out jeans, capris, shirts, tank tops, and other random clothing articles. After everything was out of her suitcase, she closed it up and shoved it under her bed. Katarina started on the shirts, folding each one and placing it in a pile. She always sorted her clothing by color and each color into order from dark to light.

She folded her last shirt as Abigail came back wearing a pair of light green shorts and a tie-dye t-shirt.

"Your turn, Kat." She placed her pajamas onto her unmade bed. "Ugh, I hate making my bed." She groaned.

Katarina waggled her eyebrows at Abigail grinning. "It better be made by the time I'm back!" She grabbed a lacy, purple tank top and tan capris and scurried out.

Abigail pulled the covers up and then plopped her pillow on top. "There. I made my bed." She stuck her tongue out at her pathetic attempt.

"Nice bed." Katarina giggled, coming back into the room and brushing her hair before braiding it.

Abigail stuck her tongue out at her.

"Let's go eat." Katarina placed her brush on her dresser. They ran downstairs and into the kitchen. On the counter were two yellow, flowered plates. One was piled high with French toast; the other held donut muffins.

"Ooh! Donut muffins! Yum-my!" Katarina dragged out the last word.

Granny smiled and poured them both cups of steaming coffee and placed them at their spots.

"Here you are, girls." She handed them each a plate. They sat down and plopped some French toast onto their plates. Granny placed the syrup, whipped cream, butter, and cream onto the table. The girls each buttered their French toast, poured syrup, and covered their toast with whipped cream.

"Yum!" Abigail smacked her lips and dug in.

They drove down the road and headed into town.

"What are we doing first?" Abigail asked excitedly.

"I can't tell you." Granny chuckled. "I'll give you a hint, though; it's something special you'll both enjoy." She winked at them in the rearview mirror.

Katarina groaned. "Granny! That's not a hint."

"I told you I couldn't tell." She laughed at them. "We'll be there in a moment, though." Granny turned into a parking lot of a strip mall and soon after found a spot to park. She turned off the ignition and they got out of the blue Honda. The three walked across the parking lot. Granny led the way to a small store on the opposite side of the strip mall.

"Ahh. Here we are." Granny pulled the door open to a small shop with the name of

"Nicole's Styles." The girls squeaked with excitement.

"Really? This is awesome!"

"Thanks, Granny."

They spent more than two hours at the store. The girls had Nicole do all sorts of extravagant hairstyles, and she was all right with it since business was a bit slow that morning. They came out with beautiful hairdos. Katarina had half of her hair up, with braids running from the front to the back. Some braids were wrapped around the bun and the rest fell down in curls, with a few braids curled with some of the hair. Abigail went with all her hair up in a French 'do.

"Let's go and find you some proper bonfire clothing, girls." Granny led them down the street to the mall. The girls hurried to catch up with her rapid pace.

"What do you mean, 'proper bonfire clothing'?" Abigail asked; she brushed her red bangs out of her eyes.

"Well, this bonfire is a huge event. The whole town will be there, so you'll need something nice to wear to it."

Katarina was confused. "For a bonfire?"

Granny chuckled, "You'll see–so stop asking questions."

"Another surprise." Abigail sighed dramatically as Katarina started to laugh. Granny playfully swatted Abigail.

"Stop that nonsense," she said, grinning.

They headed into the mall and Granny led them into American Eagle.

"Find yourselves some designer jeans, girls." They scurried away to find their size while Granny found a bench.

"Look at these ones." Katarina held up a pair of dark blue jeans with a jeweled butterfly design going from the right pocket down to mid-thigh.

"Those are so cute!"

"Think I should try 'em on?"

"Go for it."

"Okay." Katarina flicked through the rack and grabbed a pair in her size and headed for the dressing room.

She pulled the jeans on and looked at herself in the mirror. They fit perfectly. They weren't skin-tight, either. Good; she liked them, too.

Katarina came out and saw Abigail making her way through the store to the dressing room.

"Like 'em?" she asked merrily.

"Yup, I'm gonna get them."

"Sweet. Wait here?" she responded, diving into a dressing room without waiting for a response.

"Sure." Katarina smiled, folding the jeans over the arm. The door opened and Abigail stepped out wearing a pair of green jeans and a silver belt.

"Oh, that is perfect for you, Abigail! Oh my!" Katarina giggled.

"Why, thank you," Abigail said, giggling along. "I think I'll get them."

"Okay; here, you take mine and change out of yours, and I'll go get Granny."

"We're ready to pay, Granny," Katarina spoke up upon finding her sitting on a bench.

"Okay." Granny got up and followed her granddaughter back into the shop. They found Abigail at the checkout counter.

"Here are the jeans we picked out." Abigail handed them to Granny, who bought them, and they left the store.

"All right; do you want to go into Kohl's and buy tops?"

"Sure," they replied.

"All right–make it quick, then. We have to get home so I can make dessert," Granny said, sending them off on their way.

The girls went through Kohl's in record time and came out successful. They left the mall and headed back home so Granny could make dessert.

Chapter Six

Katarina glanced at the clock: 5:30. She placed her hairbrush down on the dresser after using it to brush out her curls. She took one more look in the mirror. She had, with Abigail's help, undressed her hairdo a tad. Her bright pink shirt looked just right with her new jeans. Katarina went to the hallway and knocked on the bathroom door.

"Abi, we have to go downstairs now."

The door opened and Abigail stepped out, wearing a cream top with her green pants.

"Ready!" She beamed. They locked arms and skipped downstairs. They found Granny in the kitchen, covering up a pan with tinfoil. She was wearing a floral dress with a cream, crocheted sweater.

"Do you have sweaters, girls? It might get chilly out tonight." She turned around, hearing them come in.

"Yup." They giggled.

Granny smiled and asked them, "Do you ever not giggle?"

"Nope," they said, laughing together.

She shook her head at them as Gramps walked into the room.

"Is everyone ready to go? We have to hit the road."

"Yes, we're ready," Granny responded. "Could you take this, honey?" She gestured to the pan on the counter.

Gramps picked it up and they all trooped out to the pickup truck. Granny and Gramps climbed into the truck while the girls climbed into the bed of it to ride there. They made themselves comfortable on some blankets and on their sweaters. They all departed for Green River commons, the main gathering grounds for the Green River people. On the way, Katarina and Abigail sang songs at the top of their lungs, sending many flocks of birds scattering into the air. They couldn't keep from laughing. They were right; they never really did stop laughing.

Green River wasn't like a normal subdivision. It technically wasn't one–the inhabitants just called it one. The area covered six square miles, with all the houses spread out around the common.

Five minutes later, Gramps pulled into a

parking spot and turned the truck off.

"Here we are," he said as he and Granny opened their doors and stepped out of the truck. The girls climbed out and took a look around. They saw tables laden with food, three blow-up bouncy houses, and a ton of people. Katarina could feel the atmosphere of family, friendship, and happiness.

"Wow, there's a lot of people here," she breathed out.

"Could you see our town doing this, Kat?" Abigail asked looking about, surprised.

Katarina snorted. "No way."

"They're here!"

The girls looked around to see who had arrived. The crowd suddenly surged towards them. Abigail glanced at Katarina with a look that clearly asked what was going on. Katarina shrugged back.

There was a general cry of: "Welcome to Green River, Katarina and Abigail!"

A short girl stepped forward, holding a piece of lined paper. She cleared her throat and spoke up loudly. The crowd became quiet. "I, Alana Peters, would like to welcome Katarina Anderson and her friend Abigail Dunham to Green River, Ohio. We are very excited to get to know you and are happy you are staying for the month." Alana smiled happily at them.

Everyone clapped enthusiastically and someone gave a loud whoop. The girls were slightly shocked and taken aback at such a welcome. Katarina leaned over to her grandmother and whispered, "So this was why we needed 'proper bonfire clothing.'"

Granny grinned and nodded.

"Wow; thanks, everyone," Abigail spoke, smiling.

"Yeah, thanks, guys. Wow."

"Well, now that that's over, let the fun begin!" Gramps called out. All the kids gave out a loud cheer of excitement. Alana stepped forward.

"Want to go to the bouncy house?"

Katarina glanced at Abigail. "Want to, Abi?"

She grinned. "You bet! I love bouncy houses."

Alana grinned excitedly. "Let's go, then!"

They took off running towards the farthest bouncy house; the one that looked like a castle. It had four towers at each corner and a slide on one side that you slid down to the inside. It was pink, purple, and blue.

"Wow! Look at that!" Abigail gaped at it. They tore off their shoes quickly and scrambled in as quickly as possible. Katarina took a look around and saw four other little girls.

"There aren't many people in here," she said.

"All the better," Alana cried out. She ran to the side to climb so she could slide down. Abigail and Katarina were right behind her. Up at the top of the slide, Katarina stood tall, thrust her arms in the air, and shouted, "I am queen of the bouncy house! WOOHOO!"

"Hail ye, queen of the bouncy house!" Abigail and Alana giggled as they bowed before her. Katarina grabbed their hands and they all jumped into the air and landed on the bouncy slide and flopped, shrieking, down it.

"Woohoo!"

"That was epic!" Alana yelled.

"Totally!" Abigail responded.

"You guys are *so* much fun!" Alana said happily. They continued to play until Katarina suggested they go and get something to eat. The sun was already starting to set and it was getting darker out.

"So, what do you guys do for fun here, Alana?" Katarina asked as they sat down at a picnic table with plates laden with food.

"Well, I like to go swimming and I love going to the movies or just sitting quietly at the library. I have a lot of sleepovers, usually more in the summer than in the school year. Also, there is the waterpark and the mall. Plus," she winked at them, "there's the bouncy house gym. Formally named 'Bounce the Roof Off.' But it's usually just called the bouncy house."

"They have a place just for bouncy houses?" Abigail asked, shocked. Katarina's mouth hung open. Alana nodded, grinning at their shock.

Katarina licked her fork. "Wow."

Abigail swallowed some fruit salad. "You guys are beyond lucky."

"I know." Alana winked and giggled.

"Welcome, ladies and gentleman and kids! I hope you all are enjoying yourselves on this fine summer evening." A middle aged man stood up on the stage, speaking through a microphone.

"That's Mayor Mills," Alana whispered to them. They nodded in understanding.

He continued to speak. "We have games and bouncy houses over there for the kids, plus food for everyone over there. Also, Mrs. Scott will be cutting the cake soon, so make sure you get a piece. Mrs. Jones made it, so it's bound to be good."

A laugh rippled through the crowd.

"But in moments, right here in between the tables, right here in front of me, the dancing shall begin!" Everyone began to cheer loudly.

"Who likes to dance!?" He raised his voice and the cheering grew louder and louder. They settled down quickly, though, so they could finish eating.

Five minutes later, the grass between the tables was full of people–kids and adults alike. The music was turned up loud. They danced in all sorts of styles. The music was a huge assortment from Christian to Country to Pop. Alana, Abigail, and Katarina were right in the middle of it all. They were having the time of their lives. Everyone danced late into the night till every person there tumbled into their beds at midnight.

Chapter Seven

Back home at the Andersons' house, things were moving along at a normal pace. They all admitted to the house being *much* quieter since Katarina was gone and Abigail wasn't always popping over. They kept Katarina and Abigail supplied with any tidbit that could be considered news, which was just about everything–from Antoinette and Peter Marchen dating to Therese getting braces to Benedict smashing his thumb with a hammer while building something. Plus there were things like the neighborhood baseball team winning every game so far that August and their neighbors having another baby. News of that type was what Katarina and Abigail liked to hear.

Katarina and Abigail kept both their parents well stocked with all the information of their visit, especially of the bonfire night. They'd had so much fun. They were shocked they could have that much fun in one night. Granny kept them hopping after that day. The next day was Sunday and after Mass it was St. George's parish picnic. It was almost as large as the previous night's get together, but a little smaller since not everyone in Green River was Catholic. It was almost as fun as the night before, though Alana was not there–her family could not make it–but they did meet many other kids. Some boys got a group together to play baseball and asked them to play. Abigail said they only would if they got other girls to play, so it ended up being girls against boys in rousing games of baseball and then soccer. The girls won both games.

The day ended with the girls inviting Alana over for the evening to watch a movie with popcorn. They also played Wii late into the night, until Gramps went downstairs to tell them to go to bed because it had been two late nights in a row and they were only thirteen. So that was how Abigail and Katarina had their first sleepover together in Green River, Ohio. They basically crashed into their beds after Gramps gave them a sleeping bag for Alana. The girls were all out like a light.

Monday started bright and early. The sun shone through the window into the girl's room at 6:30: too early for the girls that morning. It was so early that they rolled over and fell back to sleep until the ringing phone woke them up again at half past eight. Katarina groggily sat up and rubbed her eyes. Abigail glanced at the clock and flopped backwards again. Alana didn't even move from her spot, staring up at the ceiling. The phone had stopped ringing, so they figured that Granny had answered it and they waited to see if it was anyone special.

Chapter Eight

The door opened and Granny stuck her head through the door and looked to see if they were awake. She smiled when she saw them all lying on their beds.

"Alana, that was your mother; she wants you to come home because she has to go to the store and needs you to watch the kids."

Alana sat up and climbed out of her sleeping bag. She stood up and stretched. "Okay; let me find my clothes so I can get dressed."

"I'll go cut you some chocolate banana bread to eat on the way home, all right?" Granny said as she ducked out of the room. Alana grabbed her clothes and hurried after her.

"Oh, you don't have to do that. I can eat when I get home."

Katarina and Abigail grinned at each other as they heard Granny say that she was still going to give her some bread and she was sorry that Alana thought she could pass up anything that Granny made. They heard her laughing at her own joke, too.

Katarina laughed. "She's not going to get out of this house without at least two slices." Abigail shook her head and grinned. She climbed out of bed and headed to her suitcase. Abigail knelt down and sat back on her heels.

"I know what will be on our agenda today," she spoke to Katarina as she searched through her suitcase for something to wear. Katarina headed to her dresser to look for a shirt.

"Hey. I already started yesterday. You didn't. You have a lot to do; I just have this." She gestured to the pile clothing on the floor at the end of her bed.

Abigail shrugged and replied, "That's still a lot."

"So?"

Abigail grinned back at her and turned to find a shirt. She pulled out a royal blue t-shirt and a gray one. She held them up so Katarina could see.

"Which do you think would go better with these pants?" She gestured to the pair that was on the floor next to her. They were a light gray.

"I like the blue with it."

"Okay. Last one to the bathroom is a rotten egg!" She jumped up and ran to the door.

"Hey!" Katarina grabbed a neon pink t-shirt and jean shorts and dashed after her, almost tripping. Abigail made it to the bathroom first, but she had to wait anyway because Alana was still getting dressed.

The door open and Alana stepped out. She stopped and stepped back in surprise. Right in front of her face were Katarina and Abigail. She squeaked.

"You know, at that angle you guys look really freaky." She smirked.

Abigail laughed creepily. "Why, thank you very much." She dove past Alana into the bathroom and shut the door. Alana glanced at the closed door and Katarina caught her looking at it.

"Oh. She was just proving to me that I'm a rotten egg." She winked at her.

"Ohh." Alana nodded in understanding and winked back.

"What did you say?" Abigail called through the door, sending Alana and Katarina into peals of laughter.

Finally Alana answered her question. "Not a thing, Abigail."

The door swung opened and she glared at them. She walked out of the bathroom looking at both of them, which only made them laugh harder. Abigail grinned slyly and said, "I'll eat all of the chocolate banana bread, Kat."

"No, don't!" Katarina stopped laughing looking slightly surprised.

"I was only joking; I won't," Abigail said, grinning. "You should've seen the look on your face."

Katarina stuck her tongue out and grinned. "I'll meet you guys downstairs. I'm off to get dressed."

"Well, I should go, but I'll see you both later," Alana said regretfully. Abigail pouted.

Katarina's face turned joyful. "Hey! Do you have a cell phone? We could swap numbers–for while we are here and when we go home."

Alana's face spread into a grin. "I do!! Do you have paper? I can write my number down on it for both of you."

"Yeah. Downstairs," Abigail replied. "I know both mine and Kat's by heart."

"Okay, well, I'll see you later, Katarina. Thanks for letting me come over. Bye." She and Katarina hugged each other goodbye. Abigail led Alana down the hall to the stairway. Katarina shut the door of the bathroom to get dressed.

"Finally! I was afraid I'd have to eat your slices of bread," Abigail said; she grinned at Katarina from her stool at the counter. Katarina scrunched her nose up at her and headed to the fridge for some milk. She pulled the door open and looked around for it. Ahh, there it was. She grabbed it off the shelf and went to a cabinet to grab a cup. Katarina headed to a stool and sat down. After pouring herself a glassful, she reached over and took two slices of bread from the plate. She couldn't wait to eat it. She loved her grandmother's chocolate banana bread. Granny always put the right amount of chocolate chips in there as well as swirling some cocoa powder into the batter to make the insides swirled. Katarina took a bite and glanced at Abigail.

"So, Abi," she chewed and swallowed, "like Granny's chocolate banana bread?"

"Oh my gosh!! I love it! It's divine! So so so so so good."

"Well, thank you, Abigail; I'm very glad you like it."

Abigail's face turned bright red. Katarina's hand went to her mouth to stop the giggles from coming out. Granny walked into the room. She must have been in the hall or back from seeing Alana to the street.

Katarina ginned slyly and asked her grandmother slowly, "So, Granny, did you walk Alana home? Or did you let her make the walk by herself?"

Granny shook her head and said, "What would I do without you, you silly girl! Just like your mother, you are." She smiled and tousled

Katarina's hair.

Katarina playfully ducked out of the way.

Granny beamed. "You have a bit of your father in you too."

Abigail was laughing silently at Katarina. Katarina could tell; she could see it in her eyes.

Granny headed to the sink to wash the breakfast dishes. She turned the faucet on and checked the water temperature. Once it was hot enough she put the plug in, poured some soap in and began filling the sink up.

"When you're done with your glasses just hand them to me and go take a walk or something."

"All right," Katarina replied around a mouthful of bread. Granny gave her a look for talking with her mouth full.

Abigail smirked at her and said, "Hasn't your mother ever taught you not to talk with your mouth full?"

"Actually, she hasn't."

"Really?" Abigail asked her.

Katarina nodded grinning. "Yup. My dad taught me."

Abigail burst out laughing. She was laughing so hard she almost fell off her chair. Granny glanced at the two of them and rolled her eyes. She walked over to the counter and took their glasses.

"Would you two shoo! Out of my kitchen."

The girls ran out, giggling. They headed for the patio door in the living room. Katarina shoved it open and they went tumbling outside. Abigail fell onto the ground. She was laughing so hard. Katarina sat down on the ground and started laughing at Abigail, who was still laughing at what Katarina had said. The girls couldn't stop laughing. What Katarina had said really wasn't that funny and it wouldn't have been to anyone else, but to Abigail it just struck as hysterical. Katarina always laughed when Abigail laughed because Abigail had a very contagious laugh, which usually made anyone in the room start laughing even if they had no idea why.

"Dudes, you're disturbin' the peace, man."

The girls shot up in surprise; the laughter stopped. Abigail looked around wildly to see who had just spoken. She turned to Katarina and hissed at her, "Who was that?"

Katarina didn't answer; she was staring at the far side of the yard with a small smile on her face. Abigail turned and looked where Katarina was looking. What she saw automatically made her raise her eyebrows. Sort of lounging on the opposite side of the fence was a boy who looked to be fifteen or so. He looked vaguely familiar. Maybe he was at the picnic last night or, probably, at the party last Saturday. His hair, hanging down in his eyes, was the color of a bonfire. At least that's what it made Abigail think of. She snorted. Abigail couldn't see what color his eyes were. The kid looked tall and on the thinner side, and his face looked rather tan.

"He did." Katarina breathed.

Abigail snorted again.

"What's your name?" Katarina asked, standing up. Abigail stood up next to her.

"My name's Liam. What's yours?" Liam spoke lazily, as if he hadn't a care in the world. Katarina smiled.

"I like that name. My name is Katarina."

"Are you Mr. and Mrs. Jones' granddaughter? I think I've seen you here before." There was that lazy voice again.

Abigail rolled her eyes.

"Yeah. Around the holidays usually."

"Who's your friend?" He swung his gaze over to Abigail. He smiled faintly.

Abigail nodded back at him, trying to look polite. Liam actually looked nice when he smiled.

"Oh, this is my best friend, Abigail."

"Hey," he said offhandedly.

"Hey," she replied just as offhandedly. Abigail turned to Katarina and tapped her on the arm.

"Weren't we going to go for a walk?" she spoke in a lowered voice, glancing at Liam lounging on the fence.

He smiled at her politely.

Katarina snapped out of it and turned to Abigail. “You are right; we were.” She turned back to Liam. “We’ll see you later.”

“Yeah, see you later,” Abigail said to him, using his lazy voice.

“Bye, dudes.”

“I like the term “dudettes” better,” Abigail shot back over her shoulder as they walked around the corner of the garage.

Liam shouted back, for once not talking in his lazy voice, “It isn’t as catchy, man!”

“Whatever!” Abigail yelled back. They headed to the garage to get bikes, with their usual unspoken decision to do something. Katarina flipped up the cover and typed the code in. The garage door opened. She went to the back and pulled out two bikes. She pushed one towards Abigail, who caught it.

“Here; you can use Therese’s bike. We use them when we come to visit in the summer.”

“Cool.” Abigail looked it over. All she would have to do was raise the seat a smidgen. She was only a tad taller than Therese, but she was much shorter than Katarina. But she didn’t mind being shorter. She pushed the bike out of the garage, followed by Katarina.

Katarina hopped onto her bike and placed her feet onto the ground so she would stay put. She looked at Abigail. “Ready?”

Abigail raised the seat up and then pushed the lever back so the seat wouldn’t move. “Now

I am." She hopped onto her bike and looked to Katarina to lead the way. "This is your grandparents' neighborhood, you know the area, you lead."

Katarina pushed off and started peddling down the driveway. "I don't know it completely."

"Well, you know it better than I do. I've never been here before."

"Fine." Katarina turned right at the end of the driveway and headed up the hill. Abigail peddled to catch up.

"I just thought of a place I want to show you. I'm sure my mom won't mind. She took me here the first time when I was five and I had just broken my arm. I told her that everyone was being mean to me, when it was just me being crabby because my arm hurt."

"You never told me you broke your arm?" It was more of a question than a statement.

"Oh, I didn't? I've also broken my leg."

"When!?" Abigail asked, puffing as she pedaled hard to get up the hill.

"Oh, I'm just joking. I've never broken my leg." Katarina smiled.

"I've known you for–how many years?–and I never knew you broke your arm. How'd you ever break it?" she asked, slowing down next to Katarina as they came to a stop sign. They glanced back and forth and then pedaled across.

"Um, I don't really remember. It might have

been when Benedict shoved me and I fell down the stairs."

"Yeesh. What was wrong with that kid?"

"I honestly have no idea," Katarina said in response. "Here; we turn here."

A few minutes back they had passed the last house and were starting to just see trees on either side of them. Katarina stopped and hopped off her bike. Abigail skidded to a stop and fell off.

"Careful there," Katarina said as she held her bike up. Abigail stood up and wiped the dirt off her pants and her hands.

"Do we just leave the bikes here?"

"No. We put them right here." Katarina pushed her bike into the trees a bit and looked around until she spotted a patch of tangled brush. "Right here." She laid her bike on the ground and started to remove the branches. Abigail saw that the brambles covered up a hole large enough to put two bikes in it.

"My mom told me last year that it's not completely necessary to do this, but I remember when we first rode our bikes here when I was like six I think she said it added to the mysteriousness to hide them."

"Cool," Abigail said. Katarina pushed her bike into the hole and then turned to get Abigail's and pushed it in there as well. With Abigail's help, Katarina took the branches and covered the hole up again–so well that you could hardly tell they were there.

Starting off again, Katarina led Abigail through a twisted maze of overhanging trees, tangled brush, and weeds, as well as lots of weeping willows. The forest was silent except for their noise and an occasional bird call. Finally Katarina pushed her way through the last tree. She stood tall and proud and looked around at the clearing. It was a relatively large one. You couldn't see the sky because of all the branches, but with the sun trying to shine through the branches it gave the spot a greenish look. It was almost fairy like. Abigail looked around and saw an old, wooden table with matching chairs, and there was a bench on the other side. She looked up at the green roof and saw ribbons and scarves hanging down from different branches. When the wind blew it ruffled them, making it look ever so much like a fairy's home.

"Oh, wow," Abigail breathed out. "You put this all together?"

"No, my mom did," Katarina said, smiling, She walked over to the table and ran a finger across it. It was very dirty. "We'll have to wipe the table down. Oh! If you go through that tiny hole there, you'll step right onto the bank of the river."

"Wow. Let's go see it!" Abigail said excitedly.

Katarina took her hand and led her to the hole. They ducked under the branches and pushed through the bushes. Katarina heard a small splash; excitement and happiness surged through her and she dashed through the last barrier between her and the river. She felt a branch graze her arm and felt the sting of the cut. *Ouch*. Bright light. Blueness. Sunshine. Water. The next second, Katarina was standing on the bank of a wide river: a river so perfect it was like you just jumped into your favorite fairy tale. It had those picturesque trees and rocks along the river. There was Katarina's favorite rock out there–that huge one in the middle. Abigail came out behind her and stood quietly in awe, staring at everything. She began to breathe rapidly.

"Oh my gosh. It's all *so* beautiful," Abigail breathed out. She turned to Katarina and smiled. "Thank you so much for showing this to me, Kat."

Katarina smiled back. "How could I keep it from you? Other than my mom and me, you're the only who knows about it. At least to my knowledge you are."

Abigail grinned. "I'm glad."

"Me too."

Katarina knelt down and placed her hand in the water, letting it rush through her fingers. She looked up at Abigail, who stood next to her. "Wouldn't this place look beautiful in autumn?"

"Oh boy, yes!" Abigail squealed. She knelt down next to her best friend.

Katarina sighed and looked back at the river. "Too bad I never make it over here when we come for Thanksgiving. Usually we get here the day before and then leave on Saturday morning, after spending days filled with eating, playing Wii, and watching movies."

Abigail nodded. "Yeah, that's a bummer."

"One time I should make it here. Then I'd call you and describe every little detail to you," Katarina said, standing up.

Abigail grinned and stood up as well. "You better." She winked.

The girls linked arms and walked down the riverbank, looking at everything in silence. It was all just so beautiful, with the deep blue sky above and the turquoise blue river next to them and the green grass and trees around and the flowers of all colors. Katarina stopped and turned to Abigail, her face alight with excitement.

"Let's go wading!"

"Yes, let's!!" Abigail gasped. The two girls kicked off their flip flops and took off running. As they ran, Abigail reached down and was trying to roll her pants up, but it made her trip and fall. Katarina skidded to a halt and went to Abigail.

"That's the second time you've tripped today. A little tipsy, eh?"

"I guess," Abigail said, standing up. She wiped her hands off onto her jeans before leaning down to roll them up as high as possible. She stood up straight. Abigail grinned at Katarina and then grabbed her hand and took off running.

"Woah!" Katarina was yanked along. When she got her balance, she ran after Abigail. They dashed into the water and squealed as it splashed against their ankles. Katarina stepped in deeper and felt the water hit her legs as it rose up and down. Abigail swished her legs around in the water. She moved her leg swiftly through the water and came out, splashing the water against Katarina's legs.

She jumped back and slipped. "Hey!!"

"The first fall for Katarina Rebecca Anderson on this day, Monday, the third of August," Abigail proclaimed while grinning, not even bothering to help her up.

Katarina fell and landed on her bottom in the river, soaking her shorts. "Rats!" She gingerly stood up and looked down at her soaked clothing. "How come you didn't help me up?" She gathered her hair together in her hands to wring out the bottom half of it.

Abigail shrugged and raised her hands in mock defense. "I don't know."

"Well, I think the wise choice would be to go home. We don't need a repeat of last winter," Katarina said, walking to the shore. Abigail followed her.

"Yeah that wouldn't be good. We don't need your mom showing up."

"Exactly."

The girls pushed back through the bushes and Katarina led the way out of her clearing and back through the tangled maze of brush and trees. Katarina winced when a weed got caught on her arm and rubbed across her cut. Abigail tripped and fell again because her foot got tangled in a long, vine-like weed. It seemed to take them longer to get back to their bikes than it took them to get to Katarina's clearing. Finally they broke through the last row of bushes and uncovered their bikes. Soon they were on their way back. The bike riding part only took them a total of ten minutes and then they were turning into Katarina's grandparents' driveway.

Chapter Nine

"Hey, girls!" Gramps called to them from the front yard, where he was watering the plants Granny kept out there.

"Hey, Gramps!" Katarina skidded to a rough stop and jumped off her bike. Abigail came to a less rough halt. The girls stowed their bikes in the garage and hurried inside to find Granny. Granny was sitting on the brown leather couch in the front room. The TV was playing quietly in the background while she read her book. Katarina and Abigail popped their heads around the corner to see what she was doing. Katarina glanced down at Abigail, who was looking up at her. Good. Granny was distracted. The girls slipped stealthily past the doorway. They paused on the other side and sighed in relief.

"All right; let's get upstairs," Katarina whispered to Abigail, who nodded. They hurried across the hallway and pounded up the stairs two at a time. From the front room, Granny heard their footsteps in the hallway and looked up. There was no one there. She smiled and turned back to her book.

"Whew!" The girls flopped onto Katarina's bed in relief. Katarina looked up at the ceiling.

"Good thing Gramps didn't notice my wet clothing."

"Yup. That was close," Abigail responded.

Katarina sat up on one arm and looked over at Abigail. "You can't tell anyone about my place okay? Because no one can know." She flopped back down again and laid her arms over her stomach. "My dad doesn't even know."

"Hey, don't worry. Your secret is safe with me. I will never ever tell a soul," Abigail said, smiling.

Katarina smiled back. "Thanks."

"Now go get changed so we can put our clothing back before lunch."

"All right." Katarina jumped up off the bed and grabbed a new pair of shorts and a black t-shirt off of the piles of clothing and headed to the bathroom.

Abigail sat up and looked around. She liked this room. She wondered if this was the room Katarina slept in every time she came to visit her grandparents. Abigail glanced at the night-stand between their beds. Her phone lay on it next to Katarina's. *Oh! I haven't texted Mom!* She dove over and grabbed her phone. Turning it on, she swished her finger across the screen and clicked on her contacts. She moved her finger on the screen, scrolling through till she found her mom's number and tapped it. A blank screen appeared that she could type a message on. Abigail turned the phone sideways and began typing out a message.

Hi mom! how r u? I am good. I've been having a lot of fun. They had a party for us on sat, and then yesterday was the parish picnic for st. george's. last night our new friend came over. Her name is Alana. She is fun. We hung out last night.
luv u! kisses! <3

She hit send and as she placed her phone down, her eye caught the piece of paper that had Alana's number on it. Abigail grasped her phone again and grabbed the paper with her other hand. Glancing at the paper, she flicked back to her contacts and tapped *New Contact*. She typed in Alana's name and then the number. Katarina walked back in, holding her wet clothing. Abigail glanced up as she put her phone back.

"Here is Alana's number if you want to add it to your contacts." She held the paper out between her thumb and pointer finger. Katarina took it while she tossed her clothes onto her bed. Sitting down, she grabbed her phone and touched the screen. The screen lit up and a picture of her and her little cousins stared back at her. She pulled up her contacts and quickly added Alana. Katarina stuck her phone on her bed and stood up.

"All right; let's get started, Abi!"

Abigail groaned and flopped onto her pillow. "No!"

"Oh, yes!" Katarina grinned and pulled on her arm.

Abigail played along and stood up. "Fine." She dug out the portable speaker from her suitcase and attached her phone to it. She pulled up her browser and searched for an online music website to start her playlist. Katarina's face lit up as a song she liked came on.

"This song is so cool."

"Agreed. Now let's get started on this room."

The girls turned to the room and, to the music, they tackled their clothing, sometimes singing and sometimes just cleaning. Within an hour they were done. Katarina stood up and wiped her forehead.

"Wow. I'm warm."

"Yeah, it's warm in here." Abigail looked at Katarina. "Is the AC on?"

"Are you kidding? Granny always keeps it on during the summer," Katarina responded.

"Okay."

Katarina looked around at the room. It looked as clean as it did when they had arrived on Friday. Well, minus the unmade beds. She pointed to the beds.

"We forgot one thing." She winked at Abigail, who groaned.

"No! Don't make us do that."

Katarina shook her gently. "Nope. We must do it!" Katarina pulled a staggering Abigail to the beds.

Abigail groaned. "No no no no no no! I hate making my bed."

"It's actually not that bad. I've been doing it since I was three."

Abigail laughed sarcastically. "I highly doubt that." She placed her hands on her hips.

"Okay; fine." Katarina crossed her arms. "Maybe since I was five or six."

"Fine."

They pretended to glare at each for a minute, until Abigail looked away and lost the staring contest.

"You lost; now let's make our beds before lunch."

"All right." Abigail made a face and leaned down to tuck the sheets in. Katarina made her bed in record time. Abigail slowly made her bed while Katarina smirked at her behind her back.

"Done!" Abigail turned and grinned. Katarina clapped in praise.

"Yay!" She headed to the door. "Now let's find something to eat."

They hurried out of the room and went flying down the hall. Katarina slid to a stop and stuck her arm out to stop Abigail.

"Wait; stop!" She climbed onto the banister and held on tight.

Abigail grinned. "Can you do that?"

"Why not? I used to do it all the time. Come on."

"Okay." Abigail climbed on next to her and held on tight as well.

Katarina glanced at Abigail. "Ready?"

"You bet."

Katarina pushed off and went sailing down, followed by Abigail. At the bottom, they tumbled off and fell onto the floor.

"Lunch is ready." Granny stepped out of the kitchen to find them sitting on the floor, slightly stunned. Katarina and Abigail jumped to their feet, staggering slightly. Granny placed her hands on her hips and looked at them.

"Why were you on the floor?"

Katarina looked sheepishly at Abigail, who was shifting from one foot to the other.

"Um, nothing." She scrunched her face up into a cat grin.

Granny shook her head. "Don't think I don't know what you just did. I don't approve of young ladies flying down the banister, but your grandfather would say you're never too old to do it."

"Does he still do it?" Katarina asked, grinning.

Granny shot her a look. "If I caught that man flying down the banister, I'd send him to his room, and you know what he'd be doing as I told him to go."

"Yeah. Laughing his head off."

"Exactly; so don't you say anything about flying down banisters to him. You'll be putting ideas in the old boy's head. Understood, girls?" Granny looked at them; her expression was slightly stern. Katarina couldn't help but laugh, but she smothered it by coughing. Granny raised her eyebrows. Katarina put her arms down from covering her mouth. Granny knew her too well.

"Yes ma'am," they replied in unison.

Granny nodded, satisfied. "Good. Now come and have some lunch or it will get cold. Oh, let me get your grandfather." She hurried off to the garage.

The girls stood staring at each and grinned.

"Well, that was interesting," Abigail said as they walked into the kitchen.

"I really don't think she minds us doing it."

"Why?"

"Because we used to do it all the time when we were little. I think she is just scared we'll get hurt. Because that's how I broke my arm."

"Oh." Abigail looked up, puzzled. "I thought you said Benedict shoved you down the stairs."

"Yeah. He was going to send me down the

banister and he accidentally pushed me too hard. I fell off and tumbled down the stairs, and I landed wrong and my arm broke."

"Oh. Ouch." Abigail winced at the thought of falling down stairs like that.

Granny walked in with Gramps. "And that is why I don't like people sliding down banisters."

"Except me," Gramps teased. "She doesn't mind it when I do it."

Granny hit him on the arm and he jumped away, grinning teasingly.

"Ouch!" he rubbed his arm as if it really hurt. Granny rolled her eyes and turned to the girls.

"Take him off my hands this afternoon, will you? I need some more peace and quiet."

"Sure, Granny. We can take him to the mall for some shopping," said Katarina, doing some of her own teasing.

Gramps threw his hands up into the air and groaned. "Oh no! I'm being swamped by teenage girls who only go shopping. I must escape and go golfing!" He picked up the phone on the counter and pretended to dial it. "Hello! Joe! Save me! Too many girls!"

By now Katarina and Abigail were laughing really hard. Gramps set the phone down, chuckling.

"I'm joking. What would you girls like to do today? Fishing? Golfing? Hunting? Woodwork?"

"No!!" they shot down his ideas in an instant.

"Besides, it's not hunting season, Gramps," added Katarina. Gramps took his mug of coffee and sat down next to them. After taking a sip, he turned to Katarina.

"I thought you used to like to fish?"

"Well, it's all right but not my favorite thing to do, sorry." She cracked a smile at him.

Gramps snapped his fingers. "Rats." He winked.

Abigail laughed at him from behind her hand. Katarina shrugged as Granny placed two paper plates in front of the girls. They had a grilled cheese sandwich, some grapes and strawberries, and another slice of the chocolate banana bread from breakfast.

"Eat your lunch before you go do anything like golfing or fishing," Granny said, handing them glasses of lemonade.

Katarina lifted up her sandwich and took a bite. She chewed and swallowed. "This is really good, Granny, but you don't have to cook special things every meal. We're going to be here for a month–it's bound to get tiring."

Granny turned and raised her eyebrows at Katarina. "You think I'd get tired of cooking for my grandkids? Please."

Gramps tapped Katarina on the shoulder. "Yeah don't even mention not cooking for you girls; she won't even hear what you say."

"He's right, you know," Granny said with one

hand on her hip, the other waving the spatula at her.

Abigail held a strawberry by the leaves; she twirled it around. "Are you guys always like this? It's just so funny how much Mrs. Anderson is like you guys."

Katarina jokingly rolled her eyes. "Abi, honey, they are only getting started."

"Okay, so the worst hasn't hit yet?" she asked, grinning. Katarina shook her head vigorously.

"No it has not. Nowhere close."

"And she is right about that," said Gramps, chuckling as he took the plate Granny handed him.

"Would y'all finish up your lunch? I have chores to do."

"Yeah, yeah, yeah; we'll get there eventually," Katarina said lazily. She ducked out of the way of Granny's swat and fell off her chair.

"Besides we just started!" Gramps complained.

Abigail snorted with laughter and got off her chair to help Katarina up off the floor.

Gramps chuckled and shook his head at their antics. He stood up and stretched. "I think it *is* time we left your grandmother to clean so that we don't have anyone else falling out of their chairs. Bring your plates with you, girls."

Abigail helped Katarina up from the floor. Granny shooed them all out of the kitchen and told them not to come back till later.

Chapter Ten

"Let's play a board game," Abigail suggested. The girls were sitting on the couches in the den, waiting for Gramps to come back.

"Okay!" Katarina jumped up and led the way into the hallway to the game closet. She turned the knob and pulled the door open. Katarina stepped into the closet.

"What should we play?" Her voice was muffled slightly as she looked up at the shelves loaded with games. Abigail thought for a moment.

"Hmm." She leaned against the wall and thought hard. "Well, what about *Clue*?"

Katarina whipped around; her face was filled with excitement. "Yes!!"

Gramps walked into the hallway. "What are we doing, girls?"

"We're going to play *Clue*; want to join us?"

"Sure, why not," Gramps said; he smiled. "I always love a good game of *Clue*."

"Good!" Katarina lifted up some games and pulled out the *Clue* box. The girls headed back to the den. Katarina plopped the box onto the coffee table and Abigail yanked the lid off.

"I claim Mrs. Peacock!" She grabbed the pawn and waved it triumphantly in the air above their heads. Katarina grabbed Ms. Scarlet.

"Haha! I'm Ms. Scarlet so that means I go first! Wohoo!" Katarina squealed. Gramps looked at each of the pawns and then decided on Mr. Green. Abigail spread the board out while Katarina shuffled and dealt the cards out to everyone. She took the slightly ripped "Confidential" envelope and placed one card of each category into it. Katarina ceremoniously placed the envelope onto the center of the board. Abigail placed the extra pawns onto the board at their respective places and then randomly placed the weapons in rooms.

"Okay, are we ready?" she asked, picking up her cards to see which ones she got so she could mark them down on the sheet.

Katarina picked up her pen and quickly marked off hers. "I'm ready."

"Me too."

"Me three," Abigail chimed in. Katarina took up the dice and shook it. The dice fell and bounced onto the table. Katarina read the numbers. Four and five: nine. She looked at the board and found her pawn. She counted the squares; her finger moved across each space. Katarina took her pawn and placed it on the ninth place. She made it into the Lounge. Now she could accuse someone. *Hmm*. She moved her hand around over the board. Abigail kicked her leg, impatiently.

"Hey!"

"Just move!" Abigail urged, quickly grinning like a cat. Katarina smirked and turned back to the board and glanced at her cards. She picked up Colonel Mustard and placed him in the Lounge.

"I suggest Colonel Mustard in the Lounge with the knife." She found the knife and plopped it into the Lounge. "Anybody?" Gramps, who was to the left of her, glanced at his slip of paper and then shook his head.

"Not a thing, Kitty-Kat."

Katarina mimicked her friend's cat grin and turned to Abigail, who nodded yes.

"I've got one."

"Okay; let's see the card." Abigail leaned across the table to Katarina, blocking her cards from Gramps. She showed her the card for the knife. Katarina nodded and turned to her slip of paper.

"Thank you!" she said as she checked it off. "Your turn, Gramps."

"Okay, let's see what we have here." Gramps looked at his cards, at the board, and then he grabbed the dice and rolled it. The dice bounced loudly onto the table. A six and three. He calculated the move and then decided to take his pawn to the Ballroom. Gramps moved his character eight spaces and plunked him into the room. Then he thought, looked at his cards then the board, then he thought again. Gramps made his move. He plunked the candlestick into the room and then he spoke.

"I suggest Mr. Green, in the Ballroom, with the candlestick." He sat back triumphantly as both Katarina and Abigail checked their cards and then shook their heads no.

"I don't have anything."

"Neither do I," Katarina said. Gramps grinned cheekily at them. Abigail glanced at Katarina with questioning eyebrows. Katarina just rolled her eyes. *Gramps is up to his old tricks*, she thought. *I bet he thinks he's going to win this game, but I'll show him.* She leveled her eyes at her grandfather and smiled slightly.

"Okay, my turn." Abigail squinted and cracked her fingers. She took up the dice and shook them hard. One and Two. Three. Abigail snapped her fingers.

"Darn it! Lousy roll." She picked up Mrs. Peacock and waved her around above the board. She moved her three spaces forward. Done. Abigail sat back against the couch, hands behind her head.

"It's a-your turn, Kat Woman." Katarina gathered up the dice and rolled them, hard. She let go of them and they flew all over the table. Abigail held out her hand at the last moment, stopping one of the die.

"Ooh, that was close. You would have had to reroll them." Abigail smirked. Katarina ignored her as she gathered up both of them. She read the amount of dots. Two and three.

"See, I got a lousy roll too." She giggled at Abigail. Katarina turned and studied the board. She moved her pawn across the hallway on the board.

"I'm going to the Dining Room." She placed Ms Scarlet into the Dining Room. She looked at her slip of paper before suggesting someone. She then glanced at Gramps. He had on his "Game Face;" in other words, he was trying his hardest to look incredibly innocent while really he was processing everything super quickly in his brain. Katarina scrunched her eyes up, making them super small–so small she could hardly see out of them. Gramps looked up to see her staring at him like that. He started to chuckle. A deep chuckle.

"Yes, Kitty-kat?"

"Oh nothing, Gramps," she responded airily.

"Whatever you say, honey dew melon," he

said winking at her merrily. Katarina groaned.

"Gramps! You know I don't like that nickname!"

"Well, what about 'Watermelon' or 'Cantaloupe' or 'Apple Pie' or 'Cheesecake' or 'Pumpkin'–or make that 'Pumpkin Pie'? Oh, what about 'Smoothie'?"

By now Katarina was groaning and trying so hard not to laugh she was almost choking from the effort. Abigail was lying on the couch dying with laughter. She clutched her stomach; she was laughing so hard it hurt.

"No! No! No! No food names! Please!" Katarina chortled with laughter. Gramps' eyes twinkled with laughter; his face was all alight, and he was grinning, too.

"Well what about 'Fluffy'? Or 'Troublemaker' or 'Sparkler' or 'Piggy' or 'Hanalooloobalooloo'?"

"Stop it! You are killing me!" Abigail shouted. Katarina was laughing so hard she was making no noise at all. She gasped for breath.

"Please stop, Gramps; I can't breathe!"

"Okay, fine, Snickerdoodle." Gramps chuckled at them. "Whose turn was it?"

"I think.... Hahaha!.....it was...hehehe!!.....my t-t-turn!" Katarina gasped for breath.

"Okay; now go," he said.

Abigail finally pulled herself together and sat up, ready to continue the game. Katarina sighed and thought of who to suggest.

"Okay; got it. I suggest Mrs. Peacock in the Dining Room, with the lead pipe." She sat back to wait. Gramps looked at his cards and shook his head thoughtfully. Abigail looked at her slip of paper and shook her head as well. Katarina smiled triumphantly.

"Your turn, Gramps," she said, grinning with satisfaction. "Let's see you win this game, all right?" Her dark, brown eyes sparkled mischieviously.

"You bet I'll win this game."

"Of course; don't you always win these types of games?"

"I wouldn't be surprised if you did." Abigail snorted.

"Yes, I always do win these types of games." He smiled at her as he prepared to roll the dice for his turn.

"Okay, let's see." He thoughtfully studied the board; thoughtfully but less triumphantly. Gramps rolled the dice. He got four and three. Seven. He took his pawn, Mr. Green, and moved him seven spaces to the Kitchen.

"I suggest Professor Plum in the Kitchen with the wrench." He sat with his elbows on his knees waiting for them to check. Abigail glanced at her cards and pulled one out, cheerfully.

"I have a card!" She held it out to Gramps, making sure Katarina could not see it. Katarina grinned, *Oh yeah! He didn't fool us this time.* She glanced at the large picture window behind Gramps.

"Hey! It's raining!" She jumped up from the couch and hurried to the window. She leaned against it. In seconds, Abigail was next to her.

"It looks so pretty!"

Gramps turned around in his chair to look at them. "How can it look pretty?" He glanced at the gray, rainy sky.

Katarina responded, still watching the rain, "Don't you see? Look at the silvery clouds and the lemon lightning. Imagine thunder, if you could see it, being a dark golden color and the rain a beautiful cerulean. Now put that all together. Don't you see a beautiful image?"

"I do," Abigail answered all dreamy like.

Gramps chuckled and shook his head, muttering, "Girls and their imaginations."

"Let's go outside, Kat!" Abigail grabbed Katarina's arms excitedly. Katarina gasped.

"Yes, let's!"

"Hey! Whoa, whoa! What about our game?" Gramps said, standing up.

Katarina gave him her cat grin, scrunching her eyes up extra tight.

"What's the point of a game if you can't just randomly interrupt it when you want to go run out in the rain?"

"She has a point." Abigail crossed her arms,

standing with her feet apart. Gramps waved his hand.

"Fine, fine, go get soaked running and jumping around in the 'Picture of life,'" he said, shaking his head good-naturedly, mimicking Katarina on the last words.

The girls hurried to the hallway. Kicking off their flip flops, they ran into the large entryway. Katarina yanked the oak door open and dashed outside. Abigail dashed out after her. They jumped off the porch, not even bothering to use the steps. Katarina shrieked when she felt the rain pounding down on her. It felt beautiful–wonderful–perfectly unimaginable.

Abigail spun around, laughing with joy. Katarina saw that Abigail's hair was already soaked and her clothes were soaked too. She reached her hand up and felt her hair; it was sopping wet, too. She glanced down at her clothing; they were wet as well. Yahoo! Katarina spun around, super-duper fast. She kept spinning and spinning. When she stopped, the world spun rapidly around her. The rain, the sky, the front yard, and the house had all turned into a spinning mush. Katarina plopped down on the grass, feeling very dizzy but very happy and very much alive. Abigail stopped turning and fell down next to her.

"It's so beautifully wet!" Abigail cried out, ecstatic.

Katarina shouted loudly, "It's more than

beautiful; it's marvelous, dazzling, elegant, fascinating, bewitching, ravishing, gorgeous, stunning, superb, magnificent, sublime, and I'm running out of words to describe such works of God." She stopped for breath.

"It's out of this world! Shimmery!" Abigail hollered.

"Wahoo!" Katarina whooped with joy as she jumped up again, fully un-dizzied, as she would put it. She turned and gripped Abigail's hands and yanked her up.

"Yodel le he hoo!" Abigail screamed.

Katarina burst out laughing. "Now that was random."

"That's me: Queen of Random." She did a little dance while swinging her hips. Katarina doubled up with laughter. Abigail suddenly stopped,

"Hey! Let's go running!"

"Where?" Katarina asked, standing up straight. She wiped her forehead to no avail; it was still raining hard. Abigail pointed behind Katarina. Katarina turned around.

"There."

"Oh!" Katarina suddenly remembered that there was only one house next to her grandparents and that was to the left of them. To the right was the park: the park that had been the site of many afternoons of play for Katarina and her siblings when they were younger. She turned her head and looked at Abigail and grinned.

"Let's go."

The two girls took off running. They jumped over a patch of flowers. Katarina almost stumbled but caught herself. They climbed over the fence that separated the Jones's yard from the deserted park. It was not deserted for long, because as soon as they climbed off the wood fence the girls filled it with screams and yells of joy as well as the pounding of feet. Katarina ran as fast as she could. Feeling the rain run off of her seemed like a whole new feeling, yet it was a feeling she experienced every time it rained and she was allowed outside in it. It left her filled with joy and anticipation as well as the feeling of being alive again. She glanced over at Abigail who was keeping pace with Katarina. Abigail's face was alive. She looked like a little girl on her birthday: excited and very much independent. Abigail turned and looked at Katarina; she grinned.

Katarina stumbled to a stop and fell onto an abandoned bench. Abigail fell down onto it next to her. The girls were both breathing heavily.

"That was so much fun," Katarina gasped out, joyfully.

Abigail nodded breathlessly. "I am totally in agreement with you there." She slapped her leg. "Ouch," Abigail said as an afterthought. There was a moment of silence, then the girls exploded into giggles. Katarina almost fell off the bench, she was giggling so hard. Abigail leaned back against the bench and slouched. Her whole body was shaking with laughter.

Once the laughter had subsided and the girls had calmed down enough to talk normally, Katarina sighed.

"You know, we laugh way too much."

"True. But laughter is the best medicine out there," Abigail pointed out.

Katarina nodded her head thoughtfully and responded, "That is true; you do have a point. Laughter *is* the absolute best medicine in this whole beautiful wide world."

"Total agreement," Abigail murmured contentedly.

The girls sat in silence, feeling the rain drip down on them. Katarina felt extremely peaceful and very happy. The rain had slackened to a steady drizzle. Not the usual dreary and miserable kind of drizzle, but the kind that falls when you are feeling happy and content. It was a beautiful, peaceful drizzle. Abigail sighed peacefully.

"It's so pretty out."

"Even with those flowers that are slightly smashed, right?" Katarina teased, pointing to the patch of dahlias at the base of the tree closest to them. Abigail punched her in the arm.

"Hey!" Katarina yelped, punching her back. She missed Abigail's arm by an inch.

Abigail jumped up from the bench and took off running back to the house. Katarina dove after her.

"I'm going to get you back!" she hollered after Abigail's fleeing form.

"Haha! No, you won't!" Abigail shouted back over her shoulder.

Abigail climbed over the fence as quickly as she could, but Katarina had caught up and was climbing over the fence as Abigail was running away. Katarina jumped down and flew after her best friend. Abigail skirted around a flower bed; it slowed her down a bit. Katarina wildly jumped over the bed and was inches from Abigail. She reached out to grab Abigail's shirt just as Abigail slammed into the front door, full force. Katarina skidded to a stop on the front porch. Tripping on the doormat, she fell into Abigail as Abigail turned the door knob. They fell onto the front hall floor. Their clothes dripped onto the floor, creating a puddle almost right away.

Granny walked into the front hall to find out the source of the commotion. She was slightly shocked when she saw the girls on the floor. Granny placed her hands on her hips and stared down at the girls. Katarina and Abigail stood up, giggling; they still hadn't noticed Granny standing in front of them.

"Totally beat you that time," Abigail boasted, grinning.

"Yes, you did!"

They turned and saw Granny; they fell silent.

If this was a movie, this would be one of those moments where you would hear crickets chirping.

"Hi, Granny," Katarina said, feeling awkward.

Granny crossed her arms; she looked stern. Katarina and Abigail exchanged looks.

"Go change your clothes and watch a movie or play Wii. I don't know; just do something inside."

"Yes, ma'am," they muttered quietly. They turned and headed for the stairs.

Chapter Eleven

The days passed quickly. Some were filled with fun and laughter, others with peaceful quietness at home. The girls had already done so much; they couldn't believe there was anything else to do. They had had two more sleepovers with Alana and had gotten to know Liam. They found out that he had three older brothers and an older sister and that he hardly ever talked without that lazy tone of voice. At night, on days that they saw him, they would imitate him to the best of their abilities. It made them laugh very hard. Katarina and Abigail knew that they would always be friends with Alana even after they went home. She was just like them and fit right in. Some of their wild antics caused Granny to worry about one of them getting hurt–so much that Gramps would have to talk to them and then they would calm down a bit; well, at least until their next idea.

'Hey Mum! How're you doing? What's new?'

Katarina hit the send button; she flopped back onto her bed with a sigh. They were all taking a break. Granny was taking a nap; she had said she needed one after spending a day at the fair with them pulling her everywhere. She had laughed, though. Abigail lounged on her stomach while on Gramps' laptop. Katarina closed her eyes for a moment.

Her phone buzzed, pulling Katarina out of her dream. She sat up and took her phone. She glanced at the time and squawked in surprise. Abigail looked up at her, startled.

"What?"

"It's been half an hour since I closed my eyes!"

Abigail giggled, "Yep." She turned back to her screen as Katarina read the text from her mother.

Hello, precious i am doing wonderful. How're you? Tonight is Dad's and my date :) We miss you all. Dad says hi and so do your brother and sisters. love always.

Katarina smiled happily and quickly typed out her response.

I am doing great. So is Abi, and gramps

and granny. Ooo! yay! you guys better have fun! i miss you all too. Tell them i said hi. Love ya.'

She hit reply and placed her phone on the bed. She climbed over to Abigail's bed and playfully shoved her over.

"Hey!" Abigail protested but moved over anyway.

"What ya doin'?"

"Just lookin' at Facebook."

"Let's look at all the pictures we have taken," Katarina suggested.

"Okay!" Abigail went to her page and clicked on *"Photos"*. A ton of albums popped up. She searched for the one titled: "Just Keep Swimmin'!". Abigail grinned and clicked on it. Then she clicked on the first photo. It was of the two girls in front of "Nicole's Hair Styles." That had been the first of Granny's surprises, back at the beginning of their visit. They had their mouths hanging open in shock. It was a posed photo because Granny hadn't thought to take one till Abigail had suggested it. Katarina giggled; it was such a weird photo.

"Look at your hair!" She pointed at the photo. "Good thing we were at a hair salon."

Abigail slapped her and giggled. "Very funny."

They continued to look at the photos until they came to the pictures from the other day when they were out swimming in the pool. Abigail had taken the camera from Granny and had gone wild with it, taking a ton of photos of Katarina. Katarina's favorite was a close up of her face; her hair was blowing back in the hot wind, she was grinning, and her brown eyes were sparkling. After that, the rest of the photos were wacky ones. They passed some from last night's barbeque that Liam's family had hosted for all the neighbors on the block. Next were the photos from that day's visit to the fair. They spent an hour looking at all the photos and then going back to decide which ones were their favorites.

"Girls?" Granny leaned inside the doorway. They looked up from the computer screen at her.

"It's dinner time."

"Okie dokes." Abigail closed the laptop and put it on the nightstand. They got off the bed and left the room. Abigail and Katarina walked softly into the kitchen behind Granny. The oak dining table was already set. The plates were centered in their spots, and the silverware was not the normal, everyday utensils but the company silver. At each spot was a tall glass of raspberry lemonade. In the center of the table was large bouquet of daffodils, hydrangeas, roses, lilies, and cornflowers.

"Wow, Granny. It's pretty," Katarina breathed out.

Granny smiled and replied, "Thank you,

dear. I thought we could use a change from the ordinary."

Gramps came into the room and they all sat down to a delicious dinner of roast chicken, mixed vegetables, a tossed salad, and garlic noodles.

Later that evening, after dark, a couple drove through the darkened streets of the outskirts of Boston, Massachusetts, spotted with the light from the street lamps. They sat quietly together after an evening of enjoyment. The man turned the car on to the next street. Suddenly, a car shot around the corner. Not a moment later, the night, which was as silent as a mouse, was shattered. The screeching of tires echoed loudly throughout the neighborhood. As the man swerved to miss the car he crashed into a telephone pole. The woman in the car screamed and the man yelled; their screams were cut short. Lights in the houses that lined the street were switched on. Several doors opened and banged shut. Soon the street was filled with people. A man bent down and looked into the banged up and ruined car. He saw the couple in the front seat. With all his strength, he yanked open the bent passenger door.

"Oh my gosh!" he breathed in shock. He felt the woman's pulse. Nothing. His hand went to her nose to see if he could feel her breath. Again, nothing. He hurried to the other door that someone had just yanked open. He did the same to the man. Nothing. Nothing at all. There were suddenly loud sirens. Someone had called an ambulance or the police. Someone gasped loudly behind the man. He spun about; it was his neighbor. Her face was ashen, and she held her hand over her mouth.

"No way! Oh my gosh!" She burst into tears. The man led her away as the police stepped up to the car. After a quick search, finding the couple dead, the cop found the man's wallet and the woman's purse. He took out their driver's licenses. After reading the names on the licenses, he turned to the crowd and spoke up loudly.

"Does anyone know this couple?"

The teary-eyed woman stepped forward again. "I do. I am their friend, Andrea Dunham."

"Sergeant Andys. We can ride in my car if you would direct me there."

As the two headed to his patrol car, Andys called the station to have them send someone to take care of the situation while he went to the couple's house.

Andys pulled up in front of a stately house.

"Here we are; this is it. The older children should all be home," Andrea Dunham spoke up. They disembarked from the car and walked up the flower-lined walkway. Andys rang the doorbell hard. Moments later, the door was open by a young lady.

"Hello? Mrs. Dunham, what are you doing here at this time of night? Mom and Dad are out. Oh, who are you?" Emiliana asked both adults with a tone of surprise and then curiosity. Andys spoke up.

"I'm Sergeant Andys. I have, uh, dreadful news. I am sorry to have to tell you this, but," he spoke with sympathy, "your parents were in a accident moments ago and I'm sorry to say they are no longer with us."

Emiliana's rosy face went from curious to confused, to shocked and speechlessly ashen. Her emerald eyes filled with tears. "What?" she squeaked out.

"Em? Who's here?" Antoinette walked into the front hall. Emiliana turned and fled down the hall. Antoinette, seeing them, walked forwards to the door, confused. "What's going on?"

Mrs. Dunham spoke gently, "Your parents are dead, Antoinette, dear."

"Oh." Antoinette spoke softly. "Thank you for telling us." Nodding goodbye to them, she shut the door.

Antoinette walked back into the living room. Emiliana was curled up, sobbing, in their father's favorite chair. Therese and Benedict were trying to find out what was wrong; this was strange behavior for Em.

"Mummy and Daddy are dead," Antoinette spoke bluntly. The two turned in surprise. Benedict opened his mouth and then closed it again. Therese burst into tears. She turned to Benedict, who wrapped his arms around his younger sister. Antoinette went over and pushed her way into the chair with Emiliana. The room was quiet except for Therese and Emiliana's crying. For a moment no one spoke; they just tried to grasp what had just happened.

"Does Katarina know yet?" Benedict asked, his voice all husky. Antoinette gasped and jumped up.

"I forgot about her! She doesn't know!" Antoinette grabbed the phone and quickly dialed her grandparents' house.

The phone rang, echoing loudly throughout the house. It woke everyone up. Gramps sat up in bed and picked the phone up.

"Hello?" he spoke, sounding sleepy. "Antoinette? What is it? Why are you calling so late at night?"

Granny glanced at the clock. The red numbers shone brightly back at her: 10:58 p.m. Gramps' face went as white as ash as Antoinette told him.

"Mum and Dad are dead. They died in a car

crash on the way home from their date."

Gramps could hear the tears in his granddaughter's voice. He took a deep breath and spoke into the phone. "They are what?" he said, his voice tight and choked.

"They died. Gramps; they're aren't coming home ever again!"

"Dear? What's wrong? What happened?" Granny asked hesitantly, placing her hand on her husband's arm.

Gramps spoke quietly and reassuringly into the phone. "Don't worry darling, we'll catch a flight first thing in the morning. I will tell them. Good bye. I love you. God bless." He hung up the phone and stared into his wife's eyes. She looked worried.

"What happened?"

He sighed, placing his arm around her and squeezing her tightly. "We have lost Sarah and David." He felt her stiffen in his arms and heard the sound of her crying.

Gramps cleared his throat. "Darling? We need to tell Katarina. Now; we can't just not tell her."

"Of course. I'll go get them." Granny got up and headed down to the hall to the girls' room. She stood in the doorway.

"Katarina, honey?"

"Yes, Granny, what is it?"

"Please come with me. Abigail, you too; you

should know as well." Granny waited for

them to get out of bed and follow her to the bedroom. In the light of the lamp, Katarina saw tears glistening on her grandparents' faces.

"What is it?" she asked, worried.

"Your." Granny stopped.

Gramps placed his hand on Granny's arm. "Your mother and father are dead."

"No they aren't! They were just out on their date–" Katarina stopped and stared.

When she spoke again, her voice was empty. "How?"

"In a car crash," Gramps answered. Granny held out her arms beckoning to Katarina. Katarina shook her head.

"No, no." She turned and ran from the room. Abigail, shaken from the news, tried to stop her, but Katarina brushed her away. Granny covered her face with her hands. Gramps looked at Abigail. His look told her to go after Katarina.

Abigail hurried down the hall and looked into their room. The hump on Katarina's mattress gave away Katarina's location. She walked over to her best friend, thinking–thinking about how rapidly the day had changed. It had been a wonderful day, full of fun and laughter, and now this. It was hard to comprehend how God could allow such a thing to happen. Abigail sat down next to Katarina. She thought of the other day in the pool. They had been scheming how

Katarina could change the world. It had been a happy day. Abigail looked at the girl lying curled up next to her and thought, *Does she still have the will and the spirit to change the world now?* She sighed. *Yes, she's still that girl,* a voice in her head whispered.

"Katarina?"

"Go away" came the gruff and muffled reply.

Chapter Twelve

The next morning, everyone woke up early. Granny and Abigail took care of packing up the girls' clothing. All Katarina did was get up, eat breakfast, and go sit outside on the porch. She hadn't spoken a word since last night. Abigail watched her silently, but her eyes were full of worry. Gramps went outside and stood behind Katarina for a few minutes before speaking.

"Honey? Would you like to come with me to see if Mr. D'Heere can drive us to the airport?"

"No, Gramps." Her back was stiff and her reply was stony.

Gramps' shoulders slumped and he sighed heavily. "All right." He walked past her down the steps and headed up the street a few houses. Katarina reached her hand up and slowly brushed a tear away. She stood up and stalked into the house. Abigail was running down the stairs. She slowed to a stop, her hand resting on the railing.

"Hey." She smiled. Katarina looked at her as if she was some type of alien.

Distantly, she responded, "Hey." Katarina turned and walked away without another word.

The smile slipped off Abigail's face. Her heart felt like it was breaking. She couldn't stand her best friend being brought so low in sadness. She turned and ran back upstairs. Granny came out of her bedroom, carrying two suitcases: one for her and one for Gramps. She stopped when she saw Abigail's face.

"What is it, honey?"

"I-I can't stand seeing Kat like this! It's too much!" She burst into tears. Her shoulders shook. Granny set the suitcases down and came over and hugged her tightly.

"It's going to be okay, Abigail. It's going to be super tough for Katarina and her brother and sisters. But what you need to do is be there for Katarina. And when she is ready she will open up and you, as her best friend, should be one of the first ones by her side, okay?"

"Okay." Abigail whimpered.

Granny rubbed Abigail's back gently. "It may be a while. It may be weeks–months–years. But no matter how long it takes for her to be ready, you be there for her every day, every month, and every year." Granny placed her hands on Abigail's shoulders and looked into the young girl's eyes. "You are her best friend, her sister, her angel. She needs you. She needs you to understand her. She needs you to love her, protect her, and help her along this path. Oh." Granny squeezed Abigail as Abigail began to sob again.

"I promise! I won't ever leave. I will be her best friend. I will never ever leave her! I promise!" Abigail sobbed brokenly, gasping for breath.

"Shh; shh. I know. I know you will."

"Darling? We need to be ready to leave now. Josh D'Heere is going to drive us to the airport so we can leave the cars here. I told him to be here to pick us up at 7 o'clock and it's 6:50 now." Gramps stood at the top of the stairs. His face was drawn and his shoulders sagged.

Granny nodded and gave Abigail an extra tight squeeze. "Why don't you go and get yours and Katarina's suitcases and bring them downstairs, okay?"

"Yes, ma'am." Abigail sniffed and wiped her nose with her sleeve. She scrubbed her face dry with her hands and then headed down the hall to the girls' room.

Granny turned to Gramps. "Where's Katarina?"

He shrugged, "I think she's in the living room. Want me to find her?"

"No." Granny shook her head. "I'll see if she's there." She walked to the head of the stairs where Gramps stood. He smiled weakly at his wife. Granny sighed and bit her lip. Her chin quivered.

"Now you don't start crying. I thought you were just telling Abigail to be strong. You need to be strong for Katarina. You can cry tonight, okay?" Granny took a deep breath and nodded. She headed down the stairs and went to the living room. Katarina lay on the couch, staring at the ceiling, crying silently. Granny stood and watched her for a moment. She could see Katarina's shoulders shaking with each silent, wrenching sob. Katarina pounded the couch with her fist.

She whispered faintly. "Why? Why?" Katarina felt herself gently lifted and wrapped into a warm hug. She opened her eyes weakly. Katarina leaned her head against Granny's shoulder and cried. They sat together, hugging each other for a few minutes, until they heard Abigail and Gramps come down the stairs and go to the front hall.

"We have to leave now, Kat," Granny whispered.

"But I'm not packed," Katarina weakly protested. Granny helped her up and handed her a tissue.

"Abigail and I took care of that; we're all ready to leave now."

"Oh."

Granny took Katarina's hand and led her into the front hall, where Gramps and Abigail silently waited. Abigail went over to Katarina and placed her hand on Katarina's shoulder. Katarina smiled softly. Abigail slipped her hand into Katarina's and squeezed. Gramps and Granny took the suitcases and they all headed out of the house. Leading Katarina, Abigail followed them to Mr. D'Heere's car. Before getting into the car Gramps returned to lock and shut the door. Back at the car, Gramps climbed into the passenger side while Granny and the girls got into the back. Abigail shut the door and Mr. D'Heere backed out of the driveway. They headed to the airport.

The plane landed in Boston and the passengers all got off and retrieved their bags and headed to the pick-up zone. Gramps and Granny led the way toward where Mrs. Dunham was waiting to pick them up. Abigail followed closely behind with Katarina. Each girl pulled their suitcase behind them.

"There's my mom," Abigail said, pointing to the white SUV that was pulling up to the curb. Gramps waved to her. Mrs. Dunham saw him and pulled to a stop and got out. She hugged Abigail tightly and then turned to Katarina and hugged her just as tightly. Mrs. Dunham opened the trunk and helped Gramps put the suitcases in the back of the car. Everyone climbed in and they drove away.

Mrs. Dunham pulled up to the Anderson's silent house. Gramps and Granny climbed out of the car, but Katarina couldn't move. The tears ran down her cheeks. She didn't want to go inside; she knew her parents would not come to welcome her home. Mrs. Dunham looked worried.

"Do you want Abigail to go with you, Katarina?"

"Sure," Katarina said, all choked up. Abigail unbuckled herself and helped Katarina out of the car. Abigail held Katarina's hand tightly as they walked up to the door. Granny rang the doorbell and almost instantly the door opened. Therese stood in the doorway.

"You're here!" she cried out. She flew towards Gramps. He hugged her tightly. Then Therese hugged Granny. "Come in." Therese beckoned. Her pale, sad face was only slightly more cheerful now that they had arrived. She led them into the kitchen, where the others were.

"You got here!" Emiliana cried out, running towards them. Granny wrapped her in a large, loving hug.

"Yes, we're here." She whispered in Emiliana's ear. Gramps hugged Antoinette tightly. Katarina just stood there, not moving. Her face was stony. Benedict was watching her. His eyes looked worried as he hugged his sister. Katarina shrugged him off. Abigail reached out to grab her hand, but Katarina brushed past and headed out of the room. Her siblings stared at her retreating figure. Therese sniffed and wiped her eyes, brushing a strand of hair out of the way.

"Is she okay?"

"No, it's pretty bad. She's hardly talked at all since last night," Gramps said, choking. Abigail sighed and looked down at her hands. Granny cleared her throat; Abigail looked at her. Granny nodded.

"Remember what I told you and what you promised me?"

Abigail nodded and fled from the room after Katarina. Granny looked around at the messy kitchen. Antoinette blushed; her ash colored eyes were filled with pain.

"We haven't had a chance to clean it up yet; we just finished right before you got here."

Gramps shook his head. "No worries. Benedict, is there anything you need to get done outside?"

"Yeah." Benedict sniffed loudly. "I was supposed to clean out the garage this morning."

"Well, let's get that taken care of, shall we?" Gramps headed to the garage door and Benedict hurried after him. Granny nodded,

"He's right, girls; let's work. We'll clean up

the kitchen."

"What about Kat?" Emiliana asked as she combed her blonde hair back with her fingers.

"Let's leave her and Abigail alone for now." Granny rubbed her hands together and smiled weakly at them.

"Okay," Antoinette said. She headed to the sink and began to fill it up with water so she could wash dishes. Therese went into the dining room and began to clear the table off and Emiliana started to put the food away. Granny nodded; she found the broom and began to sweep the kitchen and dining room.

Upstairs, Katarina sat on her bed, hugging her legs to her chest. Abigail sat next to her with her hand on Katarina's shoulder. Abigail could have been across the room for all Katarina cared; she just outright ignored her best friend.

"Katarina, please! Can we talk? Please," Abigail begged Katarina pitifully. Katarina shrugged Abigail's hand off her shoulder. She spoke in a bitter tone, a tone filled with hurt and loss.

"No! I said no, so leave me alone!"

Abigail drew back, stung; she gasped. "Katarina! I'm so sorry! I just..." She stopped short.

Katarina abruptly stood up and headed to her balcony. Abigail stared with wide eyes. She watched as Katarina stepped through the doors and did what the girls had always done when escaping without wanting anyone to know. Abigail stood up and ran to the balcony.

"Katarina, no!"

Katarina raised her leg and placed it over the railing. Getting a good grip she moved the leg. Up and over. She turned around. Her eyes stared defiantly at Abigail as she lowered herself down, feeling for the corner post. Abigail raced forward to the edge; her hands gripped the railing tightly. The girls locked their eyes; it seemed as if time had slowed down. Katarina slowly slipped down the wooden post. She slipped and fell halfway down to the cement patio below. Abigail gave a shriek and raised her hand to her mouth. Katarina, shaken, stood up and took one last look at Abigail before taking off toward the maze that ran in back of the house.

"Don't go!" Abigail called after her, scared. The girls had never gone into the maze without an adult or Benedict before.

Abigail spun around fast and took off running at breakneck speed out of the room, down the stairs, and into the kitchen, her flip flops slamming into the floor. Everyone turned and looked at her. Therese poked her head around the dining room doorway. Abigail gasped for breath.

"Granny! Katarina went to the maze! *By herself!*"

"Oh no!" Emiliana groaned and sat down hard on a stool. Antoinette took her hands out of the water and shook them dry. She finished drying them off with a towel.

"I'll get Benedict," she spoke crisply and ran to the garage.

"How did she leave the house?!" Granny asked, worried.

"Over the balcony. She fell off the post halfway down!"

Granny groaned and covered her face with her hands. Therese looked worried.

"Who was it that shrieked?"

"That was me." Abigail's lips quivered. Her face was as pale as death and her eyes were as big as saucers. They heard the side garage door slam shut and through the kitchen sink window they saw Benedict hurrying to the maze.

"How come you sent Benedict?" Granny asked, watching her grandson run.

"Because," Emiliana answered, "he is the only one who has ever been able to get through to Katarina when she has been hurt, except for Abigail and Mum." Emiliana got teary eyed at the last word. Abigail slumped onto a stool.

"And I'm not doing too hot of a job." Her eyes glazed over with tears. Emiliana patted her arm awkwardly.

Granny spoke up. "Remember, words spoken in the heat of anger, or bitterness in this case, don't usually mean anything."

Abigail sighed and folded her arms on the counter and laid her head down. Antoinette and

Gramps came in.

"He went after her," Antoinette simply said.

"We saw," Therese spoke softly. Now all they could do was wait. Wait and see if Benedict would come back with Katarina soon or not.

Chapter Thirteen

"Katarina! You can't go in there! You don't know your way around it well enough," Benedict said, marching after her.

Katarina retorted as she stomped towards the entrance of the maze, "Yes I do! I've found my way all the way through before."

"Yes, but I was with you!" Benedict grabbed her arm and yanked her to a stop. Katarina turned around with a stomp. She glared hard up at Benedict. He just stood with one hand around her arm.

"Benedict Christopher Anderson! You let go of my arm!! If you don't, I'll tell Dad on you!"

Benedict's face went as pale as a ghost. Katarina gasped, she made a little choking sound in the back of her throat. She turned around and fled, straight into the maze. Benedict stared. He kicked his shoe against the ground.

"Darn it!" Benedict took off running after his younger sister.

"Katarina, please stop!" he called out. He stopped just inside the entrance and looked wildly about. Benedict threw his hands in the air and groaned. He pulled out his cell phone and dialed home. Benedict put his hand on his forehead and paced around.

"Hello? Yes, hello Nettie, it's me."

"What is it?"

"I need help. I lost hold of Katarina and she ran into the maze. I don't have a clue which way she went."

"Oh my gosh. All right; I'll call Peter."

He hung up his phone and sighed heavily. He slumped down on the ground and carefully leaned against the hedge to wait. He waited. He needed to catch his breath and formulate a plan.

Benedict jumped up quickly. He heard something; what was it? It sounded like someone was running through the grass. Peter Marchen came running up to Benedict. Help was here.

"Antoinette told me everything."

"Thanks so much." Benedict sighed with relief.

"No prob, Ben. All right; Em gave me a copy of Mr. Richardson's map of the maze for us." Peter pulled out a folded piece of paper and handed it to Benedict. Benedict took the map and unfolded it.

"Okay, I vote we split up. I know it's not the smartest maneuver, but I know this maze like the back of my hand. So you take the map." He handed it back to Peter, who took it reluctantly.

He nodded. "All right; we'll do that. Keep your cell phone on the whole time."

"Yes sir." Benedict nodded briefly. Peter smiled faintly.

"Okie dokes, let's go."

They parted ways.

Katarina ran down one path and up the next. She was sobbing so hard she couldn't even see. She stopped and stood in the middle of a path. Katarina rubbed her eyes as clear as possible of tears and looked around to see where she was. She didn't have a clue. That just made her cry even more. Benedict was right; she didn't know her way around as well as he did. She dropped to the ground and covered her face and cried. It was an uncontrollable, shaking cry. It made Katarina feel miserable. She whispered.

"How come you had to leave? I miss you! Why, God, why? This isn't fair! I need you!" She hiccuped and gulped for air. She sobbed; her shoulders shook. *Why did you go away?! Why did you die?! Oh God! Why did you let them die! I still need them. I'm not ready for them to die! I won't be for several years.* These thoughts ran through her head and many more, accusing God of doing such a terrible thing. As whispered words fell from her lips, she pounded the dry ground angrily.

She felt awful, as if she was going to be sick. Katarina jerked up, her eyes wide. She jumped up wildly and clasped a hand to her mouth, afraid of throwing up. She sat back down after throwing up shaking nervously and awfully. Suddenly, she felt an arm around her and felt as if she was drawn close to someone. Looking up, she saw it was Peter. She licked her dry lips.

"Hi," Katarina whispered in a low voice.

"You don't have to talk, okay?" he whispered softly. Peter pulled his cell phone out of his pocket and dialed Benedict. "Hey Ben. Yeah, I found her. Yeah. I'll use the map to find our way out. Meet you at the entrance. Bye." He hung up and stuffed it back into his pants pocket. Peter hugged Katarina.

"Think you can walk back to the entrance?" He could feel her shaking next to him.

She shook her head. "No, I feel like I could fall over right now," she said weakly. Peter didn't say anything; he just picked her up and headed back the way he came. Every once in a while he consulted his map, but he mostly remembered the way he had come.

They stepped out of the maze. Benedict was waiting right there for them. He hurried over.

"Is she okay?" he demanded worriedly. Peter nodded. Glancing down, he saw that Katarina had fallen asleep.

"She got sick, but I think she's just exhausted. She'll be fine."

"Oh good." Benedict sighed thankfully. "Let's go back; they'll be waiting for us." The two young men took off for the house. Walking at a brisk pace, they got there in only two minutes. The girls had been watching for them and when they saw them reach the patio, Therese instantly yanked the screen door open.

"You're back!" she cried out; then she saw Katarina. "Is she okay?"

"Yes. Just exhausted," Peter responded, stepping into the kitchen in front of Benedict. Abigail flew out of her chair to him.

"What's wrong?!"

"Don't worry; she's just asleep."

"Oh good," Granny said in clipped tones. "Let's get her upstairs then. She does need her rest."

"I'll take her up there if someone would show me which one is hers." Peter volunteered. Abigail raised her head instinctively. Granny shook her head.

"Abigail, I think you need your rest as well. Why don't you go and lie down on the couch?

Nettie can show him the way."

"All right, Granny," Abigail responded and after taking one more look at Katarina to make sure she was really all right, she turned and left. Peter turned to Antoinette for direction. She smiled and headed to the hallway. They walked next to each other up the wide staircase.

"Thanks for going out to help Benedict find her, Peter."

"It's my duty to your family," he replied softly.

She shook her head. "You don't have a duty to us and you know that; all right, Peter?"

"Yes ma'am," he said sternly as they walked into Katarina's room. Antoinette cracked a smile. He was glad to see a real smile from her.

"It's not a joking matter, Peter."

"Then why are you smiling?" he countered as he laid Katarina down on her bed. Antoinette took up the blanket that lay across the foot of the bed. She unfolded it and laid it over her sister.

"I wasn't smiling," she said once they had drawn the curtains and stepped out of the room. Peter closed the door behind them.

"Yes you were." His eyes smiled gently down on her.

"Fine; I was. And fine, if you want, you can have a duty to our family." Her eyes misted over. "Though I don't think Dad would want you to feel you had a duty toward us."

"He may not, but if I insisted he would have realized that I meant it and live with it and you know that.

"Yeah." She frowned slightly.

Peter wrapped his arms around Antoinette and hugged her tightly.

"I'm going to really miss them," she whispered into his shoulder.

He nodded. "I know. You all will. They were great parents, right?"

"More than great. They were the best."

"I bet."

"Nettie? Peter? Granny said to tell you lunch is ready," Emiliana called softly from the foot of the stairs.

"All right. We're coming," Nettie responded. They separated and, holding hands, they headed down the stairs to the kitchen. The table was set with paper plates and napkins; in the center of the table were two boxes of pizza–one cheese, the other sausage.

"When did this come?" Nettie asked, shocked.

"Gramps picked it up a couple minutes ago," Therese said, sitting in her spot at the table. Emiliana pulled out the chair next to her and plopped down in it. Therese glanced at Granny to see if she would reprimand Emiliana for sitting down so unladylike, but Granny hadn't even noticed. She sat down at the foot of the table as Gramps seated himself at the head. Antoinette and Peter walked to the other side and sat down. Gramps bowed his head and made the sign of the cross.

"Bless us oh Lord and these Thy gifts, which we're about to receive from Thy bounty through Christ our Lord. Amen."

They all made the sign of the cross. Therese and Emiliana reached forward and grabbed a slice of each pizza. The pizzas were cut in large triangular pieces. Everyone else dug in as well. Nobody noticed that Granny didn't reprimand anyone for bad manners; they were all lost in each other's thoughts.

Finally Gramps sighed and spoke up. "We're going to have to talk about this eventually, so I don't know about anyone else but I'd like to get it over with. There's more to talk about than what will be discussed at this conversation, though. But when do y'all want the wake and funeral?"

Therese started to choke on her pizza. She coughed and coughed. Emiliana just turned and hit her on her back. Therese coughed and gasped for breath. Granny looked ready to fly out of her chair.

Therese nodded her head and whispered, "I'm all right. Sorry to scare you all."

"What about this Wednesday and Thursday?" Antoinette suggested. "I think by now almost everyone important knows about what happened, don't you?"

Benedict hurried in and sat down next to Peter. Everyone turned and looked at him.

"Sorry I'm late," he said, excusing himself from any criticism. Everyone turned back to the conversation.

Therese spoke up. "Do the Marshalls know yet?" She was referring to her parents' old friends from college.

"Oh, I forgot about them," Emiliana said.

Granny took a drink from her glass of root beer. "Well, why don't we make a list of people who we think need to know this afternoon; we can talk about everything else as well."

"All right, I'm good with that." Gramps nodded and took the last bite of his pizza. He reached for another slice of sausage.

"Don't forget that Katarina and Abigail need to eat as well."

"Hopefully Katarina feels well enough to eat," Peter commented thoughtfully as he took a drink. His innocent comment caught everyone's attention. Granny looked at him sharply.

"What do you mean by that, Peter?"

"Oh." He looked at Benedict, who was contentedly eating his pizza. "She just got sick in the maze is all. She said she was okay, though."

"Oh, well you should have told me," Granny said, somewhat sternly.

"Yes, ma'am."

Lunch was regretfully but quickly finished up and chores were soon taken care of, since all that needed to be done was the table cleared and the pizza cutter washed. Everyone gathered in the living room to discuss the plans for the next couple of days.

"Okay, so, Therese, I'm going to put you in charge of writing down people you think we need to call. Do you think you'll be able to call them all?"

"Okay. I can try," Therese said quietly, nodding. She jumped up and went to find some paper and a pen. She came back, sat down, and began to write. Gramps turned to everyone else. They listened closely.

"So, you think that Wednesday and Thursday would be good for the wake and funeral?"

"Yeah. I think that's good," Benedict said. They all looked at each other to see if everyone else agreed as well. They did.

"Okay; we have that covered then. Next is this, do you all want to stay here or come back and live with us?" He saw their stricken faces. "I know, I know; it's a tough decision and I don't expect an answer right now. I know it will take you a while to decide but, I just wanted to let you know your options."

"And if you all want to stay here then we were wondering if you want us to live with you. We can talk it over with your Grandpa and Grandma-"

The doorbell rang and Benedict hopped up

to get it. When he came back he brought back Grandpa and Grandma with him.

"We've just been discussing the housing situations." Gramps informed them as they sat down.

"Ahh okay."

"Well," Antoinette said thoughtfully, "I know if we stayed here it would be nice if you guys could move closer as well. Just so we could see all four of you often. I mean Katarina's gonna need all of her grandparents."

"Yeah, she would," Emiliana said sarcastically. "We all would." She stuck her tongue out at no one in particular. Emiliana tended to get sarcastic when she was upset or stressed.

"Em." Therese looked up and spoke with a slight warning note in her voice.

"Oh, right; sorry," she said hurriedly. Antoinette smiled quietly at them. Peter glanced at his watch and sighed. He stood up and looked at them all.

"I have to go now. I promised my–uh–mother that I would go do some shopping for her, so I have to run home real quick. I'll see you all later. Let me know what y'all plan to do."

"Okay. Bye, Peter." Therese waved at him. Emiliana nodded her head.

"Bye." Benedict stood up and shook his hand. "Thanks for your help earlier."

"No prob, Ben. I do what I can."

Antoinette stood up, "I'll walk with you to the

door."

He smiled down at her. "All right."

"See you later, Peter, it was nice to meet you." Gramps shook his hand and smiled at him.

"It was nice to meet you too, Mr. Jones; same for you Mrs. Jones. Good bye Mr. and Mrs. Anderson."

Antoinette and Peter walked out of the room together. Everyone got back to talking. Emiliana looked at them all, a question in her eyes.

"Was there anything else you wanted to talk about, Gramps?"

"Um, there was. Give me a moment to think about it."

The room fell silent for several minutes until Gramps remembered. He sat forward and looked at them all.

"So, we need to figure out what everyone's doing for the Mass. Any suggestions?"

"I can do the petitions, I guess," Emiliana quietly offered from her seat.

Grandma looked at her. "Are you sure?"

Emiliana nodded firmly, "I'll do them."

"Do you want to do them with anyone else? Maybe Patrick or Alec or Marial?"

She shrugged indifferently. "It doesn't matter; if they want to do them, they can. I don't really care if I do them all myself."

"All right; that's taken care of." Gramps turned to Benedict. "You want to write down the jobs?"

"Sure."

Therese handed him a piece of paper and he fished a pen out of his pocket. He wrote down that Emiliana was reading the petitions. "I vote we get people to sing for the Mass. I don't think you girls want to do that, right?" he said, turning to Therese. She shook her head violently. Antoinette came back into the room and sat down next to Emiliana. She looked around at them all.

"What are we talking about now?" Antoinette inquired. Granny got up and left the room as Grandpa explained what Antoinette had missed.

"Well, Em is going to do the petitions. We'll ask one of the cousins to see if they want to do it with her. Also, Benedict just suggested that we get other people to sing for the Mass instead of you girls and Therese agreed with him."

Antoinette nodded her head. "I agree as well; I would rather not sing for the Mass." She smiled a little at him.

"All right now that we have that settled, who do you want to pick?"

"Eileen and Callie Hickman," Therese burst out quickly. She was louder than normal and everyone turned and stared at her. Realizing what she had done, Therese blushed a rosy red. "Oops," she whispered.

Gramps chuckled quietly and leaned over to pat her on the knee gently. "It's all right, Therese;

every once in a while we need to just speak out or say what's on our minds."

"Yeah, like how you had pizza without me and didn't think to let me know that we're having a family meeting, minus mom and dad."

Everyone turned and stared at the doorway. Katarina stood there with her arms crossed, looking incredibly irritated as well as tired. She did create an almost comical look, with her hair all messed up and her t-shirt rumpled from sleeping. Benedict made a noise that sounded like an almost laugh. Katarina turned and glared at him. Granny walked in with a tray of glasses.

"Kat," she spoke warningly to her.

Katarina huffed and uncrossed her arms. "Sorry." She turned and stalked out of the room.

Granny brought the tray in and set it down on the coffee table. She sat down in the reclining chair. She sighed. "I hope she'll be all right soon."

"We all do, Granny." Antoinette smiled weakly. Therese silently nodded the same to herself.

Emiliana looked around at her siblings and her grandparents and sighed. Her parents' death had left a huge hole in their family life and she knew it would be that way for a while. It was tearing up their lives–messing them up. Emiliana would never say that their death ruined her family's lives at all. Because it didn't. Death should never ruin someone's life. She understood that it would cause a person tremendous grief and pain and that there would be an immense, gaping hole for a while–perhaps always. Emiliana knew that; she felt it. She felt the pain and the grief and most definitely she felt the enormous hole. She placed her hand on her heart for a moment. She felt its steady beating, then she quickly took it down so that no one would see her and laugh at her. Emiliana knew it wasn't literally broken but figuratively broken. She knew in time it would heal, but it would be slow.

Only time will tell
How fast my heart
Will heal from this pain
Of unshed tears and love.

Only time will tell
How soon I will talk
Of long forgotten memories
Memories of people
So dear to me.

Only time will fill
This empty void
That once was full
But now is empty
Only time
Only time will tell.

Emiliana sighed and turned her thoughts back to the conversation, which was abruptly interrupted by loud shouting from the other room. Therese glanced wide eyed at them all. It was Katarina again. It sounded like Abigail was awake now too. Everyone looked at each other; no one wanted to go in there and break it up, but they all knew it must be done before someone went into hysterics. All eyes shifted towards Therese and stared at her. She pointed her finger at her chest.

"Me?"

"Yeah, you go, Therese; you're the best at breaking up fights," Emiliana pronounced proudly to her younger sister.

Benedict nodded his head in agreement. "She's right you know."

"All right." Therese got up from her chair and placed her piece of paper and pen on it before leaving the room.

Grandma sighed and shook her head with worry. "I think Abigail should go home. Their friendship might be ruined forever if Katarina keeps exploding at her."

"I can take her home after Therese puts an end to their argument, if you want, Grandma," Antoinette offered.

"That would be good," Gramps said in agreement.

The girls' argument was on a completely dumb matter. Katarina glared angrily at her best friend.

"You don't even care about me! You don't even bother to talk to me about anything! The last time you did that was who knows when!"

"Do you know what!? I care the whole world over for you! And you know what else!? The last time I civilly talked to you was guess what! Shock of shocks! Yesterday! Before any of this happened! When we were laughing over all those pictures we took while at your grandparents'!"

"You don't even care that my parents are dead," Katarina growled at her.

Abigail stepped back, stunned. Her face filled with anguish.

Therese walked in. She stood staring in complete and total shock at her little sister.

"Guess what. Maybe I actually do," Abigail spat back. "Next to my mother your parents were two of the best people in my entire life! Ever since my dad died five years ago your dad has been like a second father! I loved them! So yes, as a matter of fact I do actually care that your parents are dead. I miss them with my whole heart. I miss that your mom always had a special word for me. I miss that your dad always had a hug for me. I-I just miss them, okay?" Abigail broke off and burst into tears. Therese walked in and wrapped her arms around her. She whispered gently to Abigail as she glared at Katarina. She knew that Katarina really didn't deserve to be glared at, but she for once needed to actually glare at someone.

"Come Abigail, you should go home now, okay? Someone will take you home. Either Gramps or Grandpa or Benedict or Nettie, all right?"

Abigail just cried. Therese took her arm and quietly led her out of the room. They bumped into Antoinette, who had come down the hall to get Abigail.

"I'm taking you home now, all right, Abi?"

"Okay," Abigail whispered as she wiped her nose and sniffed, trying to stop the tears. Antoinette glanced at Therese, who shrugged and spoke with Antoinette through her eyes: I'll go back and see what I can do.

Antoinette nodded and turned, leading Abigail to the front door. Therese took a deep breath and bravely walked back into the den. She found Katarina pacing back and forth–more like stomping–across the room. Therese stood and watched her with her arms crossed.

"You know being mad won't help anything.

At least that's what Mom would say. They wouldn't want you to be mad over it; you know that," Therese spoke quietly but firmly.

Katarina didn't speak at all, but she did stop stomping and slowly walked to an overstuffed chair and flopped down in it. Her brow was still creased into a frown, but at least it had softened from the look of pure anger that it had moments before.

Therese continued to speak. "Mom and Dad would tell us to seek joy from all the memories we made with them–and I must say we've made a lot of memories with them. Think about that time we went rock climbing when you were seven and I was nine. Oh! And the trip we went to Hawaii and we went wakeboarding and surfing. I remember Dad was a little wild on that trip." Therese lowered herself onto the black, leather couch and kept talking quietly but comfortingly. "Remember the Christmas we spent in the backyard imagining we were Eskimos and we had lost the way to our house when we were gone on an expedition? I remember you were only three and you kept trying to take off your coat and run around. You were laughing; you thought it was the best game ever and poor Mom was flipping out because she thought you might get frostbite. Dad had to take her inside and talk to her before she finally calmed down. It was really funny. I don't suppose you remember that Christmas."

Therese stopped talking and ran her finger along the seam on the arm of the couch.

Katarina sighed loudly. "I remember it vaguely but I don't remember taking my coat off and running around without it."

"Well, trust me; you did it." Therese cracked a smile. She saw the frown slowly disappearing from Katarina's face. She got up and walked over to Katarina's chair. Therese squeezed her way in next to her. Katarina scooched over and made room for her sister. They sat in silence for several moments.

Then Therese spoke up again. "Remember the time when I was learning about the ocean for science at school and I had to write a research paper on the characteristics of the ocean profile and the shore for homework?"

"Yeah, and Dad packed us all up and hauled us to North Carolina for a vacation in February so you could get your research firsthand."

"It was freezing."

"Beyond freezing. Mom should have been more worried about me getting frostbite there than that Christmas." Katarina smiled a little at her sister.

Therese's eyes lit up a little. She giggled softly. "Yeah."

"Remember my school play? When I was nine, for drama class?"

"Oh yeah. Something about chickpeas and

lobsters."

"No! It was the *Tale of the Chickadee*—an original play by Katarina Rebecca Anderson," Katarina exclaimed, pretending to be hurt. She playfully jabbed her elbow into Therese's stomach.

"Oh! Hey!" Therese reached over and started to tickle Katarina.

"Not fair!" Katarina cried out, laughing hysterically.

Across Therese's face a large grin spread out at the sound of her younger sister's laugh. She kept tickling her. In her struggle to get out of Therese's grasp, Katarina fell off the chair and landed on the floor. Therese dove after her and continued to tickle her violently.

Gasping for breath, Katarina cried out, "Please stop! I can't breathe!! *Please Therese*!!" Katarina wriggled around on the floor, trying in vain to get away from her older sister, but Therese wasn't letting up. She wanted to let Katarina laugh for as long as possible. She hoped to lift Katarina's mood and send it flying away.

Chapter Fourteen

Love is strong
Love is dear
Love is precious

Death takes a toll on love.
It can possibly shatter it.
Ruin it all.
It can rip a hole in your heart.
Time will heal that hole.
It will last forever or a short time.
Death can strengthen love.

Don't let death cause a divide.
Between lost and living.
You will fall.
A short hard fall or a long slow fall.
Come back up and begin again.

Begin again.
Love again.
Live again.

Katarina stared at her full-length mirror and sighed. Her face was tear stained, but right now she was not crying. She knew that in a little while it would be a different story. She had woken up every night sobbing, and she had suffered through many nightmares about her parents' death the way her imagination pictured it, which meant it got pretty bad sometimes. She looked down at her lacy, black dress and sighed. It was brand new as of Tuesday. She was wearing it for the funeral today. Katarina thought back to yesterday afternoon and evening. It had been tiring and miserable. She had made up with Abigail on Tuesday by asking her to come with them to go shopping. She had even written a poem for Abigail to tell her how sorry she was. Thinking of the poem turned her thoughts to another poem she had written. That poem was going to be read today at church during the eulogy. She wrote it the other night when she had woken up from one of the nightmares. She had sobbed the entire time she had written it, but it said how much her siblings and she had loved her parents and how wonderful they had been. A certain stanza came to mind at that moment, causing the tears to prick at the corners of her eyes.

Wrapped in love
Wrapped in strength
We will never forget
The strength of their love
Come what may
We will be strong
For their love and care
Has prepared us for the fight
of life.

Tearing her thoughts away from it lest she begin to cry again, Katarina turned back to the mirror. She raised her hand and ran her finger along her hairdo, over every curve and curl. It was a simple hairstyle but fitting for what today would bring. Antoinette had done it for her after breakfast. A knock on the door startled her.

"Come in." Her voice caught and she cleared her throat. Katarina turned to the door as Emiliana stuck her head around the corner.

She glanced up and down Katarina and spoke. "We have to leave soon, so you need to put your shoes on–and oh–" Emiliana tossed her a package of black tights. "Granny told me to give these to you." She saw Katarina's face fall at having to wear tights in the summer. "Oh, and yeah; I think it stinks too, but do it for Mom and Dad." Emiliana walked in and gave her little sister a quick squeeze.

Katarina nodded and smiled. "All right. Thanks, Em."

"No problem, Kat; all for you."

She winked at Katarina, who grinned and responded, "One for everyone"

"Good. Glad you still remember that," she said and ducked out of the room, pulling the door shut behind her.

Katarina called after her, "How could I forget it?"

Katarina sat down on the edge of her unmade bed and ripped open the package of tights. Pulling them out, she stretched them the length of her right arm and then her left arm.

"That should be good enough," she murmured and pulled them on quickly. Standing up, she turned to the mirror and again straightened out her dress. Katarina went to her closet and pulled a shoe box off her shelf. Opening it up, she looked down at the black flats in it. *Black, black, black; why must people wear black to a funeral?* Katarina sighed and slipped the shoes on. She hurried out of the door and down the stairs. Everyone else was waiting in the living room. She stood in the shadows of the hallway and looked at her family and Peter sitting in the room. More black; more depression. Katarina stepped into the room.

"I'm ready, guys." She spoke so unlike her normal way of speaking. They all turned and looked at her.

Gramps stood up and straightened his annoying suit coat. "All right; everyone into the car—let's go. We have to go back to the funeral home first, then on to the church." Reluctantly they all got up and headed for the car. Once everyone was in and buckled, Gramps backed out of the driveway and drove to the funeral home for their last goodbyes.

"Come here with me, Kat, I want to show you something to make you feel better." My trusting eyes looked up at my mother. I cradled my right arm in its heavy cast and pink sling in my left arm. I grinned happily. My mom was taking me somewhere, just us two, with no mean sisters or brother to come with us.

"Where are we going, Mummy?!" I squealed happily. My mom smiled and gently took my hand in hers. My left hand that is, not my right hand.

"You must wait and see, honey precious." I stuck my tongue out. I didn't want to wait.

"Do I really have to wait?"

My mother chuckled and led me out of the front door of Granny and Gramps' house.

"You have to wait because I want it to be a surprise for you. Also," my mom knelt down in front of me, "you must never tell your sisters or brother

about this place, okay?" I shook my head up and down vigorously. A secret?! From Nettie, Benedict, Em, and Therese! Oh yes, I would keep it. My mom grinned at me.

"Katarina, it's time to go in." Katarina felt a hand rest on her arm and she was wrenched from her memories. She turned from the window that was in the funeral home door to see Abigail standing next to her. She looked as if she had been crying. Katarina's cheek suddenly felt wet. She brushed it quickly and felt a tear. It was a soft and silent storm of agony. Katarina followed her best friend into the room where the coffins were that held her parents. She walked up to the rest of her family. Abigail hugged her, squeezing her as tightly as she could. The tears rushed down Katarina's face, as fast as a horrible thunderstorm and as silent as the moon in the sky.

"No, no, no." Katarina formed the words with her mouth but not a single sound came out. She took a shuddering breath and then another. She was shaking uncontrollably. Abigail squeezed her even more, trying to stop the shaking. Katarina stared at her parents' faces. They looked almost fake–not like they did when they were alive. Gramps told her that they looked that way because it was part of the routine to prepare the body for burial. As everyone drifted out of the room, Katarina stepped toward the coffins. She carefully and gingerly touched her mother's arm one last time. Her arm didn't feel real anymore. She turned to her father. He had on a calm expression, but Katarina had no doubt that their situation when they died was anything but calm. She turned to Abigail and whispered in a low voice, "I need to go outside. I don't feel good."

"Okay." Abigail led her friend out of the room and to the entrance of the funeral home. They stepped outside into the cool, fresh air. Thankfully the day's weather was very moderate, in the low 70s. If it hadn't been, Katarina would have felt more miserable than she already did. The door was pushed open not too long after they had come out.

"There you are!"

The girls turned around quickly to see who had just spoken. It was Katarina's Aunt Marina. Aunt Marina was Mrs. Anderson's sister. Katarina's Uncle Michael and Aunt Emilie were there as well, since they were Mrs. Anderson's brother and sister. Aunt Emilie was the youngest and Uncle Michael was the oldest, then it was Aunt Marina, and Katarina's mother was between Marina and Emilie. Aunt Marina ushered the girls back inside to go to the other parking lot on the other side of the building.

Abigail looked at Katarina's aunt. "Which car

are we riding in?"

"My husband, Uncle John, is driving you two and all the little cousins to the church. All the older cousins are going with Uncle Greg. All right?"

"Yes, Aunt Marina," Katarina said automatically.

They headed through the building and out the opposite door. Katarina looked back over her shoulder. She caught one last glimpse of the room where her parents lay in their coffins. She caught their faces as the door swung shut behind them. That was the last time Katarina ever saw her parents' faces. Abigail and Katarina climbed into the large van that held all the cousins under the age of thirteen. There were several eight, nine, and eleven year olds, as well as several cousins in between the ages of seven and five and Katarina's two twelve-year-old cousins. Katarina moved into the middle seat of the front bench and Abigail sat next to her on Katarina's right. On her left sat her quiet, twelve-year-old cousin next to the window. Her cousin turned and glanced at Katarina.

"Hi, Kit Kat," she spoke quiet-like. That was how Annabelle always talked, hardly ever above a quiet tone. Katarina turned to Annabelle and smiled a tiny, weak smile. Annabelle reached over took her cousin's hand. Katarina squeezed it tightly.

"Hi, Banana."

The girl's nicknames for each other were given by Katarina's parents when they were two and one. Annabelle loved bananas and Katarina loved Kit Kats. It was the day after Halloween and that year Aunt Emilie and Uncle Greg had come to visit with Alex, Peter, and Annabelle for the week. They had just spent the last two hours sharing bananas and Kit Kats together. They had both gotten stomachaches that night. Abigail looked over at Annabelle and smiled.

"Hi Annabelle; how are you doing?"

"Not too good."

"Same here." Katarina sighed heavily and looked down at her left hand. She took her other hand and started to fiddle with the ring that she'd always worn since she had gotten it for Christmas when she was seven years old. Annabelle looked down at her own hand and saw the ring on her own finger. The rings were identical: the same silver bands with the same pink stone in the center and the same swirly words that wrapped around the bands. Those words read "Faith, Hope, Love." Katarina's parents had given the two girls the same rings because the two were buddies then and still were.

Katarina turned to Annabelle and asked her, "Sit with me and Abigail during Mass?"

Annabelle nodded her head; her eyes sparkled with unshed tears. "Yes, please, I would like that very much."

"Good." Abigail spoke softly; she smiled faintly at the two cousins. Uncle John turned the car into the large church parking lot and parked the vehicle in one of the spots for the family of the deceased. Uncle John turned to look at everyone in the back seats of the van.

"All right; listen up everyone. You all know your jobs right?"

"Daddy?" One of the younger boys raised his hand.

Uncle John nodded. "Yes, Jimmy?"

"Me, Lacey, Molly, and Joey bring up the gifts."

"Yes, you're right. Anyone else know their jobs?"

"We do, Uncle John." Another of the cousins, Spencer, nodded his head. He gestured to Tyler who sat next to him. "We are doing the collection baskets."

"Correct. All right; I think we are good. Right?"

"No, Uncle John. I'm gonna read my poem before the eulogy," Katarina spoke up quickly. Everyone turned and stared at her, especially Abigail and Uncle John.

"But I thought I was reading it for you?"

"No, I want to do it. I can do it," she replied. "See? I have the paper with me." Katarina pulled out a folded piece from her little clutch purse.

"Okay; I am fine with that. Just so you know,

if at the last minute you change your mind, let me know, okay?" he told her, looking at her slightly concerned.

Katarina shook her head. "No, I'm positive. I can do it."

"All right. Okay everyone, it's time to go inside. I expect you all to behave properly if you don't you will be dealt with later, okay?"

"Yes sir" came various mumbled responses. They all rapidly climbed out of the vehicle and walked as calmly as is possible for children eleven years and younger to walk. Katarina, Abigail, and Annabelle trailed behind Uncle John and the kids. They stepped to the side of the narthex. Katarina watched as they guided first her father's coffin into the church and then her mother's. Tearful, Abigail guided Katarina and Annabelle, who were both sobbing, up to the first pew in the front of the church. They joined Antoinette, Peter, Benedict, Emiliana, and Therese, who were already sitting with Gramps and Granny and Grandpa and Grandma. Behind them in the other pews sat Uncle Michael, Aunt Marina, and Aunt Emilie, who were sitting with Aunt Elisabeth, Uncle John, and Uncle Greg. In the pews past sat three and a half pews full of cousins and the two oldest cousins' wives.

Katarina gripped the short, wooden wall that divided the front pew from the aisle in front. The tears streamed down her face; it wasn't a silent storm but a vicious, shoulder-shaking thunderstorm of tears. She couldn't hold it all in anymore. She cried more tears at that moment then she had ever cried in her entire thirteen years. Katarina hardly noticed that the Mass had started. She didn't hear anything the priest said at the beginning of Mass. The only words conscious to her were the words that ran through her head.

Chapter Fifteen

"Kat! It's time to read the poem!" Abigail was nudging her and Annabelle whispered loudly at her. Katarina jumped and nodded.

"Okay." She wiped her hand across her face and reached down and pulled the paper out of her purse. Katarina got up and walked out of the pew and followed her Uncle John up to the pulpit. Uncle John was going to say the eulogy after Katarina read the poem. Katarina stepped up to the pulpit as Uncle John adjusted the microphone to her level. He squeezed her hand and held it while she spoke.

"I wrote this poem the other day, and my uncle said I could read it to you all." There was a catch in her throat and she cleared it and blinked her eyes fast. Then she spoke.

"One day
Two lovers pledged their love
To each other.
This pledge would last years
Years they promised.

Soon they had children.
Five lovely, young children
They taught them the best things
The best things of life
And the sad things of life

They were blessed abundantly
The family did so many things
Wonderful things
They had fun times
The time of their lives.

That pledge granted the children
Wonderful gifts.
Gifts of love and kindness.
It was helping them prepare for the world
But that love was cut short.
Cut short by the knife of death.
Never to be loved again
Those children were alone.

Wrapped in love
Wrapped in strength
We will never forget

The strength of their love
Come what may
We will be strong
For their love and care
Has prepared us for the fight
of life."

Once she was done reading, Katarina stepped down from the pulpit. The entire church was in complete and total silence. Not a soul was stirring. Not a voice spoke. The only sound that you could hear was the sound of people crying. The church was filled with pain and sadness. Katarina herself was crying again. Only this time it was her silent storm. The tears rolled quietly down her face and onto her dress. It felt to Katarina like her heart was ripping in two and then into shards and then into tiny pieces. The pain was so intense that Katarina felt like crying out; it was almost as if she was dying herself. She sat down again between Abigail and Annabelle.

"You sounded like a true speaker," Annabelle whispered to her. The twelve year old was immensely proud of her cousin.

Abigail squeezed her best friend's arm gently but proudly. "You sounded proud."

"I am proud. Proud of my parents. Proud of who they were and proud of what they taught me. I am proud–very, very, proud."

"I bet," Abigail whispered back and nodded.

They sat in silence, listening to Uncle John speak of Sarah and David Anderson.

"I remember the day my wife, Marina, brought me home to meet the Jones family. And when I met Sarah, I remember I was instantly struck by her beautiful personality. How caring she was; how absolutely loving and kind she was to everyone. I could see she loved her family very much. I firmly believe that she never spoke an unnecessary harsh word to anyone in her entire life. That was just not her style. Then the day she brought David home, well, that's a memory. I remember that he fit right into the family. He always had a joke and a hug for you. He was that sarcastic, funny, kind of guy. He knew when something was bothering you. I know they loved each other very much. They were such strong Catholic people, very well-grounded in their faith. You can tell just by looking at them that David and Sarah put that same strong faith into the children." He paused for a breath.

Katarina turned to Abigail and whispered to her softly, "I can't listen anymore and I need some air."

"Okay." Abigail nodded, understanding Katarina perfectly. Abigail turned to Annabelle and whispered to her so that she knew where they were going. Annabelle nodded, her eyes glistened with tears. Thankfully the three girls sat on the end of the pew so they didn't have to climb over anyone and make a scene. Katarina and Abigail quickly left the pew and walked hurriedly down the aisle towards the back of church. Every word that Uncle John spoke echoed loudly in her ears. She felt short of breath. Katarina looked down at her hands and saw that they were visibly shaking. She clasped them both together to stop the shaking. Abigail pushed the doors open and they stepped out into the Narthex. The door swung shut behind them, muffling Uncle John's voice. Abigail took Katarina's hand in her own and the two walked silently across the narthex and out of the church doors. Outside, the two girls went and sat down on the steps off to the side. They just sat in silence for a little while until Katarina decided she couldn't stand the silence anymore. She spoke up.

"It just doesn't seem right, Abi."

"I know it doesn't. I felt the same when my dad died

"How could God plan this? Such a horrible way to ruin our lives."

"He planned it this way because your parents' time on earth was up. It's been like this since the beginning of time. God planned everything out perfectly, and for different people he decided to give them a shorter lifetime than others. But–" Abigail stopped and looked down at her shoes. Katarina turned to Abigail; her face was in pain.

"But what, Abi?"

"You're lucky, ya know."

"What do you mean? How can *I* be lucky?" Katarina asked her indignantly.

"You're lucky because you got your parents for thirteen years of your life and I only got my dad, my wonderful dad, for eight years. Just eight short years."

"But Granny would say you were lucky as well for getting eight amazing years with your dad. You may not have had fun every single day for all those eight years but the joyful, happy times overrule the sad or angry times in those eight years."

"I guess you're right," Abigail admitted, biting her lip.

Katarina sighed. "I miss them. A lot. Sometimes it feels like my heart is dying inside of me."

"Yeah, mine did too; sometimes it still does. Though when my dad died I didn't quite fully realize what had happened until everything was over. Then everything hit me."

"Does it ever lessen?" Katarina asked, picking at a mosquito bite on her arm.

"Sometimes, but it won't for a while. You'll be living with this same aching pain for months. Mine didn't start to lessen very much until I started taking voice lessons with your mom and then I finally found peace from singing. It helped to relieve my burden of memories."

"Really? It took that long?" Katarina squeaked

out. She sounded scared of the thought that it might take such a long time.

Abigail smiled softly at Katarina. "Yeah it took two years to lessen it for me."

"Gosh, that sounds scary, Abi."

"It is scary at first. Especially when it comes to all the little things a person used to do."

"Oh." Katarina realized that not only her life but each day from now on would be altered with the death of her parents. Now there would be no mother to wake her up in the morning by singing her favorite song, no father to have dance parties with, no parents to take just her out for ice cream when everyone else was gone for the evening.

Abigail waved her hand in front of Katarina's face frantically. She had seen the look of pure agony and loss come over her friend's face. Katarina let herself be distracted and turned back to Abigail.

"What?" Katarina asked.

Abigail shrugged and answered, "I just–you were just scaring me with the look you had on your face. That's all."

"Oh." Katarina sighed. She took a strand of her hair and started unconsciously twisting it around her fingers. Abigail sat in silence, thinking back to the day her own dad died of brain cancer. She remembered the long, hard months during his treatments. She hadn't understood what was going on back then. She hadn't gotten why her once happy and active father was spending so much time in the hospital and then he died. It had come as a shock to Abigail; she hadn't understood what was going on even after her mother had explained it to her.

"I miss my dad lots at times like this. Even when I hear about someone who died, like through the newspaper or people's friends or relatives on Facebook; I miss him a ton."

"I'm sure; your dad was pretty cool."

"Not as cool as your dad," Abigail said, smiling as she playfully shoved Katarina. Katarina almost fell off the step.

"Hey!" She seated herself again and fixed her skirt. "My dad was pretty cool." She winked at Abigail. "No; he was awesome."

"Totally. Your mom was cool too!"

"My mom was just beautiful and that sums her up entirely. She was cool, but beautiful."

"Yeah, that's right." Abigail agreed, nodding quietly. A door swung open and they heard footsteps.

"Girls! It's almost time for Communion. Therese sent me out to get you two." Abigail and Katarina jumped up quickly and hurried after Annabelle back into the narthex. They slowed before entering the inner part of the church. Katarina listened silently as Father Vincent spoke the words of the Mass.

After Mass was over, both families, Andersons and Jones, along with all the cousins, filed out after the pallbearers who had the coffins. Behind the families was the rest of the congregation. Once outside, everyone got in their cars to head to the cemetery. The whole trip to the cemetery was filled with silence. Nobody spoke a word. Not even the little kids. Everyone was wrapped up inside their own thoughts of who knows what. Katarina placed her chin on her hand and leaned forward, staring out the front window of the van. She thought back to the last week. She was exhausted from so much misery. A whole week filled with trials surrounded by the sign of death is not good for a thirteen-year-old girl—or for anyone, for that matter. Katarina sighed and bit her lip. She really was going to miss her parents. A tear trickled slowly down her cheek. She brushed it away, thinking nobody had seen it, but Uncle John was watching her in the rearview mirror, his eyes full of gentleness and love. *The poor girl; so much pain and sadness for her to deal with*, he thought wistfully. Someone else had seen that tear. God knew the pain she was dealing with as well; He just was waiting for her to bring it to Him. And would she?

A little girl came dancing down the stairs. She was dressed all in blue. Her shirt was blue with little bits of ribbon on the ruffled sleeves; she wore a puffy, blue tutu, and in her hair was a large, blue, flower clip. Her face was beaming with happiness. She ran to her father and grabbed his hands, jumping up and down.

"Daddy! Daddy! I'm ready for our dance party!!"

"Are you sure you're ready?" The little girl's father chuckled heartily. Her father was a handsome, young man, always ready to have a fun time or create a fun time for his five young children. "Well, if you are ready, then let's get started." He led his little girl into the living room. The two had cleared the floor earlier so they could dance. The father hooked his iPhone up to the large speaker set on the shelves in the room.

"What song shall it be first, my sweet petunia?"

"Play 'Overcomer,' Daddy!" the little girl clapped her hands excitedly.

He smiled and scrolled through his music to find his daughter's favorite song. As she put it, a dance party couldn't end without him playing that song.

"Is Therese joining us?" he asked, speaking of his second youngest. The little girl shook her head.

"No, Daddy, remember Mummy took her to get her hair cut?"

"Oh that's right! I forgot." He playfully slapped his forehead as if it was the wildest thing to forget his wife had taken his daughter for a haircut. The

little girl giggled at her father. She bounced up and down excitedly.

"Can we start the dance party, Daddy?"

"Why, of course we can, my impatient, little nugget!" He chuckled and patted her head.

The girl shrunk back. "No, Daddy! Don't touch my hair!"

"Oh, my! I am sorry; will you forgive me, your royal highness?" he said, grinning at her indignation.

She grinned up at him.

"All right. Let's get this party on the road, shall we?" he said cheerfully, pressing play on the song.

"Yes! Yes!" She jumped up and down wildly as her favorite song started to play.

"Here we are," Uncle John said, pulling in through the cemetery gates. He followed the cars in front of him, driving up the long, winding road through the cemetery. He pulled up next to the curb, close to the spot where David and Sarah Anderson were to be buried. The kids and Uncle John all piled out of the car and hurried toward the crowd of people standing around the coffins and the holes that were dug in the ground. The whole crowd was silent except for a crying little baby. They all listened to Father Vincent as he prayed the prayers of Christian burial. His voice resonated loudly; it rose high above the crowd. To Katarina, it seemed like it was soaring with the birds. Once he was done, Father turned to Mr. and Mrs. Jones and Mr. and Mrs. Anderson and spoke his condolences to them. Then he turned to Antoinette, Benedict, Emiliana, and Therese and spoke softly to them. Father Vincent turned one last time and laid his eyes on Katarina tenderly. She squirmed uncomfortably under his gentle gaze. She had a feeling of being greatly pitied by him. Father Vincent stepped towards her and smiled. *How could he smile at a time like this?* she thought in a slightly sneering tone.

He spoke to her gently, "I am very sorry about your parents. If you have questions about anything or would just like to talk, you know that I am here. That is what priests are for." He nodded slowly and then stepped away.

Katarina mentally raised her eyebrow as he walked away. *Really?* she thought. *You think I'm going to talk to you if I need to?*

"Kat, it's time to leave now and head to the luncheon," Abigail whispered into Katarina's ear.

"Okay. Let's go eat!" she said in an attempt to be merry; she failed miserably. She, herself, didn't even laugh.

Katarina walked to the car; Abigail and Annabelle followed behind her. Abigail watched her friend with worry. She noticed how Katarina's shoulders slumped, how she held her head low. They got to the car and climbed in. Abigail glanced casually at Katarina. Katarina's face was pale and drawn, there were dark circles under her eyes, and she looked very tired. Abigail sighed. *Too bad we have class schedules and placements tomorrow; that means she has to wait till Saturday to sleep in, and she needs it more than anything right now*, she thought. *She can take a nap later, though, too. I'll see if she wants me to go home with her or give her the evening to rest.*

Katarina pulled her knees up to her chest and leaned her chin on them. It was uncomfortable to do on a car bench, but she did it anyway. Her eyes gradually drifted shut, closing off the world from her vision. Katarina bounced up and her eyes flew open. Her legs slid off the bench. They must have hit a bump. Sluggishly, she pulled her legs back up, rested her chin again, and closed her eyes. Succumbing herself to sleepiness, she drifted off. Abigail glanced over Katarina's head to Annabelle. She caught Annabelle's attention.

"When do you guys go home?" she whispered under her breath.

"We go home tomorrow."

"Okay; where do you live again?"

"In Canton."

"Oh, cool. So not extremely far away," Abigail commented.

Annabelle nodded in agreement.

Abigail smiled. "Okay so, can you explain everything to me? Katarina's family is kind of confusing. Who are your parents?"

"My parents are Emilie and Greg, and I have six siblings. They are Alec, Peter, Lacey, Joey, Greg, and Jason, and I'm between Peter and Lacey."

"Cool; okay."

"Then Uncle Michael and Aunt Elisabeth have Brian, Hayden, Ryan, Zachary, Molly, Lizzie, and Rylee. Aunt Marina and Uncle John have Marial, Patrick, Lucas, Sallie, Tyler, Jimmy, and Grace and Anna. You of course know the order of Katarina and her family." Annabelle suddenly got a thoughtful look on her face. "Ya know, Aiden would be the same age as Sallie by now."

Abigail looked confused. "Who's Aiden?"

Annabelle looked at Abigail as if she had lost her brain. "Don't you know who Aiden is?"

Abigail shook her head. "Nope; never heard of him."

Uncle John looked at the two girls through the rearview mirror.

"How long have you been friends with Kat, Abigail?" he asked her.

She answered, "Nine years. Since we were four."

"Yeah. Annabelle, it's not like they always talk about him; you don't even talk about him a lot, right?"

"No," Annabelle answered, "but sometimes I

think about what he would have been like."

"Who's Aidan?" Abigail persisted out of curiosity, a little louder than she meant.

Katarina sat up, slowly rubbing her eyes. "Yeah, who's Aiden?" she asked groggily. Then Katarina remembered as she shook off her grogginess. "Right; that Aiden."

Abigail looked from Annabelle to Katarina's uncle and then at Katarina. Uncle John sighed as he stopped the car at a red light.

"Katarina and Annabelle, please don't interrupt while I tell Abigail, unless Katarina you would like to tell your friend who Aiden is."

"May I?" Katarina asked pitifully.

He nodded yes.

Katarina cleared her throat and began to speak. "Fourteen years ago, on August fourteenth of 1999, a little baby boy was born and his name was Aiden Luke Anderson. He seemed like a healthy baby to his loving parents and faithful siblings, but five days later on August nineteenth, early in the morning, he died in his sleep. And that is who Aiden is. He is my big brother."

"Wow," Abigail spoke softly. "That's sad."

"Totally. I never-got to meet him." Katarina sighed again. "But now Mum and Dad are going to get to see him."

"Yup."

They continued to the drive in silence, Katarina trying to think through the possibility of it all. Abigail was so surprised that she even forgot to ask Annabelle about the rest of the family members. Uncle John turned into the parking lot of the banquet hall, where the luncheon was to be held. He pulled up in front of the door and dropped off all the kids, then drove off to find a parking spot.

"There you are, Kat." Emiliana came out of the door and hurried up to them. "We saved you a seat. We're sitting with Granny and Gramps and Grandpa and Grandma."

"Where do I sit?" Abigail asked quietly.

Emiliana turned towards her and answered, "You are going to sit with us next to Katarina." They all followed Emiliana into the banquet hall and down the hallway to the room in which the luncheon was being held. It was a large room and on the ceiling were several huge chandeliers. The room was crowded, and it seemed like everyone one was talking at the exact same time as everyone else.

Chapter Sixteen

Katarina pulled her bed sheets back on her and rolled over. She didn't want to wake up; she felt completely exhausted. If she woke up that meant she would have to get ready and go to school, and she so did not want to go to school today. She didn't want to do anything except sleep away the day, but she knew her sleep would be punctuated with nightmares just like her night had been. Vaguely through the fogginess of sleep, Katarina heard the door swing open and the sound of feet walking across the floor to her bed. She groaned and opened her eyes. It was Antoinette; she looked just as tired as Katarina felt. Antoinette smiled down at her and sat down on the edge of Katarina's bed.

"Hey."

"Hey," Katarina mumbled. She reached up and rubbed her eyes and sighed, staring up at her pink and cloud-covered ceiling.

"Good morning." Antoinette smiled again.

"Good morning," Katarina repeated then asked her sister, "Did you need something?"

"Yes," Antoinette said softly as she looked down at Katarina's bed. Out of the corner of her eye she saw the color purple. She looked down at the floor and saw Katarina's limp, bright purple teddy bear. Antoinette picked it up and laid it gently on Katarina's blanket.

Katarina clasped it in her hands. "Thanks. What was it that you needed?"

"I need you to get up for breakfast and school. Therese and Emiliana are almost ready and they'll be waiting for you."

"Oh, all right." Katarina sat up and groaned. "I really don't want to go to school. Why do they have to start so early? It's August 23rd–and at the end of the week?"

"Today isn't really school, and you know that. It's just for finding out where your classes are and to meet new people and get to know them."

"There are never new people," Katarina said sarcastically as she got up and headed to her closet. She stared blankly at her clothing. "I don't know what to wear," she said lamely as she violently kicked a shoebox, sending it flying into the depths of her closet. Antoinette got up from Katarina's bed and walked over to her. She put her arms around her. Katarina was breathing deeply from the effort of trying not to cry.

"Want me to help you?"

Katarina nodded. "Yes please."

Antoinette looked through Katarina's closet. She flicked through the skirts, through the pants, and through the dresses. Antoinette stopped when she came across a sweater dress. It was purple and had a cowl neckline. She pulled it off of its hanger and handed it to Katarina. Then she headed to Katarina's dresser and pulled out some black leggings and a wide, black belt. She held it out to her younger sister.

"Here you go. Get dressed and then I'll do your hair, okay?"

"Okay; thanks, Nettie." A small smile skipped across Katarina's face.

Antoinette smiled back and headed out of the room. Katarina quickly got dressed. After pulling on the dress, she looked at herself in the mirror. She pulled the belt on and buckled it on the second to last hole, to make it tight enough to fit properly. It looked just perfect. Antoinette was good at that; every time you asked her or she offered to pick out an outfit for you, she always seemed to pick out the most perfect outfit for that day. It made you wonder why you didn't think of that outfit first. Grabbing her hairbrush from her dresser, Katarina ran out the door and hurried down the stairs to the kitchen. She found Antoinette making her some scrambled eggs and bacon. She looked around.

"Where's Granny and Gramps?"

"Don't you remember they went home with Grandpa and Grandma?" Antoinette took the skillet off the hot stove and filled Katarina's plate up and placed it on the counter.

"Oh, they must have decided that after I went up to bed."

"Oh, right."

Katarina sat down on the stool in front of her and took the fork. "Here's my hairbrush." She placed it on the counter.

Antoinette took the pink hairbrush in her hand and stepped around behind Katarina. She slowly and soothingly brushed through Katarina's tangled mane of hair.

"Fishtail sound good, Kat?" she asked.

"Yes, I like fishtail braids." Katarina took the last bite of eggs and then took a large gulp of her chocolate milk. She picked up her two slices of bacon and held them each up in front of her. They were brown, slightly burnt, and extremely crispy. Just the way she liked it. Katarina took a bite from each and chewed slowly. If she sat still, she could feel the movements of Antoinette's hands as she braided Katarina's hair. Katarina felt as her braid bounced against her spine. Antoinette wrapped her arms around Katarina's shoulders and gave her sister a squeeze.

"There you are." She grabbed Katarina's

empty plate and glass and whisked them off to the kitchen sink, which was full of dirty water. "Therese got your backpack together with all your supplies that, um, Mom got you last Monday."

"Oh." Katarina began to cough as she almost choked on her bacon. She got up from her chair. "I'm done." She headed to the hallway.

Antoinette called over her shoulder as she finished washing the dishes, "Don't forget to brush your teeth."

"Yes, ma'am," Katarina called as she took the stairs two at a time.

Benedict ran past her down the stairs. "Good morning and goodbye, Kat! See you this afternoon." He bolted out the front door. Benedict went to a different school than Emiliana, Therese, and Katarina did. The girls went to West High School while Benedict went to Sheldon's Boys Academy. Sheldon's was ten blocks away from their house, so he usually car pooled with their neighbors. The girls took the bus to school. Katarina went into the bathroom where Therese was at the counter brushing her teeth.

"Hi, Therese." Katarina quickly washed her hands, grabbed her toothbrush, put toothpaste on it, and began to brush her teeth. Therese nodded at her sister and continued to brush her own. They both finished at the same time because Therese always took forever while it only took

Katarina, at her fastest, a minute and a half (she had timed herself once). Emiliana poked her head around the corner just as Therese and Katarina were about to walk out of the bathroom.

"Whoa!" Emiliana yelped, not expecting them to be right there. She recovered herself quickly and said what she had come to say. "The bus is here and we have to go now."

"I have to get my backpack!" Katarina exclaimed, indignant over being told it was time to go. Therese grabbed her hand and yanked her down the stairs after Emiliana.

"No you don't. It's by the door."

"Thanks." Katarina huffed as she stumbled after her sister. Emiliana already had the door open waiting impatiently.

"Don't expect me to always wait for you guys." She spoke tartly.

Antoinette walked into the hallway. "See you guys at lunch right?"

"You won't see me; I'm going to Cassie's house for the afternoon," Emiliana reminded her.

Antoinette nodded. "Right; okay. Just be home for dinner."

"Yes, ma'am." She rolled her eyes and let the door slam shut behind her. She ran after Therese and Katarina. Katarina was the first one to climb on the bus. She smiled at the driver. It was the same super nice guy as last year.

"Hi, Mr. Jordan."

He nodded his head at her. "Hi, Katarina."

Katarina looked about for Abigail. Mr. Jordan knew exactly who she was looking for. He smiled at her and jerked his thumb to the back. "She's in the back."

"Thanks, Mr. Jordan." She flashed him the biggest grin she had given anyone in the last week. She hurried down the aisle, pushing her sisters out of the way. Katarina made her way to the back of the bus and plopped down next to Abigail who was sitting in the second to last bench of the bus–before the one that went all the way across the back. Abigail looked up to see who had sat next to her. Her face lit up excitedly and she grabbed Katarina's arm.

"Hi! I didn't realize we had already gotten to your house!"

Katarina suddenly grinned again and giggled a small giggle. Abigail started to giggle too.

"How're you?" Abigail asked her happily. Her face was lit up, happy that Katarina had grinned and was giggling.

"I am doing okay," Katarina said putting her backpack down at her feet.

Abigail smiled, encouraging her to continue.

"I had nightmares all night last night. I hardly slept at all."

"Yeah, you look pretty bad," Abigail admitted, patting her best friend's arm.

"They were awful and sca–"

Abigail waved her hand, cutting Katarina off. Abigail put her finger to her lips and whispered, "I'd keep quiet or The Careless Kiddos might hear you and tease you about the nightmares." Abigail pointed across the aisle.

Katarina looked over and saw the group of boys the girls had nicknamed The Careless Kiddos last year in eighth grade. They were giggling amongst themselves, and she was almost positive she saw one of them point a finger at her and Abigail. Tossing her head around, she turned back to Abigail and to their conversation.

"They were awful and super scary."

"What were they about this time?" Abigail asked as they grabbed the back of the seat in front of them as the bus lurched down the road to the next street.

"I was dying this time; I was falling off a cliff and you, Nettie, Benedict, Em, Therese, and my parents were standing at the edge just watching me fall. It was like you didn't even care that I was falling off a cliff to my death."

"What else?"

"I don't really want to talk about it," Katarina mumbled and looked down at her hands.

"My mom says that sometimes telling people about certain things, just getting it off our chests, can help us feel better."

"Well, when I hit the ground at the bottom of the cliff, it was like I broke into a million pieces but I was still one whole body."

"Whoa. That's weird," Abigail said with a shudder.

Katarina nodded her head. "Yeah, it was. Then I was standing in this extremely foggy and dark place. Above me was darkness and below me was fog. I happened to look down at the fog and it looked as if it was moving towards me or like there was something in it that was moving towards me."

"Oh wow," Abigail breathed quietly, listening patiently to Katarina's retelling of her dream.

"Then suddenly out of the fog jumped this huge, monster-type thing. It attacked me, knocking me into the fog. It was ravenous and was ripping me to shreds with its mouth. Again I felt whole still; it was weird. Then suddenly I didn't feel whole–I felt the intense and extreme pain of being ripped apart by this insane monster." Abigail looked like she was getting ripped apart herself by the look of pain on her face. Katarina's face was expressionless and motionless. She continued the narration of her dream.

"I started screaming and then it was like it bit the last part of me apart and I like shattered, my heart stopped, and then I found myself lying on soft, warm ground, except it wasn't ground, it was a cloud. I looked up and I saw two people walking towards me."

"Your parents?" Abigail asked breathlessly.

Katarina shook her head sadly. "No, it wasn't. It was Aiden and God. I don't know why God appeared to me."

"How'd you know it was Aiden?" Abigail asked, slightly confused as to Katarina's last statement. They had always talked of how cool it would be for God to appear to them even if it was a dream.

"I don't know." She shrugged. "I just knew, I guess. When they got close to me, God reached out His hand to me and at first I just looked at Him and then He beckoned to me again. Then I woke up."

"Wow. That is one intense dream," Abigail said in wonder.

"Extremely. I'm surprised nobody heard me last night, since in most dreams when I laugh or scream I do it out loud too."

"Yeah, maybe you didn't actually scream loud enough," Abigail said, shrugging in wonder.

The bus lurched to a stop, slamming the girls against the back of the bench in front of them. The Careless Kiddos burst out laughing.

Rolling their eyes, Abigail and Katarina slung their backpacks on their shoulders and got up. They headed down the aisle towards the door and were the first ones off the bus. Katarina looked up at the large, tall school building in front of her.

“Ahh, Westie,” she breathed, using the favored name that all high schoolers used. “We meet for the first time.”

Abigail grinned at her and pulled her through the front doors into the large hallway. “You sound like you’re old friends.”

“Well, we are! Or almost! I do have two sisters who go here and one that did!”

“Fine.” They followed the crowd that was heading towards the auditorium to find out their classes.

“Ya know,” Katarina continued.

“That you have hardly stopped talking since you got on the bus this morning,” Abigail teased, grinning at her friend.

Katarina rolled her eyes. “Did you know! That we’re extremely lucky to be here and not in eighth grade again?”

“Yes, you are right. You’d think after last year they would have held us back since we totally stunk.”

“Yo, what are you kids doing here?” a tall senior guy asked them, sauntering along next to them. Abigail grimaced at what he had called them. “By the way, how old are you?” He looked down at them like they were weirdos.

“We’re thirteen,” Abigail said proudly.

“Dude! You’re babies.”

“But! We are smart babies.” Katarina winked at him and he chuckled.

"How come you're freshmen when you are thirteen?"

"Our mothers started us young," Abigail said, grinning. The senior held the door open for them as they walked into the loud auditorium filled with talking teenagers.

"Dude." He gaped. "Nine years ago you would have been four!"

"Dude! The old guy can do math!" Katarina gasped at Abigail. The senior chuckled and rolled his eyes at them jokingly.

"Hey, dude! What ya doin' talking to the freshmen? C'mon Matt," another tall senior shouted over the crowd. Matt sauntered off toward his buddy. Katarina called after him.

"We were in first grade when we were four."

"Cool, dude." He grinned over his shoulder at them.

Therese ran up to them. "What are you doing? You didn't wait for us!"

"Em wasn't going to help us find our way."

"Why were you talking to Matt?" Therese spoke the last word as if it was special.

Abigail gave her a strange look. "What do you mean?"

"I mean he's like the most popular guy of the senior class and you were *talking* to him? How!?"

Abigail and Katarina looked at each other and grinned. They had just held a conversation with the most popular guy for at least two minutes.

"He just asked us a question."

"Guess what the most popular guy ever did for us," Katarina said triumphantly.

"What?!" Therese was gaping wildly at them by now. Abigail was giggling behind her hand at Katarina.

"He held the door open for us." She winked at Abigail.

Therese gasped. "You are so totally joking, right? Please tell me you are."

"We aren't," Abigail responded, giggling hysterically.

Therese looked at them with pure wonder. "Wow. You're lucky. Now let me show you where you sit."

Therese led them through the crowd, weaving back and forth between people. She led them up to the front. Looking about, Katarina noticed that all the chairs that were set up in the big auditorium were divided into sections by color. The freshmen section had red chairs, the sophomore section had blue chairs, the junior section was yellow, and the senior section was green. Therese directed them to two chairs in the front row.

"You can sit there. Or anywhere, really–in your section, that is," she said. Katarina and Abigail linked arms and headed for the two seats Therese had pointed out. They sat down just as two other kids walked up to the seats; they turned and headed into the row behind the girls.

Chapter Seventeen

"Welcome, ladies and gentlemen, to the 2013 and 2014 school year. Are you all excited for some more learning?" The principal stood on the stage and spoke through a microphone.

Some of the kids groaned loudly and others booed.

The principal smiled at them all; Katarina thought her face looked kind and welcoming. She looked about mid forty. "I am Principal Munson. I can promise you that this year all of the teachers have some fun things planned; age appropriate, too, so you seniors won't have to endure the same things as the freshmen. So don't fret, my seniors." She chuckled quietly. "Now, starting with the freshmen, I will divide each grade into two separate classes. Once you are told what class you are in and what number your homeroom is, I would like all of you to please exit the auditorium and head to your official homeroom for the year. Thank you." Principal Munson rifled through her papers to find the list for the freshmen. She placed it on the top of her folder.

"Freshmen with last names beginning with A through M, please head to homeroom fifty three on the main floor. You have ten minutes to exit the auditorium."

Every single freshman with those last names jumped up out of their seats and clattered down the aisle to the door in the back on the left. Katarina heard a chair knocked over and several burst out laughing, but she and Abigail just headed towards their homeroom.

Katarina leaned over and whispered to Abigail, "Hopefully we get nice teachers."

Abigail nodded and muttered in agreement with her best friend. All the kids were jostling one another, trying to be the first one to their homeroom. Each one wanted to be first so they walked as close to each other as possible, shoving others out of the way. Abigail and Katarina walked behind the crowd at a distance.

"Hey, aren't you Katarina Anderson?"

Katarina whipped around to see who was talking to her. It was a girl about her age; Katarina assumed she was in her class for the year. The girl had curly, blonde hair and black eyes; she was wearing mascara and some lipstick and eye shadow. Abigail thought she looked familiar, but she couldn't place where she would have seen her.

"Um, yeah, that's me; who are you?"

"I'm Monica. I've seen you around the mall sometimes." Monica chewed her gum noisily. She flicked back some hair out of her face. "I heard about your parents."

"Oh," Katarina said abruptly.

Monica scrunched her nose up a little. "I'm sorry." She turned and hurried past them down the hall to their homeroom. Katarina smiled a little as Monica ran past her. Abigail wrinkled her nose up and stuck her tongue out as Monica turned around the corner. Katarina grabbed Abigail's hand and took off running.

"Come on," she called as she ran down the hallway, "or we'll be late."

"Oh, fine! Can't I please inflict pain on a girl who deep down really does not care a cent whether your parents are dead or alive? I've never even heard of a Monica, have you?!"

"Yup, her mother, Mrs. Helen Lenowski, is in the Home Gardening club. My mom was in it; that's how I know the name."

"Oh, you're smart. My mom should join that club."

"Yeah, and be forever called Sarah Anderson's friend."

"Why would she be called that?" Abigail asked as they slowed down and neared their homeroom. The girls paused to catch their breath before entering. Out of the corner of her eye, Abigail saw a man approaching. She silently motioned to Katarina to hurry up.

"She would be called that because every new member is called so and so's friend–the friend that invited them to join the Home Gardening club. My mom was called Helen Lenowski's friend for like two years and finally they called her Sarah."

"Let's go." Abigail pushed the door into the room and yanked Katarina in behind her just as the man that had been walking towards them got to the door. Luckily, two seats toward the front, right by the door were open and they slipped into them as he pushed the door open all the way and walked in.

"Hello, y'all! I am your homeroom supervisor. Yes you still need a supervisor." He winked at them all and chuckled. All the kids nervously chuckled with him. He clapped his hands and stared them all down for a moment. Everyone glanced at each other like this guy was a nut.

Abigail quietly leaned forward and whispered to Katarina, "Too bad he's only for homeroom and not any other classes; he would be an amazing teacher."

Katarina nodded in response. He turned to

the two of them and saw Abigail sitting back in her seat.

"What were you telling your friend? No secrets in homeroom!" He grinned and winked at Abigail.

Abigail blushed and spoke up in obedience, "I just said it was too bad you are only in homeroom and don't teach any other classes–and that you would be an amazing teacher." Abigail dropped off after the last word.

He grinned and pointed a finger at Abigail. "That's where you are wrong. I will be teaching y'all science in the mornings at eleven."

"Awesome, dude!" one kid said ecstatically.

Behind Katarina and Abigail, a girl raised her hand.

"Yes?" He looked at her.

"What's your name, sir?" It was Monica Lenowski. You could hear her chewing her gum again.

Abigail rolled her eyes. Katarina giggled at the look on the man's face as he realized he had completely forgotten to introduce himself. He blushed a bright red.

"I'm sorry. My name is Ryan Gaire, but you can either call me Mr. Ryan or Mr. Laughing. I'm Irish." He spoke the last words proudly.

Katarina, curious, raised her hand up high.

Mr. Gaire called on her, once again swiftly pointing his hand at her and grinning. "Yeah?

Fill in the blank—I don't know your name yet."

Katarina giggled and responded, "I am Katarina Anderson. But my..." she drifted off as the room filled with silence. She looked around the room as everyone, including Mr. Gaire, stared silently at her. Some faces were filled with pity, other's surprise that she'd actually be in school that day, and others were blank. Abigail was looking at her hands, not wanting to look at Katarina's face.

"Yes?" she asked them, knowing exactly why they were staring her but dreading the answer anyway.

Mr. Gaire responded awkwardly while repeatedly clearing his throat, "It's just, ehem, we are surprised to see you here, ehem, since you are Katarina Anderson and, ehem, your parents' funeral was yesterday."

"So?" She stared back at him, leveling her eyes at his.

Mr. Gaire became flustered and began to fiddle with the button on the sleeve of his cuff. "Well, we expected you to stay at home today."

"Oh, well, I am better now and besides, it's God's fault they died, not mine," Katarina said defiantly with a lifted chin. There was a collective gasp from any Christian or Catholic in the room—and that was over half of them, including Mr. Gaire and Abigail.

"Katarina!" Abigail said loudly.

"What? It's true," Katarina insisted.

"I'm sorry that you think about it that way," Mr. Gaire said quietly. He glanced down at his shoes. "But I think that's enough talk; let's go on to your class schedules." He spoke crisply and efficiently. He headed over to the desk that sat in the front of the room. He picked up a stack of papers and walked to the far row, away from the door. He handed part of the stack to the guy in the front seat, then he moved to the middle row and handed some more papers to that girl and then he handed the rest to Katarina.

Mr. Gaire didn't look at Katarina; she sighed and took her paper and handed Abigail the rest of them. She glanced over the schedule quickly. She had four classes in the morning and three in the afternoon. In the morning was History, then Math, English, then science with Mr. Gaire. Lunch was at noon, for an hour. Between one o'clock and one forty-five was The Arts, and at two o'clock was study hall, and then Writing.

Fun. Katarina inwardly groaned. She was going to have a ton of homework this year, but as her dad would have said, it was high school so of course it would be harder than eighth grade. She glanced over her shoulder at Abigail. Abigail was clutching her head between her hands and her teeth were clenched tightly together. Katarina knew that was the "Oh my gosh, will I live through this?" look. Abigail looked up and saw Katarina looking at her; Abigail smiled and looked at her schedule again.

Katarina sighed. *Why can't I just keep my mouth shut sometimes?* she asked herself. Mr. Gaire handed out some more papers. This one was titled "Class Etiquette." Katarina raised her eyebrows. When had there ever been class etiquette handouts? She had never seen Therese or Emiliana come home with anything like this. She glanced over it quickly.

Mr. Gaire handed out several more papers. Then, after giving them a basic idea of what each day would be like, Mr. Gaire sent them back to Principal Munson and to the auditorium. They were joined soon after by the rest of the freshmen.

Principal Munson welcomed them back. "Hello, Freshmen! I'm glad to see you all back here with me. Briefly I will go over the rules for the hallways and in between classes. Once I am through, feel free to go hang out by the front doors and get to know each other until you are picked up." She flipped through her folder quickly and pulled out the list of rules. There was some shifting in the seats, as if some kids were getting impatient. Principal Munson looked up at them and it instantly stopped. She smiled.

"It's not long, don't worry; just a few rules." Katarina heard several relieved groans. She smiled.

Principal Munson cleared her throat and spoke up, "There are six official rules of the school. Number one is no teasing or bullying allowed at all. This rule always applies. If we see anyone being bullied, the bully will be talked to by me and probably be suspended. Rule number two: no littering is allowed on the school grounds. We want to keep this place a clean and safe school. Rule number three: no garbage or foul language. Rule number four: all meals must be eaten either in the cafeteria or out on the lunch patio. No food in the halls, unless it's little snacks that you need–and those must be kept in your lockers at all times. You may find this rule very silly, but it's there to coincide with rule number two. We're trying to create a safe and happy school for all of you. I know it won't be perfect and we will have our ups and downs, but if you all choose to help, I believe we will slowly get there. Now for the final rule, rule six; it's a very unofficial rule and it's up to you to follow this one. We aren't forcing you to, we're asking you and hope you will with your whole heart." Principal Munson grinned at them and her eyes sparkled. "Rule six is be happy and enjoy your time here at West High School." She smiled at them again and then shooed them out of the auditorium. "Now go get to know each other."

Everyone looked at each other awkwardly, not wanting to be the first to get up. Katarina was sick of everyone looking at each other today, so, grabbing Abigail's hand, she stood up and marched to the door. Slowly at first and then quickly, everyone stood up from the seats and hurried out. Now they didn't want to be the last one left. Monica Lenowski caught up to them and was yanking on Katarina's arm. Katarina, rolling her eyes, stopped and spun around.

Now that she was going to talk to Katarina, Monica felt nervous. She glanced down at her feet. Katarina sighed and looked around in irritation. She put her hands on her hips and looked at Monica and raised one eyebrow. "Yes, Monica?"

"I just was wondering if you would want to hang out at the mall with me sometime." She looked at Abigail and added, "You too."

"Um, we'll have to see. We don't get to the mall often." Katarina glanced at Abigail, daring her to contradict.

Abigail looked down at the ground. Sometimes they went to the mall every Saturday just to look around.

Monica looked upset. "I think we would have lots of fun together," she insisted.

Abigail glanced cautiously at Katarina to gauge her attitude, then she turned back to Monica and replied, "We'll have to see our schedules, but I think it would be nice to hang out with you sometimes. Well, we'll talk to you later; we have to go in a moment. Bye, Monica." Abigail gave her a smile and steered Katarina around to the door.

Katarina glanced over her shoulder and called to Monica. "See ya later, Monica. Sorry that we have to go and sorry Abigail was so abrupt."

They hurried to the door as Abigail complained to Katarina. Katarina just sighed.

"Me? Abrupt? Talk about yourself! Oh, whatever." Abigail sighed. "Just pull out your phone and text Nettie and tell her to come pick us up, please?"

"Yes, ma'am," Katarina whined sarcastically. She pulled out her cell phone, tapped Antoinette's name, and typed out a message to her.

Come pick us up?

She hit send and slipped her phone back into her pocket and headed to the door and pushed it open, stepping outside. Abigail dove after her to keep up with her best friend.

"Wait up!" The door slammed shut behind her and she hurried after Katarina, who was still walking. Katarina headed to the steps and sat down on the top one. Abigail skidded to a stop and fell down next to her. She looked at Katarina silently. Katarina swung her head towards Abigail. She put her arms around her legs and stared back at Abigail as Abigail stared at her. Finally Katarina looked away.

"Yes?" She knew Abigail was waiting for her to start the conversation. Abigail sighed and opened her mouth to speak. Katarina's phone buzzed loudly and they both jumped. She pulled it out of her pocket and glanced at the screen.

"Nettie's on her way."

"Okay," Abigail said stiffly.

Katarina looked at Abigail a little awkwardly and spoke up, "If you want to talk to me about something, just say it, okay?"

"Fine," Abigail answered. Her voice was pitched higher than it normally was and she sounded slightly offended.

Katarina turned to her best friend and stated plainly and truthfully, "I am not trying to be mean or anything. I just want you to talk to me instead of these half-hearted looks and tiny smiles."

"Fine." Abigail stared fixatedly at a large stain on the stone steps. "Why did you say it was God's fault that your parents are dead?"

"Because it's true and I said that already," Katarina stated slowly and plainly.

Abigail jumped up from her seat and turned to Katarina. "You know that it's not true! You know that! Your parents taught you that! Every good Catholic knows that it's not God's fault if someone dies. That's just what happens. Everyone dies, but it's not *God's* fault!" she exclaimed loudly, getting all excited and worked up.

Katarina turned and look out across the parking lot. "There's Nettie." She stood up and walked quickly down the steps to wait by the curb. Abigail stared after her then she threw her hands up in the air and spun around in frustration. *Why? Why? Why, why, why?!* She stopped and hurried to the car where Antoinette and Katarina were waiting. Abigail climbed in and slammed the back door shut. She buckled up quickly as Antoinette drove away.

"Are you coming to our house, Abi?" Antoinette asked as she pulled out of the parking lot.

Abigail shook her head. "No, my mom wants me home this afternoon."

"Okay; that's alright with me."

Chapter Eighteen

Katarina walked into her room and flopped down on her bed. She was ready for a nap but first she deserved a trip to the computer downstairs in the office. She sat back up again and headed down the stairs. The office was a small room; it had three desks, a small armchair, and two bookshelves. Katarina glanced at two of the desks. They were pushed together so that the two occupants of the chair could look at each other face to face over the tops of their laptops. Sadly, the owners of the laptops would never sit in those well-worn chairs again. Katarina turned away from the desks; it was too sad of a thought to think about right now. She sat down at her desk and stared at the closed laptop that sat on top of it. She smoothed her hands over it.

"Too long," she breathed out. Katarina had not been online in about a week, and she had not used her laptop in several weeks. She flipped open the laptop, turned it on, and waited for it to finish loading everything. Katarina clicked on the internet and pulled up Gmail and Facebook. She typed in her password–she always did it first– then typed in her email address: katmeow45. She had thirteen emails. Most of them were sympathy emails about her parents' death. She skimmed all of those, not wanting to dwell on them too much. She looked at the last three emails to see what their subjects were. Two of them just said hi and the other didn't have a subject at all. She clicked open the first one and read it.

> "Hi Katarina!
> How're you!? I should probably introduce myself. I'm Laila Bender; I am one of your followers from your blog. I decided it was finally time to contact you and say hi! :) Since you say we can do that. I hope everything is going awesome with you. How is your family? I haven't seen any new posts on your blog lately, what's up?
> ~Laila~"

Katarina clicked back to her inbox; she would respond back to Laila in a little bit. She glanced at the "sent from" of the other email; it was from her dad from the day he died. She had been gone at the fair so she hadn't checked her email that day. Her mouse hovered over it, but she was afraid to click on it. Katarina couldn't do it. She reached into her pocket and pulled out her cell phone, her eyes glued to the screen. Automatically she dialed Abigail's number and put the phone up to her ear. It rang three times before Abigail answered.

"Hello?"

"Hi, Abi," Katarina said quietly.

Abigail could sense something was wrong with her best friend. "What's wrong, Kat?" she asked, sounding worried.

Katarina sighed and answered, "Log into my email and look at who sent the email second from the top. Now, please!"

"Okay; one sec!"

Katarina waited rigidly while Abigail logged into Katarina's email on her own computer.

Abigail's voice came flooding back to Katarina. "I'm logging in."

Katarina could hear her best friend gasp on the other side of the line. "Oh, wow. That was the day we went to the fair, right and it was *that* day, right?"

"Yeah." Katarina sighed.

Abigail spoke to her gently. "I know it's going to be really weird for a while. I know you always said he would occasionally email you and I know that it's going to be strange not to receive those anymore, but you'll make it through somehow. We all do. I've made it through slowly. We all have our days, but we also need to keep on living. That's what they would want you to do, okay, Kat?"

"Okay," Katarina said meekly. She suddenly felt like she wanted to open it up and see what her father had said that day that seemed so long ago. "I'm going to open it now."

"All right. Well, I have to go eat lunch now. Let me know if you want to talk about what's in the email."

"Okay. Bye, Abi."

"Bye, Kat; love you." Abigail hung up.

Katarina placed her phone down on the desk. She squared her shoulders and moved her mouse over the email again, ready to click it, when Antoinette called her.

"Kat! It's time for lunch!"

Katarina resisted the urge to jump up and go eat without opening it but instead she yelled back in response, "I'll be there in a moment!" Without letting herself pause in hesitation one more time, she hastily clicked on the email. Her eyes automatically squeezed shut. *No! I don't want to read it! Don't make me!* Katarina slowly opened her eyes and stared at the message in complete silence.

"Hi Kitty!!

How're you doing, sweetie? How is Abigail? Are you girls enjoying your vacation at Gramps and Granny's? What have you been doing, honey? I can't wait till you get home. I miss my little princess. We should have a dance party when you get back, okay? It's been a while since we've had one. Well, your brother is dragging me off to go get ready for your mom's and my date. I will talk to you soon! Don't stop sending us messages! Love you with all my heart, darling!
Love,
Dad"

Katarina felt something wet slip down her left cheek. She reached her hand up and swiped away the tear. She squeezed her eyes shut against the threatening pressure of the tears bursting out.

"Kat? It's been longer than a minute." Antoinette poked her head around the corner of the doorway and looked at her sister. Katarina stiffened and moved her mouse and signed out of her email quickly so Antoinette wouldn't see. She took a quick shaky breath.

"Coming, Nettie." She closed the internet and then shut down her laptop, closing the lid. Katarina hopped up and followed her older sister back to the kitchen for lunch.

Abigail walked back into the front hall after running to check her computer when Katarina had called her. She kicked her flip flops off and dropped her purse and papers onto the floor.

"Hey, Mom! I want to talk to you! Where are you?" Abigail called as she wandered down the hall to the kitchen.

Her mom called back to her, "I'm upstairs, honey!"

Abigail smiled, grabbed an apple from the fruit bowl on the table, and ran down the hall and up the stairs. She found her mom in her bedroom, sitting on her bed. Mrs. Dunham looked up from the book she was reading and smiled at her lovely daughter. Abigail walked into the room, jumped onto the bed, and crawled up next to her mom. She flopped back against the pillows, letting out a huge sigh. Mrs. Dunham closed her book and placed it on her bedside table. She turned and looked her only daughter in the eye.

"Is there something wrong, Abi?"

Abigail didn't answer right away; she just picked at a loose thread on the comforter. Mrs. Dunham placed her hand on her daughter's slumped shoulders.

"Something *is* wrong; tell me what it is, darling."

"Oh, Mom! Katarina said something today at school that I didn't like."

"Honey everyone says stuff sometimes that other people don't like," Mrs. Dunham said, speaking reassuringly. "Sometimes it's on accident, but other times it's not."

Abigail shook her head vigorously, "No, this was very different."

"How different?" she asked Abigail.

"Super different. She said, in front of the whole class, that it was God's fault that Mr. and Mrs. Anderson are dead." Abigail spoke the last word abruptly. Mrs. Dunham inhaled sharply; her eyes misted over.

"Well...." She trailed off, not having a clue what to say. "What did you say back?" she asked, finding her voice.

Abigail shrugged and answered, "Nothing; just her name. But Mr. Gaire, the man in charge of homeroom and my science teacher, said that he was sorry that she thought it was like that but he spoke very gravely like he had expected much differently from a girl who just lost parents."

"I'm sure he did. I know Mr Gaire–he goes to our church. He was at the funeral."

"Oh, I didn't see him." Abigail snuggled up next to her mother, trying to block out everything.

Mrs. Dunham placed her arm around her

daughter as she spoke thoughtfully, "No I don't suppose you would have seen him." She paused, thinking and chewing her lip like she did whenever she was thinking really hard.

Abigail reached over to the end of the bed and grabbed the apple she'd left there. Abigail looked at it hard. It was round and fat like an apple should be. It was slightly yellowish green on one part of it, but the rest was such a rosy red; it was beautiful. She was positive that's what an apple from *Snow White* would look like, minus the yellowish-green part. Abigail rubbed it on her shirt to make it shiny. She rubbed really hard so that it would be really shiny so maybe she could see the dark outline of her shadow on the apple. It worked. There was the dark, vague outline of the shadow of her head. Abigail smiled faintly at it.

"Are you going to eat that apple or just stare at it all day?" her mom asked her. Mrs. Dunham's voice was edged with laughter.

Abigail giggled, blushing a faint pink, and took a bite of the apple. Her mom went back to thinking hard and chewing her lip. Abigail continued to eat the apple quietly. The bedroom was silent except for the curtains stirring in the gentle breeze and the quiet crunch of Abigail's eating. Mrs. Dunham quickly sat up straight.

"I know what we're doing this afternoon, Abi!" She got off the bed and headed towards the door. Abigail jumped up and followed her mother.

"What?"

Her mother turned around and answered as if she had just won a grand prize or a battle against a horrible enemy.

"Visiting!" Abigail looked at her mother as if she had gone bonkers. Mrs. Dunham turned and walked calmly down the stairs and into the kitchen. Abigail followed her mother, looking confused.

"Mom? Why and who are we visiting?"

"We're visiting Katarina's grandparents" was the answer, as if they always visited Katarina's grandparents.

"But why?" she asked her mom.

Mrs. Dunham turned around and looked at her daughter. "It's time for lunch." Mrs. Dunham pulled open the door of the fridge, looked at the shelves, closed it, and picked the phone up. Abigail watched her dial the phone and put it up to her ear. She crossed her arms and watched her mom.

"Hello, is this the Anderson home?" Mrs. Dunham spoke importantly into the phone. Abigail sighed, walked to the table, and sat down on a chair. She really hated one-sided conversations; they always drove her nuts. There's no point in listening and growing aggravated. She got up and went to the fridge and took out lettuce, turkey, hummus, and tortillas. She plopped everything on the counter, then turned to a drawer behind her, opened it, and took a butter knife out to spread the hummus onto the tortilla. Abigail began to assemble her lunch and her mother's lunch as well, all the while trying to ignore her mother on the phone. She folded up both wraps, took out two paper plates, and placed the wraps on the plates. Her mom hung up the phone and walked over to the counter and placed her palms face down on it.

"So, Mom, who did you call?" Abigail asked as she reached again into the refrigerator and pulled out two glass bottles of pink lemonade. She walked to the table and set them down and returned for the plates.

Mrs. Dunham did not say a word. Finally she answered her daughter's question. "I called Antoinette and told her that I had something to talk to her about but I wanted to talk to her grandparents as well. So, I told her we'd pick her up since both Therese and Katarina are old enough to stay at home by themselves." Mrs. Dunham sat down next to Abigail at the table.

Abigail pushed a plate towards her mother.

"Thank you, dear, for making lunch."

"No problem. So can I come with you?" Abigail asked after taking a swig of her lemonade.

Mrs. Dunham looked at Abigail as if she was crazy. "Of course you're coming with me! You told me about it."

"Oh! That's what you are going to talk to them about," Abigail said as the truth dawned on her. She took a bite of her wrap.

"Excuse me. Prayers before you eat. What have I taught you?"

"Oops." Abigail chewed and swallowed quickly. She made the Sign of the Cross with her mother and the two silently prayed the meal prayer. Once they finished praying they continued to eat.

"When are we going to her grandparent's house?"

"Eat quickly and we leave as soon as we're done" was the reply. So mother and daughter both ate their meal as quickly as they could. As soon as they took the last bite of their wraps, they jumped up from the table, threw out their plates, then dashed to the door after Abigail grabbed her bottle of lemonade.

Therese walked in the door as Antoinette grabbed a rag from the kitchen sink and said, "Therese, Katarina: I have to go out for a little while. Em should be home in an hour or two. If I don't get back by four thirty, please get dinner started. Any questions, call Grandma and Grandpa's house. Please don't fight!" Antoinette ordered as she speed-wiped the counters and the table off. Katarina looked up from washing the dishes.

"What are we having for dinner?"

"I don't know; think of something. I just need to go," Antoinette replied vaguely, grabbing her purse from the island and hurrying to the front door as the Dunham's pulled into the driveway. As she shut the door, she heard Therese and Katarina arguing over whether they should order pizza from Pizza Hut or deli sandwiches from Jimmy John's. She rolled her eyes at them and opened the front, passenger-side door in the Dunham's car and hopped in.

"Why can't we just order pizza?" Katarina argued pathetically.

Therese squeezed her head, groaning with frustration. The stress and pain from the last week was catching up to her. She needed someone other than her younger sister to complain to.

"Fine; just order pizza, Katarina." With one last half-hearted glare, Therese dashed out of the room and flew upstairs to the den. Grabbing the phone, she flopped down on a pile of blankets and a beanbag chair slightly hidden behind a couch. She dialed the number of her best friend. Therese, never really having fit in at school as she grew up, had never really had a best friend until she had gotten a Facebook account and had met this girl from California. The two were extremely similar in personality and likes. Therese raised the phone to her ear and listened to it ring. Once, twice, three times. Yes; someone was home. Therese smiled a little as she heard the phone on the other end being picked up.

"Hello?"

"Hi, is this the Marlone house?"

"Yes this is; who am I speaking to?" It sounded like a guy to Therese, but she didn't recognize the voice; maybe it was her dad.

"This is Therese Anderson, Meredith's friend. Is she available to talk?"

"Let me see. One moment please."

"Sure." Therese waited as the man went to go see if Meredith could talk to her.

"Hi, Therese!!" Meredith's voice was like a longed-for breeze on a stifling, hot day.

"Meredith!! Hi!" Therese was happy again. She felt like grinning now, so she did.

"How're you? What's up? How're you guys doing with everything?" Meredith asked. She spoke the last question with slight cautiousness.

Therese responded slowly, "I am doing all right, I guess. Better now that I am talking to you!" she spoke honestly, her voice rising at the end. "Not much is up, except today was the first unofficial day of school."

"Ahh, yeah, we had that today too," Meredith said, speaking with just a tad bit of distaste in her voice. Therese giggled.

"We're all doing okay, I guess. Well as best as can be expected. I haven't really talked to anyone except for a good morning and goodbye to Nettie this morning and when she dashed out of the house a couple minutes ago, and then a small argument with Katarina."

"Ahh," Meredith said in understanding.

"I just–" Therese took a deep breath before continuing. "It's so weird right now. I mean, every time you turn the corner you expect to run into them but you don't, and now there's no one to joke with, no one to talk to when you're upset. No one to just be there."

"Yeah, I know what you mean. I felt the same way when my grandma died two years ago. I was really close to her since I'm the oldest grandkid; I've been around the longest and I've hung out with her more. We did all sorts of stuff together. We watched movies, baked treats, just sat together, and we had long talks. When she died I felt like my life was over because there was no one to do any of that stuff with me. But there was my mom and I didn't realize that at first. We never used to be close, but since my grandma died we've grown closer and now we do all that stuff together and I'm glad I've found a new friend."

"Wow. Yeah," Therese said softly.

"So maybe–I know it was both of your parents so both of your grandparents are dealing with the loss and not just one set–but maybe you can find a new friend in one of them?"

"Yeah," Therese said. "Granny has always been there for us, but it's been kind of hard to get close to either of them because they live in Ohio. They gave us the choice of either moving out to Ohio with them or them moving in with us. I personally don't want to move to Ohio, but we haven't really talked about it yet as a family."

"Where are your grandpa and grandma from Ohio staying right now? With you?" Meredith asked.

"No. They are staying with my other grandparents who live a couple blocks away."

"Oh, okay," Meredith answered. "When do you think you'll talk about it?"

"I don't have a clue. Probably sometime soon, I would imagine. For some reason Nettie went there today. I don't know why she went, though, but she said if we needed anything to call Grandpa and Grandma's. Katarina's friend's mom picked her up, but we don't have a clue why she went."

"Do you need her at home?" Meredith asked.

"No."

"Do you want her at home?"

"No–sort of...I don't really know."

"Therese, what are you doing?" Katarina shyly walked into the room and knelt on the chair in front of Therese.

"One second," Therese spoke into the phone

and then took it away and covered up the mouthpiece. "I'm talking to Meredith. Is there something you need?"

"Want to watch a movie with me?"

"Scared to go upstairs?" she asked, smirking the tiniest bit.

"No. Just miserable and lonely." Katarina turned around and flopped against the chair. "But I guess if you don't want to watch a movie with me you don't have to." It was silent behind the chair for a couple minutes. Then Therese put the phone back up to her mouth and spoke into it.

"Hey, Meredith, Katarina wants me to watch a movie with her, so I'm gonna go now. Thanks for taking the time to talk to me, though."

"Sure; no problem. Chat with you later?"

"Yeah, sure. Bye!"

"Bye!" Therese hung up the phone. She reached forward and placed it on the table. Katarina's head popped back up over the back of the chair. She smiled softly at Therese.

"Thanks, Reese."

"You're welcome, Kat." Therese smiled back at her sister.

Chapter Nineteen

"So Mrs. Dunham, what was it you wanted to tell me?" Antoinette sat back in her seat and glanced over at Abigail's mother. Mrs. Dunham didn't answer right away, so Antoinette looked at her again. Abigail saw her second look and giggled a little.

"Oh, Mom's been doing that a lot today, so don't be surprised if she keeps delaying her answers."

"Shush, Abigail." Her mother blushed a little bit, but it got her to answer Antoinette's question. "I think it would be best to just wait a couple minutes so I can tell your grandparents as well and we can all talk it over once." She turned quickly to Antoinette and looked at her sharply. "Your grandparents are Catholic, right?"

"Yeah," Antoinette answered.

Abigail muttered about the questions just getting "randomer and randomer."

"Name only?"

"No, Both sets are pretty devout." Antoinette was starting to think Mrs. Dunham was going slightly crazy with this weird conversation.

"Okay." Mrs. Dunham pulled into the Anderson's driveway. They all climbed out of the car and headed to the door.

"Is this future conversation connected to me or my siblings in any way?"

"Oh, yes it is!!" Mrs. Dunham answered vaguely.

Abigail, getting slightly frustrated with her mother's vague answers, quickly jumped in and said, "It has to deal with Katarina and her faith."

"Shush, Abigail!" Mrs. Dunham said as they walked up to the front door. She was about to ring the doorbell when Antoinette stepped in front of her, her hands on her hips.

"What's up with my sister that I don't know about?"

"Abigail!" her mother exclaimed.

Abigail shrunk back a little, looking sorry.

"You'll find out soon; really. Just a couple of minutes," Mrs. Dunham promised.

Satisfied enough, Antoinette stepped back so Mrs. Dunham could ring the doorbell. They heard it ring inside and moments later they heard the steady sound of footsteps coming into the front hall. The door opened and Gramps stood in the doorway. His face lit up a little when he saw Antoinette standing there. Some of his old self came back.

"Hello, why are you all here?" he asked them curiously. Antoinette took the liberty of answering it for fear Mrs. Dunham would say something weird.

"Mrs. Dunham has something to tell us–I don't know what it is, but apparently it has to do with Katarina and faith."

"Oh, okay. Well, why don't you all come in? Go into the living room and wait; I'll find everyone and we'll be back in a moment." He ushered them inside and closed the door behind them. Mrs. Dunham and Abigail followed Antoinette, taking off their shoes before going into the living room. Antoinette led them into the sitting room and they all took a seat on one of the couches.

A few minutes later, Grandpa, Grandma, Granny, and Gramps walked into the room. All four sat down and looked expectantly at Mrs. Dunham and Antoinette. Abigail, sitting in the middle, looked a little awkward.

"May I get a drink, Mrs. Anderson?" she asked, directing her question to Katarina's grandma. Abigail knew both grandparents pretty well, but today, in this situation, she felt awkward.

"Yes you may, sweetie." Grandma smiled at her and nodded. "You know where the kitchen is; you can have water or there's some juice or milk in the fridge."

"Thanks." Abigail smiled and hopped up from the couch, hurrying out of the room.

Mrs. Dunham looked to Antoinette to take to the lead. Antoinette sighed and introduced her to her grandparents. "This is Mrs. Dunham; she is mom's best friend and she has something she wants to discuss with us about Katarina."

"Hi, okay, so I was just curious about something. Abigail told me that at school this morning Katarina said in front of their class that it was God's fault that her parents, your children, are dead. Abigail said that she, and over half of the class, was completely shocked by what she said."

"Oh my gosh," Antoinette breathed out quietly. Her grandparents looked equally shocked as well. Abigail walked back in the room holding a glass of milk.

"She said that after Mr. Gaire expressed his surprise at her being there today. Since it's the day after the, uh, funeral." Abigail sat down again. Mrs. Dunham looked at her daughter.

"You didn't tell me that."

"I forgot; sorry" came the answer and Abigail took a drink of her milk. Mrs. Dunham turned back to everyone else and their conversation.

"So my question is this: Is Katarina very strong in her faith?" They all looked at each other, considering this question carefully. Antoinette spoke up first. "I would say she is relatively strong; maybe not super strong in her faith, but maybe moderately."

"Do you think that it's a possibility that she is on the lower side of moderate so that when she experiences grief and pain she grabs at the biggest thing or person in her life to blame for the cause of her grief and pain?"

"Katarina isn't like that, Mom," Abigail spoke up adamantly.

"Are you sure?" Antoinette questioned Abigail, feeling suddenly that this thirteen-year-old girl knew her baby sister better than she herself did.

Abigail nodded, insisting. "I am positive. Why would I lie about that?"

"I don't know," Antoinette said doubtfully, a little taken aback by Abigail's response. Abigail chewed on the edge of her finger.

"But maybe she used to not be like that but now is," Granny suggested calmly. "I have noticed in the last week, in all its hustle and bustle, that she has changed a little."

"Yeah, I noticed that too. More irritable, more grumpy, more defensive, I guess," Gramps put in.

Grandpa nodded.

"Well, if she is acting like that, then something is up."

"But do you all really believe Katarina would blame God for David and Sarah's death?" Grandma asked them all, staring them in the eyes. "She could be all jumbled up and hurting from the pain and loss of everything. I think that's the problem."

"Yeah, and she needed to blame someone."

"But why God?" Antoinette asked them all solemnly.

Mrs. Dunham sighed and shrugged her shoulders. "I honestly don't know," she said quietly.

Everyone sat back dejectedly.

"Wait!" Abigail jumped up from the couch excitedly.

"What?" Grandma asked her curiously. Everyone was looking at her in expectation.

"She had no one else to blame! I mean there was no one else in the car crash and she obviously couldn't blame us, right?"

"No, she couldn't have," Grandpa answered quickly. He was catching on. "So she picked the next closest person in her life." He was speaking quickly; he was getting excited as well. By now he was standing up too.

"God!" Abigail and Grandpa exclaimed excitedly in one voice

"We've figured it out!" Abigail sang out joyfully.

Mrs. Dunham pulled her daughter back down onto the couch. "Could you please explain in a slower fashion for the rest of us?"

"Sure," she responded and proceeded to explain their find. "Katarina is blaming God because no one knows who was involved in the car crash and obviously she couldn't blame us because it's not our fault and she knew that so she blamed the next closest person in her life."

"Because." Grandpa continued the explanation. "From everything that she knows, her faith has taught her that God is everywhere and with everyone."

"God. She picked God to blame because there was no one else to," Antoinette spoke slowly in sudden understanding.

Everyone just sat quietly, thinking. Abigail was sucking her thumb violently–something she had not done since she was two. Antoinette twirled a strand of her hair between her fingers thoughtfully and slightly defiant, but hard. She was twisting it harder and tighter with every twist. Twist. Harder. Twist. Harder. Twist. Harder.

"Would you stop twisting your hair, Nettie? It's driving me nuts," Granny spoke abruptly, interrupting the stillness. Antoinette suddenly felt a sharp pain from twisting the hair too hard.

"Ouch," she muttered and rubbed her scalp painfully. Her hand slowly fell down from the top of her head. She got up and started walking towards the front door.

"Abigail, come on; you're coming with me. I need your help." Antoinette left the room and turned towards the front door. She was still walking slowly and slightly automatically. Everyone else stood up as well. They followed Antoinette out toward the door, asking questions.

"Where are we going, Nettie?" Abigail asked.

"You can't go and talk to Katarina. It's not right," Gramps put it.

Grandma shook her head in agreement.

"Yes, you can't go talk to the dear Kat!"

"I'm not going to!" she said in a raised voice. She looked slightly aggravated. She looked at their slightly stunned faces. She dropped her voice to just above a whisper. "Sorry, guys. I'm just going to Barnes & Noble, okay? I need Abigail's help."

"Barnes & Noble?" Grandpa asked, looking at his granddaughter as if she had just lost her mind.

Granny looked at Antoinette curiously and said in a slightly funny voice, "Barnes & Noble is a very random place to go."

"Random indeed," Mrs. Dunham added.

Antoinette put her hands to her head and spun around, slightly irritated. "You'll understand later after I tell you! Can I borrow someone's car?"

"Here." Mrs. Dunham pulled out her keys and tossed them to Antoinette.

She was prepared and caught them neatly in her hands. "Come along, Dunham!" she called out as she opened the door and hurried quickly out. Abigail ran after Antoinette while rolling her eyes. They both climbed into Mrs. Dunham's car and drove off.

"Barnes & Noble?" Gramps asked no one in particular. Nobody answered verbally, but they all shrugged and turned back to the living room. All five were prepared to wait and find out Antoinette's sudden idea and whether or not it was connected to Katarina's situation.

"What are Katarina's favorite colors, Abi?" Antoinette asked the young girl as they hurried through the doors of Barnes & Noble. Abigail raised an eyebrow as Antoinette turned and led her toward the notebook section.

"You don't know your own sister's favorite colors?"

"Shut up and tell me."

"Yes, ma'am. They are periwinkle, aquamarine, and purple."

"She sure likes blue," Antoinette commented as they reached the notebook section and she scanned the shelves.

"Doesn't everyone?" Abigail snorted sarcastically.

"I like green and yellow" came the answer. "Okay; find a leather-bound journal you think Katarina would like and let me see it."

"Yes, ma'am."

The two girls both began searching the section with leather-bound journals to find the one that would spark Katarina's interest. It took them no longer than five minutes. Abigail jumped and pulled it off the shelf.

"You could have asked me to get it," Antoinette said as she took the book that Abigail offered her.

Abigail smirked and squinted her eyes. "I like to do some things on my own."

Antoinette rolled her eyes and looked the journal over. It seemed satisfactory. Good sturdy binding. It would do. She checked the price. Whoa. Her eyebrows shot up, but then she reminded herself that it was worth it. Who cared what the price was. Antoinette turned and headed for the check out. She paid for the notebook and left the building.

"Where to next?" Abigail asked as they climbed back in the car.

Antoinette answered as she buckled herself in and started the engine. "Walmart to get some pens for Katarina."

"All right."

The trip to Walmart took a matter of minutes and they were back on the road and were heading home in no time. Abigail held the bags in her lap and she glanced over at Antoinette.

"Are we going back to your grandparents'

house?" she asked.

Antoinette nodded. "Yup. I'm dropping you and the car off and then I'm walking to my house."

"Why can't I come with you? Katarina's my best friend."

"Yeah, but I don't even know how I'm going to tell her what the journal is for and that when she is done she has to give it back to me, okay? So I don't need you around–it might just fluster me even more."

"Fine."

Antoinette dropped Abigail and the car off and walked home. It only took five minutes to walk from her grandparents' house to her own house. But Antoinette was speed-walking today and got there in just a little over three minutes. She turned the knob on the front door and walked in. It was way quieter than when she had left. But when she had left the girls had been arguing. She checked all the rooms on the main floor and then hurried upstairs. Antoinette heard the quiet sound of a movie playing upstairs, so she dashed for the attic steps and ran upstairs. When she came up, the girls had just paused it and Therese was getting up.

Antoinette slowed to a halt. "Whatcha ya doing?"

"I'm going downstairs to use the bathroom," Therese responded and took the stairs two at a time. Antoinette held the notebook and the pens in her hand. There were three pens: a blue pen, a pink pen, and a purple pen. She sat down next to Katarina.

"Hey, Katarina."

"Hey."

"I have something for you."

"Oh?"

"Here." Antoinette handed the journal and pens to her younger sister. "It's to write down how you feel about everything. I mean the last week. I want you to fill all the pages up, okay? And then so if there's any possible way I or anyone else can help you feel better, I want to read it when you're done, okay?"

"Why? It's a journal for my thoughts. Why would you read it?"

"Because I want to help you and I'm your sister and I love you."

"Oh. All right. Thanks."

"You're welcome. What movie are you watching?"

"*Captain America.*" Katarina was speaking quietly, in clipped tones. That wasn't normal for her–but then again this last week hadn't been normal for anyone, Antoinette reminded herself, so they wouldn't all be normal anymore. Therese came back up then and they started the movie again.

Katarina looked at the journal. It was leather

and on the front outlined with midnight black embroidery thread was a butterfly and a large flower: a daffodil. It had a key along with it and the key was on a gold chain. She fingered the key and then unlocked the latch on the journal. She lifted open the cover and looked at the empty, lined pages. The pages were tinted with purple and there was a small floral design at the bottom, outside corner. She was going to use it, whether or not Antoinette wanted to read it when she was done. Katarina would start later today. She locked it back up and then put the chain around her neck. She placed the journal down next to her.

Chapter Twenty

Dear Diary, Friday, August 23, 2013

Antoinette just gave me this journal today. She told me to write down my thoughts and how I feel about everything that has happened in the last week. There are five of us. I have one brother and three sisters. I do have another brother, but he's dead. He died a couple days after he was born. So I never got to meet him because he is older than me. His name is Aiden. My other brother is Benedict and my sisters are Antoinette, Emiliana, and Therese. I sometimes wish I could be an older sister, but it's not possible anymore. It's not possible because I don't have any parents anymore because they died a week ago today. I miss them a lot. But I know it's

God's fault. I don't care what people say, because I know it's His fault because there is no proof of it being anyone else's fault. I mean there was no one else involved in the car crash that killed them and no one else was around to like shoot them or anything. So it has to be His fault. I mean, my mom and dad always told me that God is everywhere at the exact same time, so He had to be there when they died and He did nothing to stop them from dying. He did nothing. Nothing. I must go to bed now, Antoinette said I have to. It's only nine o'clock though. Oh well. Goodnight.

~ Katarina Rebecca Anderson

Dear Diary, Saturday, August 24, 2013

We had to make the decision today. Abigail begged me all morning with texts, telling me to vote for staying here and not moving to Ohio. I told her with every single message in return that I was already planning on doing that. She wouldn't believe me so I ended up calling her up and telling her that I promised with my whole heart that I would vote for staying here and I would do everything it might take to make it happen. I'm not about to lose my friendship with that absolute darling of a girl! I mean who would want to move three states away from their best friend? I certainly do not. Well when I told her we had all voted in favor of staying here in Boston she got super excited. I am glad everyone wanted to stay here and not move. I mean I guess it still means that Granny and Gramps have to move out here and we have to figure stuff out and everything before they do that. Apparently Grandpa and Grandma are good with this. Gramps asked if we wanted to move to a new house but stay in Boston, but we all shot that down. I'm glad. I don't want to leave this ol' house. Some people might wonder why with all its memories we would stay, but we don't want to leave because of those very memories. Memories hold pain and sadness but also joy. Lots of joy. Joy that I want to grasp with my fingers and hold close to my heart. Maybe that would bring my parents home to me and my siblings. We need them. We need them ever so much. They were taken from us at the wrong time. The wrongest time ever. Why? Yeah, that's the question I keep asking myself and all these ghosts of memories. Maybe one of these lonely, long and forgotten days I will get a positive and sure answer. One that speaks truth to me right away. I have to go to dinner now. Goodbye.

~ Katarina Rebecca Anderson

Dear Diary, Saturday, August 24, 2013

I am back, Dinner was very quiet. Every meal has been as quiet as if we all were ghosts living in a haunted house by ourselves. I do not like the silence. It gives you too much room for thinking. Yes, thinking. Thinking of memories. Memories. Memories and replays of an incident you didn't even witness. Yeah, I know I didn't witness my parents' death and I am eternally grateful for that, but that still doesn't mean I don't replay what it could have been like. How it had happened. How it played out and everything. From the scream of pain to the silence of death, it is as loud to me as if I really was there. I can't write anymore; I'm starting to cry. Goodbye.

~ Katarina Rebecca Anderson

Dear Diary, Monday, August 26, 2013

Today was the first day of school. The official first day. Monica was bugging Abigail and me again about going shopping with her. But today it wasn't just her; she roped her twin into helping her. There's always pluses in stuff like this, I guess, because we have already met two people we'd never met before school started. Monica's twin's name is Brookelyn. Yup, bombarded by the Lenowski twins, Monica and Brookelyn. They are identical twins. You could almost say they were carbon copies of each other. They both have the same blonde, curly hair that reaches just past their shoulders, the same mascara-lined black eyes, and matching eye shadow and lipstick. They probably did it on purpose so people would get them confused. Oh well, maybe we should just say yes and go shopping with them–see what it's like.

School is going to be incredibly hard. I wish Dad was still here because he always helped me with my homework if I needed it. And if Mom was here she would help me calm down if I flipped out over the big HW. Seriously, I really, really, really miss them and I want them back now! I feel like going and pounding on something. Or maybe ripping something up. Maybe I'll find some paper to rip up or something. I just feel like screaming, crying, and hiding in a big dark pit. I want to go away. Somewhere. Somewhere far away from this misery and pain. I want to be happy and I want to hug Mommy again and I want to hold Daddy's hand again. I need to go run this off before I actually decided to pound or rip something.

~ Katarina Rebecca Anderson

Dear Diary, Wednesday, August 28, 2013

School was awful today. I didn't get my homework done on time, so I got an F for my grade in like every class. At least I am sure I did. The teachers have already made it clear that high school is different than grade school. I don't know if I like high school or if I can even do it. I just don't want to go back to school tomorrow. I can't do it! I know I can't, It's too much for me. I wish that Mom was here! I miss her soo much, so much that sometimes I can't breathe because it's like I'm missing half of my body. It's really weird, I know. Sometimes it's so hard to breathe that I feel like I'm about to faint. I haven't told Abigail or anyone about it. Maybe I should. I don't really know; it's not that bad. I wrote this poem today:

I feel lost.

Lost and broken
With nowhere to go
No one to find you
The pain rips my heart
In two it feels like.
I don't want to feel lost
or broken.
I want to feel whole
Whole and complete.
No pain for me do I want.
I want them back now.
I need them.
I miss them.

I think it looks all right, doesn't it? It's a really good one. It tells how I really feel. I feel lost and broken with no one to tell me what to do. With no one to show me the right way. No one to lead me and no one to hold me. I have to go now. Antoinette insists we talk about what we we're doing with the bedrooms so that Granny and Gramps can move in. I'll write more later.

~ Katarina Rebecca Anderson

Dear Diary, Thursday, August 29, 2013

It's all figured out. We are redoing Antoinette's room for Granny and Gramps. Yes, that means she is moving in with me because none of us feel comfortable sleeping in Dad and Mom's room. I don't get to have my own room anymore. Benedict's the only one with his own room now because Em and Therese share a room. I guess I have to make the best of these very new bedroom arrangements. We aren't moving anyone around till Saturday afternoon and Sunday afternoon after Church. I'm going to do a little surprise for Nettie. While she starts moving stuff around in her room I'm going to be in my room doing the surprise. I'm going to need some help, though. Abigail is very good with art too, and I wonder how good Monica and Brookelyn Lenowski are? I'll talk to Abigail about it. It's going to take a while. I'll need lots of paint and lots of tarp to cover everything. I should probably talk to Mrs. Dunham about it, 'cause I don't want to tell anyone that is living in this house or Grandma and Grandpa. I talked to Abigail today at school today. We'll have to get the stuff this afternoon or evening because I want to be ready to start when I get home tomorrow or tonight if possible. Oh well; Nettie is calling me. I think it's time to leave for school. I promise I'll write when I get home and I'll see when we can get the paint.

~ Katarina Rebecca Anderson

Dear Diary, Thursday, August, 29, 2013

Mrs. Dunham is going to help me out!! Abigail is going to help me paint it, too! She said it was fine if I asked Monica and Brookelyn. Well, she looked fine and I know her very well so I think she really was fine. I also even texted her afterwards when I got home, and she told me she was positive that she is fine with it. I'm going to paint the large sun from Tangled on the ceiling. Nettie really likes it a lot. Like she likes Tangled, but she really thinks that the sun is pretty. So I called Monica because she gave us her number the other day when she was begging us to go shopping again. I asked her to come paint with us, and she said yes for herself and for Brookelyn. Mrs. Dunham said she would pick me and them up and drive us to the painting store. We need gold, yellow, and purple and some glitter gold paint. I want it to cover the entire ceiling as much as possible and I think I want to repaint the walls as well. Maybe the same purple as the ceiling and then we can have Tangled flowers all over the walls too because that uses gold too. It's going to be so cool! Oh, Mrs. Dunham is going to be here real soon and I want to change and get a snack so goodbye!

~ Katarina Rebecca Anderson

Dear Diary, Friday August 30, 2013

I'm so excited! Abigail, Monica, and Brookelyn will be here soon to help me paint the ceiling. We got some really cool paints! I am very glad that they have glitter spray-on paint! And they had it in gold! We got two containers to be on the safe side. Mrs. Dunham is so nice for paying for all of it. When I asked her, she seemed genuinely happy about helping and had this mysterious smile on her face. Who knows what it was for. School is out for the day. It's been going all right, I guess. Not much different; still a ton of homework that I need to get done on time. I have to read a chapter for history and it's like thirty pages long! I have some math homework to go over and then some other stuff that I'm sure I'll get done, but I want to get the room finished soon. I already got all the furniture covered up before I went to school, and last night when I was supposed to be asleep I dragged a ladder from the garage up into my bedroom through the balcony and I outlined the entire sun on my ceiling with a pencil. It took over two hours to do it and I almost fell off the ladder twice. I'm glad I have a reputation of making noises and talking in my sleep so nobody came to check in on me. It was a close call though, especially when Nettie came upstairs to bed. She has very keen hearing, like they always say a cat has. But it's done and ready to be painted. I hope she likes it because if she doesn't I just wasted a ton of Mrs. Dunham's money to make Nettie happy about losing her own room and having to share with me. At least we don't have to share a bed. Ugh! I am forever thankful my room is big enough that we don't have to share a bed. I've already moved some stuff around to make room for her dresser and such. I moved my desk over next to my bed so she could put her dresser there by the door and I moved some sweaters and such out of my closet and some pants as well to make room for her stuff. I also moved my bookshelf to the end of my bed, but Gramps told me he was going to get a loft bed for me so that I could put stuff in there. A loft bed will be really cool. He is out getting it now. I think that's where he is, since that's what Em told me.

She said that Benedict went with him and so did Grandpa. Oh, they are here! I have to run! Bye!! I'll tell you all about it later, dear diary!

~ Katarina Rebecca Anderson

Chapter Twenty-One

"Katarina! Your friends are here!" Emiliana called from the stairs. Katarina slapped her journal shut and quickly locked it and dashed out of the room, almost tripping over the ladder in the process. She ran down the stairs past Emiliana, who glanced at her.

"Guys! Hi! You're here!! Thanks for coming!" Katarina giggled in her excitement. She gave all three girls big hugs, sort of surprising Monica and Brookelyn. She looked at them all with a huge grin. Each girl felt a large grin spreading across her own face as well.

"Are you ready?" she asked them. They all nodded enthusiastically.

"Yes!" Abigail squealed.

"You bet, girlfriend!" Monica said grinning.

"Of course!" Brookelyn cried out, giggly.

Emiliana stepped into the hallway and looked at them with a raised eyebrow and crossed arms. They stopped grinning and giggling when they saw her.

"What's going on, girls?"

"Uh, nothing," Katarina said awkwardly not sure how to keep Emiliana from finding out. "Let's go to my room, girls. We need the space to get away from inquisitive eyes and curious questions." Katarina grabbed hold of Abigail's hand and ran for the stairs, yanking her along. Monica and Brookelyn dove after the two girls. Katarina led them all up the stairs and into her room at top speed. She slammed the door behind her and grinned while dancing a jig.

"This is going to be awesome, to say the least! Ahhh!" Katarina squealed, rising up on her tippy toes.

Brookelyn looked up at the sketch on the ceiling in awe. "Wow. Did you do that, Katarina Anderson?"

"Yes, I did!" Katarina grinned. "I did it last night after bedtime. I actually almost fell off the ladder twice." She grinned sheepishly at them.

Abigail gasped and exclaimed, "No way! You should have been more careful! Sheesh!"

"Calm down, Abi; it was an accident. I didn't do it on purpose," Katarina said hugging her arms to her chest in worry.

Abigail glanced out the window and took a

deep breath real quick. "Sorry, I didn't mean to panic that bad," Abigail replied and smiled weakly.

Monica stared at the two friends. "Do you want to start now?" she asked nervously.

Katarina nodded and stepped over to the table in the middle of her room that had all the cans of paint, the two cans of spray-on glitter, and various other supplies. She placed her hands on the table and smiled at them all. She lifted up two paintbrushes.

"I have all the supplies laid out on the table and I got Benedict to bring up three more ladders for us to use. Granted, we must all be careful because–trust me–it's hard to do stuff on the ceiling while standing on a ladder," she informed them all importantly.

Brookelyn grinned and giggled. "It sure looks like it."

Katarina giggled along, her eyes scrunched up with laughter. Abigail grinned and looked at them all.

"So are we ready to begin?"

Everyone looked at each other and nodded. With that one nod, the excitement started up quickly. They opened the first can of gold paint while Katarina explained her plan. She had printed out several pictures of the sun so that they would know what to do. She also gave them the explanation of everything and she said that she was going to do the glitter part because it would be kind of hard to explain how she wanted it done. After a few more instructions, they grabbed their paintbrushes and climbed up on their ladders and—following the pictures—they began to paint the ceiling of Katarina's large bedroom. They were all having a good time. The four girls worked well together; they kind of just fell into a steady, rhythmic pace. They figured out the safest way to stand so they could paint without feeling like they were going to topple off the ladder. From beneath the paint-covered brushes, the impressive painting gradually appeared. Nobody spoke at all. It wasn't an awkward silence that settled over them but a comfortable, relaxed silence. The minutes and the seconds slipped away from them; they became so absorbed in painting they lost all track of time. A knock at the door surprised them all from the silent painting. Katarina climbed down from her ladder and carefully laid her brush down on the supply table. Brookelyn looked around at them.

"What time is it, guys?" she asked curiously.

Katarina took a quick search around for her clock but then remembered that she had unplugged it. She looked down at her watch and raised her eyebrows. "It's almost six o'clock."

"Wow," Monica breathed out in surprise. Abigail looked up at the ceiling; they had gotten a quarter of it done. Not bad for four girls who were only thirteen and fourteen years old. Katarina opened the door a crack and stuck her head out. It was Therese who had knocked on the door.

"What's going on in here? Did your friends leave? You all have been really quiet in there."

"Oh, um, no, they are still here. One second." Katarina ducked back into the room and mouthed to them: *It's just Therese, want to let her in?* They all looked at each other and nodded. Katarina turned and pulled the door open. She beckoned for her sister to come in. Therese walked in and stopped in complete shock.

"What kind of catastrophe are you girls doing!?" she yelped. They all shushed her loudly and Katarina clamped her hand over Therese's mouth.

"We're redecorating my room for when Antoinette moves in." Katarina pointed up at the ceiling as she quietly explained the situation to Therese. "Want to help?"

Therese stared up at the ceiling. Then she stared at all four girls and replied, "Are you nuts!? Let's do this!" All four girls' faces broke into giant grins. Abigail, Brookelyn, and Monica all turned back to the ceiling and started painting again. Katarina handed her older sister a paint brush and set up another ladder for her.

Abigail looked curiously at her best friend. "Where'd you get the other ladder?"

"I brought up an extra one just in case Therese came looking for us to see what was going on." Katarina winked at Therese, who grinned back.

"Let's get started again then!" Therese said excitedly.

They continued to paint long into the night and didn't stop when Antoinette came to tell them it was dinnertime or when Gramps, Benedict, and Grandpa came home with the bed. They just sent them away, saying they were busy and they couldn't stop to eat or to let them set up the bed. Therese did sneak down later in the evening and rounded up some snacks and juice boxes for them all. The painting began to spread across the ceiling underneath their brushes. Every time they finished a new section, Katarina would go to the previous section and spray on the gold glitter paint in all the right places. Their arms were getting tired, but they kept on working and working. Towards midnight they neared the opposite wall. It seemed like the closer it got to midnight the faster they worked, but instead of their painting getting sloppier it almost seemed to get a tad neater. In the last several hours of painting, nobody had ever talked more than a few words–like, "Can you get me more paint?" or an occasional yelp as someone almost fell off their ladder. A comfortable companionship settled between Katarina, Abigail, Monica, and Brookelyn almost without them realizing it at all. Therese noticed it, though, and smiled a bit because she knew Katarina really had only ever had one best friend and never had any other types of friends. Well, she'd had several through the years but never any real ones worth keeping. Katarina took her paint brush dripping with purple paint and brushed it across the last bare white spot on her ceiling. Another brush–now two more brushstrokes. She sighed and smiled with content. Her once pink, cloud-covered ceiling was now beautiful and finished. Everyone carefully climbed down from their ladders and set the brushes on the table to be cleaned up. They all looked at each other in silence. Good thing they had all worn old clothing because Abigail's shirt was covered with gold paint splotches and a few purple drops. Monica had some paint on her shorts and her face and Brookelyn had a little in her hair and lots on her shirt. Therese had some up and down her arms and some on her shirt. Katarina looked down at her own shirt and saw that it had stripes of gold and purple and it was very sparkly. She giggled a little and then Brookelyn started to join in. Soon everyone was giggling at how everyone else looked.

"I vote we go crash on the couches downstairs," Therese said, still giggling. Everyone nodded and headed towards the door. Katarina stopped.

"Wait! We have to clean the brushes up and

close the paint cans."

They did so quickly. After restoring them to Katarina's room, they walked downstairs to the living room–the home of the comfiest couches. They all crashed onto the couches, but they did not fall asleep right away because they were just so excited to have finished the painting on the ceiling so quickly.

"Do you think she will like it, guys?" Katarina asked as she lay propped up on pillows with her feet on Abigail's lap. Abigail was slouching comfortably in the squishy, leather couch. It was so soft and squishy you almost literally sunk into it. Brookelyn was slumped in a large, leather comfy chair. Monica and Therese were lounging together on another couch. Therese shook her head and smiled at Katarina.

"Nettie will love it. Trust me, honey."

"I'm sure she will," Abigail said, smiling softly. She slowly moved her hand forward and started to tickle Katarina's feet to get them off of her lap. Katarina jerked her feet away and tucked them underneath her. Therese flipped to her side and curled up so Monica would still have room on the couch.

"I vote it's time for us all to go to sleep, since it's twelve thirty. So goodnight, y'all." Therese closed her eyes.

"Oh, fine," Katarina muttered and closed her eyes as well. Abigail, Monica, and Brookelyn followed suit and soon all that could be heard in the room was the sound of their steady breathing.

Antoinette woke up quickly. She reached over and shut off her alarm clock. Why hadn't she turned it off? Now she was awake on a Saturday at six thirty. She threw back the covers and got out of bed. Antoinette threw on a pair of track pants and a tank top. After brushing her hair, she stepped out into the hallway. She stopped suddenly, remembering. *Right! That's why my alarm is set! I'm moving into Katarina's bedroom today! Rats!* She stuck her tongue out slightly then shook her head as she continued to walk down the hall to wake her siblings and Katarina's friends up. It wasn't Katarina's fault that she had to share a room with her. It was no one's fault. Antoinette had noticed herself saying that to herself a lot lately. If she didn't, she was afraid she would end up in the same fix Katarina was in. Antoinette stopped at Katarina's door and knocked on it softly. There was no answer. Antoinette turned the knob and pushed it open quietly. She looked at the bed–no one was in it–then she noticed that there was a tarp covering it. She looked around the rest of the room and saw all the other tarp-covered furniture. Her eyes traveled to the table in the middle that held paint cans and paintbrushes. Antoinette walked into the room with a confused look. What on earth was going on in here last night? The smell of fresh paint pulled her head up towards the ceiling. What she saw made her gasp out loud.

"What on earth?!" She stared at the picture on the ceiling. *What will that girl think of or do next?!* She turned and ran down the stairs to find Katarina. She looked in the kitchen first and then in the office. Nope. Antoinette decided to check the living room. Maybe Katarina and her friends were watching a movie with the volume down. Antoinette walked into the living room to find Therese, Katarina, Abigail, Brookelyn, and Monica sound asleep on the couches and a chair. Antoinette crossed her arms over her chest.

"Katarina, Therese! What happened last night in that bedroom upstairs?" she spoke loudly and firmly.

Therese, who always slept lightly, flew up from the couch at the sound of Antoinette's voice. "Who's there!? Guys! Call the cops!" Therese rubbed the sleep out of her eyes as the other girls slowly came out of sleep. When her eyes focused on Antoinette, she breathed a sigh of relief. "Oh, it's just you." She paused. "Wait–what did you just ask?"

"I asked what happened in that bedroom last night. The ceiling?"

"Ahhhh!! Katarina, wake up!!! Don't ever

believe what I say again!! She doesn't like it!!" Therese pulled Katarina up off the couch and shook her to wake her up. Katarina jerked awake.

"Wha–? What's going on, Therese? Why did Antoinette ask what happened to my bedroom?" After asking that, Katarina fully woke up. "Oh no!!" She fell back into the couch.

Abigail groaned and covered her face with a pillow. Brookelyn and Monica both looked like they wanted to sink into the floor. Therese's face was panic stricken, and she looked like she wanted to sink through the floor as well. Antoinette still stood in the doorway with her arms crossed, waiting for them to answer. They heard the front door open and the sound of someone walking into the kitchen.

Benedict walked up to the door and looked at them all. He had running shorts and a t-shirt and gym shoes on. He had taken up running after his parents had died. He said it helped him relax and everything.

"What's going on?"

"Um, the girls painted Katarina's ceiling with purple and gold paint," Antoinette informed him. Her voice held a crisp tone to it.

"What? What does it look like?"

"The sun from *Tangled*," Therese answered in a choked voice. They heard a stifled sob from the couch where Katarina was hiding.

"Wow. What were you thinking?" he asked,

not knowing he was pouring oil onto an already-kindling fire of anger in Katarina.

Katarina shot up from the couch, her eyes filled with anger and hurt. "I did it because I was trying to make the best of having to share a room with you. I mean, who wants to share a room with their sister after getting to have their own room for their whole life?" Katarina shouted.

Abigail stepped towards her, reaching out her arms.

"Who wants to have to share a room with their sister when there's a whole big reason behind it–a reason that hurts? Why?! You wouldn't be moving into *my* room if Gramps and Granny were not moving into yours! And they wouldn't moving into yours if God hadn't killed *my* parents!!"

Katarina was sobbing by now and Abigail tried to put her arms around Katarina but Katarina shrugged her off. Therese was crying silently and Benedict was staring at his younger sister; his face was like a stone–no expression showed. Antoinette looked hurt.

"God did not kill Mom and Dad, Katarina. And you know that," she said, speaking as levelly as she possibly could. Her voice was filled with hurt.

"Yes He did!"

"No He did not!" Antoinette replied again, in a louder, slightly angrier, voice.

"What on this earth is going on!? Can't a person get some decent sleep in this house!?" Emiliana stood in the doorway. Her hair was all messed up and she looked half asleep. She was awake enough, though, to be mad about getting woken up.

Abigail sighed and rolled her eyes. It was time for her and Brookelyn and Monica to leave. She gestured to the twins and pointed to the door. They nodded and followed Abigail as she slipped past the Andersons. They left Antoinette, Emiliana, and Katarina all glaring at each other. Benedict went and sat down on the couch and Therese was still crying. Katarina finally broke down and began to sob hard. All the anger was diminishing from her.

"I just wanted to paint it for you. I wanted you to be happy about moving into my room. I wanted to make the best of it. So I decided to paint the ceiling for you. That's why it's the sun from Tangled–because I thought you liked the sun." Katarina dropped onto the couch, still sobbing her heart out. "I did it so you would be happy; I didn't want you to get mad. You weren't even supposed to see it till everything was done in the room." All the anger seemed to have drained out of Katarina and she looked like a helpless, pathetic child just wanting to do good. Antoinette couldn't look at her little sister. She didn't like her looking like that–it hurt her too much. Antoinette felt a lump rise in her throat.

"I'm sorry, Katarina. I didn't mean to get mad at you. It's just..." Antoinette sat down on the arm of a chair. "It's just with everything going on I'm just so stressed out and I'm exhausted and..."

"Okay, we get it. We get how you feel. We all feel that way, okay? Stop trying to make us pity you," Emiliana said in a tight, biting tone. They all looked up and stared at her.

Benedict gave her a look of annoyance. "You can be stressed out and tired, Em, but you cannot take it out on us; all right?"

"Who said I was taking it out on you guys?" she asked sarcastically. She leaned against the doorjamb with crossed arms and an irritated look.

Therese rubbed the tears off her face before replying. "It's quite obvious."

"Oh, well, that's your guys' problem. I am not taking anything out on anyone." She glared at them all. "I'm going back to bed if anyone really cares." She turned and stomped out of the room.

Chapter Twenty-Two

"So is everyone ready to help move Antoinette's stuff to Katarina's room?" Gramps and Grandpa walked into the living room, where they all still were after Emiliana had run out of the room. They all just stared at the two of them. Grandpa raised his eyebrows.

"Okay. I guess not. Have you all had breakfast yet?"

"No," Therese said quietly. Katarina brushed past them all, sniffing.

"I'm not hungry. I'm going to go clean up *my* room." She marched upstairs. They all heard the emphasis.

"We aren't ready at all. Sorry, Gramps and Grandpa, I know we told you we would be, but we aren't," Antoinette said. She looked distressed; Grandpa wondered why they all looked miserable.

"Okay," Grandpa said. "What if we build Katarina's bed first?"

"Oh no! I guess her room is a disaster. There isn't any room to build it," Benedict said quickly. Therese got up from the couch.

"I should go help her. I helped make it." She brushed past them too and ran upstairs. She walked into Katarina's room, where she found Katarina slamming and shoving stuff around as she cleaned up. Therese walked over to her sister's bed and started rolling up the tarp and then moved onto another. Katarina finally noticed that her sister was helping her. She stopped, holding a box in her hands.

"You don't have to help me; you know that, don't you?"

"Yes, I do." Therese insisted, "I helped paint the ceiling last night."

"Oh, thanks."

The two sisters continued to clean up and move stuff around. It did not take them very long since a lot of the stuff was ready to be moved and had already been shoved into boxes. Once they were done, the entire floor was cleared and there was a large space for Grandpa and Gramps—with Benedict's help—to build Katarina's new loft bed and take down her old one. Katarina stared around at her room.

"Where is this bed going? Do you know,

Therese?"

"I think it's going up in the attic, but I'm not sure. They might put it downstairs and take it apart."

"Oh. I like the attic idea better."

"Yeah, me too," Therese agreed. They looked at each other and smiled.

"Well, let's go tell them that they can set up my bed," Katarina said as she sighed heartily. Therese took her younger sister's hand and squeezed it. They turned and left the room to go find their grandpas, who were in the kitchen with Antoinette and Benedict.

"Hey guys," Katarina said as they walked in. "We're ready to help move stuff. My room's all cleaned up and stuff."

"Okay, sounds good." Gramps smiled at his granddaughters. Grandpa ruffled Katarina's hair while she playfully tried to duck out of the way.

"So let's go put some rooms together!" he spoke cheerfully.

"Off we go," Benedict said, heading to the garage with his two grandpas to get the box that held Katarina's new bed. Katarina went into the front hall to the closet where they kept shoes and coats as well as bins for each of their little things. She opened the door and reached into her bin and pulled out her cell phone. She smiled a tad; her parents would be proud that she was keeping her cell phone in the bin or on her dresser more often and not carrying it with her all the time. She was leaving it in the bin because she was hanging out with Abigail ten times more than she used to. Abigail had been over almost every single day the last week and they had already had two sleepovers together, not including last night's with Brookelyn and Monica. She turned her phone on and tapped out a new message to Abigail, Brookelyn, and Monica.

"Hey girls! sorry about us all getting mad and you having to see it :P I didn't expect Nettie to get mad like that. Sorry. I hope I see you all soon. <3"

There, that was done. She walked into the kitchen and set the phone on the counter. Therese was still in there cleaning up. They had had to make a chore schedule because they were so used to Mom and Dad doing half the stuff that nothing was getting done. Katarina glanced at the schedule on the bulletin board that hung on the wall. She had lunch clean up.

"Kat, want to help us with the bed?" Benedict stuck his head into the kitchen.

She shook her head in response. "No, I'll just watch." Katarina smiled and followed her brother up the stairs.

"Benedict?"

"Yes?"

"Have you ever wondered what life would be like if Aiden hadn't died?"

He said after hesitating a few moments. "Yes, but not very much recently,"

Katarina looked at him as they paused on the top step. "It would be very different, right?"

"I don't know." He shrugged honestly.

"Maybe Mom and Dad wouldn't have died."

"We can never know," Benedict said, preparing to continue walking to her bedroom.

"Or it could have been the same just with a brother?"

Benedict stopped again and turned on his heel and looked at her, "Kat it's not worth wondering because one will never know. Ever."

"Oh, okay," Katarina said quietly. She reached forward and slipped her hand into Benedict's. He squeezed and they continued to the bedroom, where their grandpas were. Gramps and Grandpa had already gotten the boards and such out of the box and had spread them out over their workspace. Benedict went over to help them out and Katarina went and sat on her other bed.

"Guys, am I using the same mattress or did you get another one?"

"I think we're using the same mattress and just taking down your bed and storing it either in the basement or the attic, all right?" Grandpa replied as he looked over the instructions. Katarina banged her legs on her bed as she swung them back and forth. "All right. Do you want me to unmake my bed then?"

"Yes please," Gramps responded as he got all the tools separated and ready and all the screws in piles.

"Okay." She hopped off the bed and began to unmake her bed. She rolled up each sheet in a ball and folded up the comforter so it was a nice size that would be easy to carry. She plopped her pillow, her decorative pillow, and her three little heart pillows in a towering pile on the floor. She had already put her several stuffed animals into a box so they would be out of the way of painting and everything. Katarina only owned six stuffed animals. She had seven or eight at various times when she was younger, but she either lost the other two or got rid of them for some reason. She never could quite remember where they had gone or what she had done with them. Once she was done, Katarina sat down on her mattress to watch them build her new bed while she imagined where it would go and what would go underneath it. While Katarina daydreamed and watched, the bed grew up before her eyes. Soon it was done and it looked really cool. Katarina walked over to look at it. The bed had a built-in ladder on the side and railings wrapped all the way around. She walked underneath it to test the height. Good; it was still taller than her. She wouldn't bonk her head trying to stand up straight under it. Katarina smiled. She would like her bed.

"Okay, where is this bed going, Kitty Kat?" Gramps asked his granddaughter while he stretched his back. Katarina pointed to the wall next to the balcony doors. It was a good-sized section of wall and there was window in it.

"But then it would be in front of a window, Kat," Benedict pointed out.

Katarina nodded her head. "Of course. That way there will be extra light under it besides lamplight."

"Oh, good point, honey," Grandpa said, nodding his head in agreement.

Gramps nodded as well. "You are right about that."

"Then let's do that," Benedict said as he walked over to the bed to move it. They carefully lifted the bed across the floor and moved it into the spot that Katarina wanted it. She nodded her head in satisfaction. *Good thing my desk is a smaller one because I know exactly where it's going.*

"What are we moving next?" she asked.

"I say we move from top to bottom," Grandpa said as we he walked over to the other bed. "Let's get this mattress up there and then you can remake your bed." The men moved and grabbed the bulky, awkward mattress, moved it across the room, pushed it up over the rails, and popped it into place. The mattress only fit because they had gotten a bigger-sized loft bed. Katarina grabbed her sheets and hopped up the ladder the first time and as quick as wink put the sheets on. Benedict tossed up the comforter and she tucked that in real quick as well. Next he sent up her pillows and her stuffed animals and then her special blanket that she always kept on her bed. Katarina moved that all around and made her bed presentable for the day and then climbed down.

"What do you want underneath the bed?" Benedict asked. He stood with his arms crossed and his feet apart.

"I want my desk and my beanbag chair. But I can move the beanbag chair," she responded. The men moved over to the desk and took out all of her drawers, moved her chair out of the way, and picked it up. They gingerly moved across the floor, trying to be careful so they wouldn't drop it on their feet.

"I want it on the side. Between the wall and the ladder. It should fit," Katarina directed as she looked doubtfully at her desk. They set it down under the bed and pushed it into the right spot. It fit perfectly. Katarina moved her beanbag chair and shoved it into the open spot and plopped three more fluffy, large, lounge pillows and two more blankets on top of it. Suddenly she got an idea and ran out of the room while Grandpa, Gramps, and Benedict began to take apart her old bed. She hurried to her mother's linen closet. She remembered the chiffon-type curtains that had been in the living room and sitting room. They were a light blue, if she remembered correctly, but that went with her walls and her purple and gold ceiling. She stood on tippy toes and reached around on the second to the top shelf. She felt something soft; was that them? Katarina grabbed onto them and yanked them off the shelf, pulling several sheets with her. They toppled down on her head and Katarina knocked them to the floor.

"Oops."

She heard a giggle and turned around; Abigail was standing behind her.

"You're back!" Katarina cried out, running to give her a big hug, in the process trampling the sheets and the curtains she had just knocked off the shelf.

Abigail giggled again. "Of course I came back. When I saw your text, I knew that everything was fine. Besides, you always yell at me for leaving when you say I'm technically part of the family."

Katarina giggled and grinned at her friend. "Of course you are! You've basically been through almost all of our 'ups and downs.' Remember the time I got sick with the chicken pox and your mom had to literally drag you out of my room because you wanted to stick around and entertain me—but your mom didn't want you sick because she was too busy right then with work?"

"Oh, yeah! I ended up getting sick anyways."

"Yeah."

Abigail looked down at the sheets and curtains on the floor. "What were you trying to do when I came up?"

"Oh, I was getting these curtains for my new bed." Katarina held up the chiffon curtains. She had remembered correctly. Katarina turned and shoved the sheets back up on the shelf, then shut the closet door.

"Awesome! Can I help you put them up? How're you doing it?"

"Well," —they walked back to the bedroom—"I'm going to put one of these on the curtain rod." She held the curtains up. "And the rest I'll put around my bed somehow to make it a little curtained-off area."

"Neat!! I love it! Oh, what are they doing with your old bed?"

"They are taking it down and putting it away in the attic or the basement," Katarina answered as they stepped back into her bedroom. Her brother and grandpas were almost done taking down the bed. Katarina led her friend over to her new bed in the corner.

"That's such a cool bed!" Abigail squealed excitedly and danced around a little. Katarina nodded; her eyes were lit up in excitement.

Abigail clapped her hands together. "Let's put the curtains up!"

Katarina dropped all of the curtains onto the floor and then separated one from the pile. "Here, Abi, want to go up on my bed and take down the other curtain?"

"Sure." Abigail climbed up the ladder and went over to the wall side of the bed. The bed was far enough away from the window that she could reach her arms down and unhook the curtain rod from the window. She pulled it up and gathered the curtain up onto the bed, then she handed it down to Katarina and climbed back down. Katarina handed the new curtain to Abigail and replaced the old one before putting the rod in the window and positioning it at the right length. Good; it was still long enough but not too long. She pulled back the curtain and hooked it on the left curtain hook. Abigail called Benedict over and he helped them unscrew the right curtain hook.

Next the girls worked together to hang up the other curtains all around the lower part of the bed to make it similar to a tent. Two of the curtains were for extra wide windows, so she used one of them on the end of the bed and it made it all the way across. Then they used the second one for half of the side of the bed. After looking at the bed, Katarina decided she didn't need the third smaller curtain because there was the perfect, little spot to get under the bed. Abigail stared thoughtfully at the bed.

"What if you actually use the curtain and hang it up on the inside of the bed–like, here, behind the ladder." Abigail waved her to the ladder as she spoke.

Katarina nodded, thinking about what Abigail was describing.

"Hey girls, we're going to start bringing in Nettie's bed so make sure you stay out of the way, okay?" Gramps stuck his head into the room and looked at them. The girls nodded and Katarina looked around the room and realized her old bed was gone and there was an empty space where it had been just half an hour ago. She turned back to her new bed and and the two girls hurried to put up the last curtain and find the curtain hook Benedict had taken down from the window frame. They borrowed tools and screwed the hook onto the ladder so Katarina could hook it open if she wanted to. Once they were done, while staying out of the way, they moved her bookshelves next to Katarina's bed and arranged everything else so she had half of the room for her stuff; she left the other half for Antoinette. Having the loft bed helped Katarina out a lot in trying to condense her things. Antoinette and Emiliana came in, carrying some of Antoinette's stuff. Katarina and Abigail left the room and headed to Antoinette's to grab more things. They were heading back to Katarina's room with a load when they passed Antoinette and Emiliana.

"Where's Therese?" Katarina asked as she struggled to hold onto the large box in her arms.

"She's preparing lunch for us," Emiliana responded as she ducked back into Antoinette's room.

"Oh." Katarina hurried after Abigail to drop her box of stuff off in the room.

Katarina pushed the door open and walked into her–and now Antoinette's–room. She paused and her eyes roved over the room. She liked the new look. She glanced at her side of the room. It looked homey and cozy. Her eyes drifted to the ceiling. It looked gorgeous and it had worked! The light did reflect off the glitter closest to the ceiling light. A shudder ran through her, thinking what had happened this morning after Antoinette had seen it.

Everything was fixed and everyone was happy now. Antoinette had forgiven her for painting the ceiling without permission and had told her she liked it too. Emiliana had apologized for yelling at them all for waking her up, and Katarina had forgiven both of them. Neither Gramps nor

Grandpa had said a word when they had come into the room to move stuff around, but Katarina had seen a raised eyebrow from Gramps. She giggled a little. Katarina's eyes drifted back toward her bed and she took off running and climbed up the ladder and bounced onto the mattress just like a little girl. She giggled again. Katarina turned and sat crossed-legged on her bed. She stared down and around at the room around her. She had a skyview now. Katarina turned her head and looked at the wall. On it she had moved her calendar and her bulletin board as well as a framed picture of her whole family with Abigail and her mother. Katarina reached under her pillow for her diary and a pen. She opened it up and began to write.

Dear Diary, Saturday August, 31, 2013

It's all done. Antoinette has officially moved in, and it has become not just my room but Antoinette's and my room. I really like my loft bed. It is super cool. My view of the room is from above now. Abigail helped me finish up my side of the room and then we helped Antoinette with her side. It looks pretty cool too. She asked me for advice on how I thought I should arrange some things. I'm glad; I like to help people organize and arrange stuff. I just wish Mom and Dad could see our new room. But I guess if they were here Antoinette wouldn't have moved into it. Oh well. I wish Abigail could have slept over tonight, but she was just over last night and I guess Mrs. Dunham wanted to go to the movies with her. A mother-daughter thing. I wish Mom was still here so we could go on mother-daughter dates. I did go on some with Mom and I am very glad. Oh! I just realized that because Gramps and Granny are moving in I'll never get to go to my secret place! I'm going to miss that place really bad! I'll have to tell Abi...

Chapter Twenty-Three

Seven Years Later

Katarina turned the knob and pushed open her front door. Pulling her rolling suitcase behind her, twenty-year-old Katarina walked into the front hall of her old house. She lived with Emiliana and Therese. They had all decided to keep living in the house instead of moving to an apartment. Antoinette and Benedict were both married. Antoinette to Peter and Benedict to a girl he had met through church. Antoinette already had a little boy and a darling baby girl, and Benedict and Caitlyn were expecting a baby but didn't know the gender yet. She only had one grandmother and one grandfather left; Granny and Grandpa. Granny had been in the hospital for the last couple weeks and Grandpa was living in a small apartment a couple blocks away. Katarina left her suitcase by the bottom of the stairs and headed into the kitchen. School was out for the summer; she had just finished her second year of college. It was going good—well, truthfully it was going all right—not the greatest, but all right. It was better that Abigail went to the same school as she did because then she at least had a piece of home with her. Therese would be home from school today too. Emiliana would be home in about an hour—she had just texted Katarina. Katarina looked around the large kitchen and all the old, familiar things. Everything was just like it had been when she had come home for Christmas break. She hadn't come home for spring break because the three sisters had gone to Antoinette and Peter's house. Katarina sniffed a bit. The air smelled stale. This house needed some fresh air. Katarina hurried around the house, upstairs and downstairs, shoving open windows and doors and letting the fresh, summer air blow in. She even aired out the attic. By the time she was done, she was ready to have a snack. The slim girl walked back to the kitchen in search of food. Katarina paused.

"Wait; there's no food in the house," she said, remembering, and then paused again. "Nope, Mrs. Dunham said she bought some food for us yesterday; right," Katarina spoke aloud again. She had recently slipped into the habit of talking to herself. Abigail, who shared a dorm room with her, was finding it a little creepy and had ordered her to stop, but Katarina always forgot. She pulled open the fridge door and looked at what was on the shelves. Hmm, there were some containers of yogurt, some milk, eggs, cheese, and deli meat. Katarina reached in and grabbed a container of yogurt and went to a drawer and pulled out a spoon. She sat down on a stool at the counter and opened up her yogurt and began to eat it.

"Yum; strawberry and chocolate." She smacked her lips together. "Oops, good thing Abi's not here, I'm doing it again." She rolled her eyes at herself and continued to eat. Once she was done she dumped the container and put her spoon in the sink to wash later. She headed to the stairs, grabbed her suitcase, and brought it up to her room. She had her own room again. Katarina looked up at the ceiling. It was still painted purple and gold with the *Tangled* sun on it. She chuckled; she had done all sorts of wild things when she was growing up. Katarina set the suitcase by her bed and went down to get the rest of her bags from her car. She shut the trunk and carried in her backpack and two more rolling suitcases. She carried her bags upstairs and dropped them by her other suitcase. Katarina knew she should unpack her bags now, but she didn't feel like it. After debating with herself, out loud, she decided to just unpack and get it over with. She searched in a bag for her iPod speakers and hooked her phone up to them and put some music on. It was a pretty song. The song was on the slower side but Katarina still liked it. She sang along with it.

"You look at me and you see right through me. Not seeing anything at all-all. That's just how I want it. I want it that way. For I want to be invisible. Completely, fully, invisible." She opened up her other bags and began to pop things into drawers and into her closet. She was basically shoving things away for now; sooner or later she would have to organize her drawers but for now this was good. By the time she was done unpacking Emiliana arrived. Katarina heard the door open and Emiliana walk into the hall. Katarina jumped up and ran down the stairs to greet her sister.

"Hey Em! How're you?" Katarina said, jumping down and skipping the last two steps.

Emiliana shook her head with a sigh of disappointment. "Will you ever grow up, Kat? You're twenty!"

"Who wants to grow up too fast? I want to take it slow," Katarina responded, gigging merrily.

Emiliana hugged her sister tightly. "Well, who cares? I'm still glad to see you and I'm glad it's summer!" Emiliana said, sighing dramatically.

Katarina looked at her sister weirdly. "When

did you get so dramatic? I can't remember when you ever were dramatic growing up," Katarina said.

"What about all those plays we'd do with Peter and Abigail when we were little? I was dramatic in those."

"Ridiculously dramatic." Katarina rolled her eyes dramatically as if to show Emiliana the proper way to be dramatic.

Emiliana playfully hit her. "Now who's being ridiculously dramatic?"

"No, I'm being properly dramatic," Katarina retorted and stuck her tongue out at her sister.

Emiliana set down her suitcase and looked around. "You already opened the windows?" she asked.

Katarina nodded her head yes. "Yup; it's all taken care of. Oh, and Mrs. Dunham bought us some food supplies, so there's bread in the cabinet and some stuff in the fridge, like yogurt."

"That's like the only food you think of: yogurt," Emiliana spoke sarcastically and rolled her eyes as she walked to the kitchen.

Katarina skipped after her sister. "But yogurt's so good! I could live on yogurt! Besides, the yogurt Mrs. Dunham gets is healthy for you."

"Hah, can't convince me about that. Is there any candy in here?" Emiliana asked, grinning.

Katarina shrugged and replied, "I don't know. There might still be some left from Christmas."

"Hah. That's really old." Emiliana grinned as she searched the cabinets for candy.

Katarina groaned. "If you don't eat something healthy, I'm going to call Nettie right now and make her tell you to eat some yogurt."

"No!" Emiliana protested loudly. The phone rang loudly, interrupting their antics.

"Maybe that's Nettie," Katarina said, diving for the phone before Emiliana could get it. She read the name on the phone. "Hey! It *is* Nettie."

"Just answer it before you miss her!"

"Fine." Katarina answered the phone and spoke into it, "Hey!"

"Hey, Kit Kat," Antoinette said.

Katarina shot a look at Emiliana. Antoinette's voice sounded funny. "What's up?"

"Did Benedict call you yet?" Antoinette asked.

"No, he hasn't. Why? What's wrong? Is something wrong?" Katarina gripped the phone in fear of what could have happened. She hoped it was nothing extremely awful; she had seen too much of that in the last seven years.

"You need to get to the hospital now; they think something could happen to Granny in the next couple hours. Uncle Greg and Aunt Emilie, who are visiting Granny, called me and said we should probably go there."

"Okay; we'll leave now. Bye."

"Bye." Antoinette hung up the phone.

Katarina turned and stared at Emiliana; her face was pale with fear and heartache. Emiliana turned around from looking in a cabinet.

"What happened?"

"She said that Uncle Greg wants us to go to the hospital because Granny is worse and the doctors aren't sure if she'll get really bad or not. You want to drive?"

"Sure." Emiliana followed her sister out of the kitchen. Katarina ran upstairs to her room and grabbed her purse while Emiliana got her phone and keys from her backpack in the front hall. Katarina came hurrying downstairs and the two sisters quickly left the house, locking the front door behind them, and climbed into Emiliana's car and drove off.

"Does Therese know yet?" Emiliana asked as she carefully guided the car down the busy main street of town as fast she dared to go.

Katarina shrugged and answered quietly, "I don't know; Nettie didn't say. I should probably check, though, and see where she's at." Katarina reached down for purse and pulled out her phone. She dialed Therese's number and waited for her to answer.

"Hello, Therese," Katarina said.

"Hi, Kat; what's up?"

"Have you left school yet?" Katarina asked.

"Yeah; I'm almost home, why?"

"Don't go home!"

"Why not?"

"Why don't you just tell her?" Emiliana asked.

Katarina looked over at her sister with raised eyebrows. "Oh, um, you need to go to the hospital 'cause Granny is worse and Uncle Greg wants everyone to be there."

"Okay, I'll see you there." Therese's voice was softer now. "Bye."

"Bye."

The two sisters rode in silence until they reached the hospital. Once there the girls hurried inside and went to the reception desk. The nurse behind the desk looked up from her papers.

"Hello, can I help you?"

"Hi, can we see Mrs. Eileen Jones?" Emiliana asked politely.

The nurse smiled and replied, "Oh yes, I remember you; you're some of her granddaughters, right?"

"Yeah, that's us. I'm Katarina and this is my sister Emiliana."

"It's nice to meet you both officially; my name is Leah Mason. All right let's see." Leah checked her computer and then smiled sweetly again and nodded. "Yes, you may go see Mrs. Jones."

"Thank you, Leah." Emiliana smiled and nodded her thanks. Katarina smiled to the sweet nurse as well. The two girls head down the hallway toward the elevator and stepped in. Emiliana pressed the button for the fourth floor. When they stepped out of the elevator they met up with Peter and Antoinette and Benedict and Caitlyn. They had come to see if they were there yet. Antoinette looked as if she was going to start crying. Katarina went pale with fright.

"How is she? Bad?"

"Yeah. The doctors don't expect her to live past tonight." Peter nodded in response to her question as he informed them of what the doctors had told them. "She is deteriorating very rapidly. She just has no strength to fight to stay alive."

"Oh, is–is she awake?" Katarina asked as she took a deep breath trying to be brave.

"Yes, but she is a little out of it sometimes, all right?" Benedict warned them. They nodded. The group set off to head towards Granny's room when the elevator door opened behind them and Therese stepped out. She looked up and down the hallway before she saw them and ran in their direction.

"Hi. I came as fast as I could," she said softly and slightly out of breath.

"Good. We should go see her now," Antoinette said, a little stiffly from the effort of trying not to cry. Antoinette turned and subconsciously fell in line with her siblings. All five Andersons walked in a line down the hallway towards their grandmother's room. Behind them walked Peter and Caitlyn. The group walked in silence; nobody felt like saying a word. As they walked, Katarina heard a crash behind them as if something had fallen or had been dropped behind them but she just kept walking with her family until they reached her grandmother's room. They paused in front of the door. Antoinette turned and faced her younger sisters, hand on the door knob behind her.

"I just want to warn you, girls, Granny does look very much different than she did at spring break, okay? It's been a gradual change, but it may seem drastic for you, okay?"

"All right." Emiliana nodded, looking as if she was ready for anything.

"Okay," Therese spoke in a whisper. She looked scared and upset.

Katarina only nodded that she understood; she couldn't make herself speak–she was afraid she would burst into tears if she did.

Antoinette, positive that her sisters understood, turned around and opened the door to the hospital room. Katarina walked into the stark white room behind her sisters and brother. It even smelled sterile and clean. She wrinkled her nose without thinking. Antoinette and Benedict stepped back a little to let their younger sister step forward to see Granny. Even though Antoinette had warned them that Granny looked completely different, Katarina was still so shocked she could hardly move. She forced herself to walk towards the bed. Granny was extremely pale and looked exhausted. She seemed incredibly small compared to the last time Katarina had seen her. Katarina took a deep, shaky breath. Granny slowly turned her head and saw her granddaughters standing next to her bed. She smiled faintly at them and tried to speak. It came out frail and very quiet.

"Hello, Em, Therese, and Kat. How're you girls doing?" She paused for a breath and then continued. "How's school? Are you home for the summer?"

"We are all doing good, Granny," Emiliana spoke up first.

"School's going all right," Therese added half-heartedly.

Katarina just nodded her head.

Granny noticed her quiet granddaughter, and she slowly and weakly moved her hand over to the side of the bed where Katarina stood. She gripped her granddaughter's hand feebly. Granny's grip had weakened. Katarina felt a tear roll down her cheek; she squeezed Granny's hand tightly. Granny smiled at them all. Katarina needed to leave, just for a moment.

"I'll be right back, guys," Katarina mumbled as she brushed past Peter and Caitlyn and out the door. Once outside of the room, Katarina leaned against the wall and took some deep breaths. Once she had recovered herself, she pulled out her cell phone from her purse and dialed Abigail's number and waited for her to respond.

"Hi Kat, what's up?" Abigail sounded cheerful.

"I–I want to talk to you about something; can you come to the hospital? I'm here because of Granny."

"Sure, I can come." Abigail sounded less cheerful now. "Where should I meet you?"

"The fourth floor. I'll be by the elevator."

"All right; see you in a few."

"Oh, and Abi, thanks."

"Hey, no problem. Bye."

"Bye." Katarina hit end and looked up from her phone. Her attention was brought to a young man about her age standing across the hallway. He was leaning against the wall staring at her. He just smiled at her and turned and walked down the hallway. Katarina shrugged her shoulders. Weird. She turned and headed back into the room. Granny was talking to her siblings. Katarina paused and stayed back in the shadows and listened. Granny was talking like she knew she might die tonight. Katarina didn't like it. She listened quietly.

"If I go tonight, or when I do go, I want you guys to take care of Katarina because after the last seven years, she is very different. I've noticed. She has not been herself. She has turned quiet on us. She hasn't been her normal, happy, contented self since before your parents died."

Katarina felt her eyes tear up again. The sadness and pain of her parents' death had not softened at all over the last seven years–in fact all the pain had doubled with Gramps' death and then Grandma's death. She couldn't listen anymore; she slipped back out of the room and headed to the elevator to wait for Abigail. Katarina looked around at all the doctors and the nurses as she walked. They all had a job to do. A job that helped people. She stopped and sat down on the bench next to the elevator to wait. Katarina looked around and continued to wait. The elevator door slid opened and she jumped up, expecting it to be Abigail. It wasn't; it was the guy who had been watching her. He stared at her. There was something about his eyes. Katarina blushed a bright red. She mumbled as she sat down again, "Sorry."

"No problem." From under her eyelashes she could see he was still looking at her. She was starting to want to disappear through the floor when the elevator doors slid open again and she looked up. Her eyes lit up ecstatically.

Chapter Twenty-Four

"Oh good! You're here!" Katarina jumped up and hurried toward her best friend; they had just seen each other several hours before. Katarina dragged Abigail with her down the hall closer to her grandmother's room just so they would be near if anything happened. Abigail glanced over her shoulder.

"Who is that guy? He's been watching us ever since I got off the elevator."

"Oh." Katarina glanced over her shoulder as well. "Him? I don't have a clue. I noticed him when we first arrived."

"Oh," Abigail said as they paused outside the door. "Okay, so what was it you wanted to talk to me about?"

"Well." Katarina slid to the floor and leaned

against the wall.

Abigail followed suit.

"You remember after my mom and dad died? And how when I did talk about it I would blame God for it?"

"Yeah. But then after a few months we stopped talking about anything." Abigail nodded her head. "I remember it all."

"Well. I've realized it wasn't God's fault that Mom and Dad and Gramps and Grandma died—and it isn't God's fault if Granny dies." Katarina took a deep breath. "And I am sorry I ever said it was His fault."

"Really?" Abigail asked breathlessly. The door flew open next to them and Therese ran out. The two girls jumped up from the floor. Katarina grabbed Therese's arm because Therese hadn't seen them yet. Therese whipped around, her eyes wide.

"What's wrong?" Katarina gasped out, her face pale with fright.

Abigail reached down and slipped her hand around Katarina's and gave it a squeeze.

"You need to come in right now." Therese turned around and yanked the door open again and ran back in, followed by Katarina and Abigail. Katarina glanced down at her watch as they hurried into the hospital room. They had only arrived half an hour before. She looked around at her family—or what was left of her family. It seemed like every time she looked around, another person was gone. She saw Antoinette crying softly, and Emiliana was trying to be strong and not cry; Benedict was teary-eyed and Therese was sobbing. Her eyes trailed to her grandmother; she already looked different from when Katarina had seen her just moments ago.

The door burst open again and a nurse rushed inside as Granny started to breathe shallowly and quickly. It felt like the tears were being ripped from her eyes. Abigail was crying too as she gripped Katarina's hand as tightly as she could. Peter held Antoinette in his arms as he let his wife cry. Caitlyn held Benedict's hands and stood with her eyes shut, praying. Uncle Greg and Aunt Emilie stood across from them on the other side of the bed. Uncle Greg held Aunt Emilie in his arms. Before their eyes, Granny went into cardiac arrest. Katarina couldn't watch anymore; she closed her eyes and let the tears roll down her face. *I'm so sorry! I'm sorry for blaming You, God, for killing all of them! It wasn't Your fault. I don't understand why You are taking Granny away from me now too. I'm going to miss her really bad and You know that. But I know it's time for You to take Granny, so go ahead and take her. I think I'm ready. I know—seven years too late and I'm finally ready to release someone. Go on; do it.*

Abigail squeezed Katarina's hand again and she opened her eyes and looked at her grandmother one last time. Granny suddenly stopped breathing; it happened so quickly and it seemed to Katarina as if she took one last look around the room at the part of her family that was there and then she sighed deeply and closed her eyes. The nurse watched Granny then checked her pulse. There was nothing. She leaned down to see if she could hear her breathing. Nope. Mrs. Eileen Jones, mother and grandmother, was dead. The nurse stood up and straightened. He looked at them all with a grave, silent look.

"She is dead. I am very sorry for your loss. It must be quite a shock as we all expected her to have several more hours. I am sorry. I will leave you for now." He smiled gently and then turned and left the room quietly.

Katarina walked up to the bed. She reached down and touched her grandmother's hand. It was already starting to grow cold. She whispered in a soft voice, "Bye, Granny. I love you."

"Bye! I love you!" Therese sobbed out jerkily.

Emiliana stood at her spot at the end of the bed and stared at her grandmother as she spoke in undertones, "Goodbye, Granny; I will miss you."

Benedict stared mutely at his grandmother; he spoke a silent goodbye to her in his head. Antoinette murmured a goodbye as well. Aunt Emilie was sobbing hysterically. She had no parents now, and she was missing a sister.

"Goodbye, Mother. I will miss you with all my heart. I love you," she said, speaking as softly as she could while crying.

Once they had said their goodbyes, they left the hospital room in a wordless procession. Katarina sniffed as she felt the tears on her cheeks. She hung her head in sorrow until something in the corner of her eye caught her attention. She glanced to her left and there standing against the wall, looking sad, was the same young man who had been watching her when she had been on the phone with Abigail and when she had waited for Abigail to get to the hospital. He gave her a look that said he was sorry for her loss. Katarina gave a small smile of thanks and turned her head away and continued to walk with the rest of her family.

"How're you doing, Kat?" Emiliana asked as she climbed into the window seat with her younger sister. It was a week after Granny had died. They had already gone through all the funeral and wake business, and she had been buried. Katarina shrugged.

"I'm okay. How do you expect me to be doing?" she responded a tad sarcastically.

Emiliana sighed and responded, "I didn't mean it like that; sorry."

Katarina turned her head to her sister; her face was changed now–it was penitent. "No, I'm sorry. I didn't mean to be sarcastic." Katarina wrapped her arms around her older sister and squeezed.

Emiliana smiled and forgave her sister. They sat together like that quietly for a few minutes. Emiliana moved her legs and climbed off the window seat.

"Come on, Kat, it's time we left for Nettie's house for Leroy's birthday party."

"Oh, right." Katarina climbed off the window seat. "Let me go fix my hair and grab my purse." Katarina headed for the stairs. She was quiet. She had been extra quiet in the last week. There was too much to think about. Katarina preferred not having a lot of time for idle thinking because she tended to think of things that stressed her out. She wandered into her bedroom. Finding her hairbrush on her bed, Katarina walked to her mirror and stood looking at herself as she brushed her hair out. In truth she was not staring at herself; she was really staring into memories of times long gone. Reflected in the mirror were glimpses of parties, Christmas Eves, cozy evenings by the fire, warm hugs, and lots of laughter. A tear ran down her left cheek.

"Oh, Katarina, you are just the absolute most adorable little girl in the world!"

"You think that because you're my mommy!" little four-year-old Katarina cried out, squealing happily as her mother tickled her making her laugh.

"No, you really are the most adorablest girl ever!" her mother continued to insist as she laughed at her daughter.

"I don't believe you!" Katarina giggled, grinning at her mother's face above her.

Her mother gave a fake gasp and spoke in a mock hurt voice, "Really?! You don't believe me!?"

"Mummy!" Katarina giggled; she reached her hand up and patted her mother's pretty cheek. "I believe you with all my heart!"

"Oh, good!" her mother replied, chuckling.

Gramps took his enthusiastic seven-year-old granddaughter's hand and led her outside. She was all bundled up in her winter coat, snow pants, boots, and a hat and gloves. Katarina loved the snow, and she most especially loved going out in it with her grandfather. She reached down and grabbed a handful of snow. Grinning excitedly up at Gramps, she tossed it in his face.

"Oh!" He chuckled as the cold, soft, white snow flew into his face. He reached down and grabbed some and threw it back to her.

Katarina burst into giggles. Her whole face was lit up and her eyes were—

"Katarina, we really need to go now." Therese stood in the doorway with a sad look in her eyes. Katarina turned from the mirror and looked at her sister. Therese hadn't really changed much in the last seven years. She had grown a few inches taller but not much; she was still the shortest person in her family. Her hair had darkened quite a bit. It was more of a deep, dark red than a brown, and her eyes seemed darker as well, like deep sapphire wells of water. She was just as quiet as she had been, though she was more open and livelier with her family than before. Therese's face was soft and pretty and she had gotten a small sprinkling of freckles too. Katarina shook herself.

"I'm coming; sorry if I delayed us," she responded, grabbing for her purse and dropping her brush onto the dresser. Katarina hurried after her sister and the two girls ran down the stairs and out the front door. Therese climbed into Emiliana's car on the passenger's side and Katarina got into the back. Emiliana backed out of the driveway and turned down the street. Katarina stared thoughtfully out of her window. She sort of wished she could drift back into her memories again, but she knew from past tries she had to just let it happen. She couldn't force herself to remember things from her childhood. It just came by itself.

Thankfully, Antoinette and Peter lived in a house that was only a few minutes away from the girls, so it was quick trip. Emiliana parked the car on the side of the road in front of the house and they quickly got out. Therese grabbed the present that was on the floor by her feet. Katarina opened her door and got out. She glanced around to see who was here based on the cars. She smiled a bit when she saw that Aunt Emilie and Uncle Greg were there–that meant that Annabelle and everyone else in their family was probably there too. With a swift glance, she could tell that several of her aunts and uncles were there, as well as Peter's parents and his sister and brother. Katarina slammed the car door shut behind her and followed her sisters up the front walk.

The doorknob was being opened clumsily and then the door swung open and Katarina, Emiliana, and Therese were enthusiastically greeted by an overly-eager little two year old.

"Hi!!! It's my birthday!!" Leroy grinned ecstatically.

Katarina giggled. She stepped inside after her sisters and knelt down in front of him and gave him a big, bear hug.

"How are you doing today?"

"Good!" he said firmly, with a huge smile.

Leroy looked past her with a curious look on his adorable face. “Is Gwanny comin’?” He looked slightly hurt that his great grandmother hadn’t shown up yet. Katarina sighed and looked up at Therese who was still standing next to her, Emiliana having already walked into the kitchen. Therese shook her head.

“He doesn’t understand, Kat.”

“I know that,” she replied before turning back to Leroy. He looked up expectantly at his young aunt. Katarina sighed and replied to her nephew’s question, “I’m sorry, Leroy, but Granny won’t be coming tonight.”

“Oh.” His face fell. His lip started to quiver.

Katarina stood up and held out her hand for him to take. “Wanna come with me so I can tell Mommy and Daddy hello?” Katarina asked him.

Leroy just nodded and took her hand and skipped along with her. Therese followed the two into the kitchen and found Antoinette and Peter talking with Peter’s sister and Uncle Greg.

“Hi everyone,” Katarina said, smiling and looking at them.

Antoinette came over and gave her younger sister a hug. “Hey. How’re you?” she asked, looking at Katarina.

Her sister just gave a small shrug and responded, “Fine.”

“Hey, Kat,” Peter hailed her.

Katarina smiled and nodded. “Hey,” she said

back.

"Kit Kat!"

Katarina spun around, letting go of Leroy's hand. Her eyes lit up when she saw her favorite cousin in front of her. "Banana!" She hugged her cousin tightly. It felt like ages since they had talked, especially because Annabelle and her family hadn't been able to get back from out of town fast enough for Granny's funeral and wake, much to everyone's distress.

"Do you really still call each other that?" Emiliana asked sarcastically as she rejoined the family with a cup of Pepsi in her hand.

Annabelle giggled and answered, "Of course, Em." She winked at Katarina, who laughed out loud.

Antoinette smiled happily; she was glad Annabelle was here because no matter how upset or sad Annabelle was herself, she always seemed to make Katarina laugh hysterically.

Leroy threw his little chubby hands in the air and exclaimed loudly, "Auntie! Pwease pway with me! It's my birthday and I miss you!" His loud and unexpected outburst caused them all to burst out laughing because it took them so much by surprise. Leroy stared in shock that they were laughing at him; his two-year-old mind couldn't come up with a reason why they were. His lip quivered and his eyes squeezed shut tightly. A tear trickled out.

Antoinette smiled and stopped laughing. She went over and picked up her little boy and hugged him, giving him a big kiss on his chubby cheek. "It's okay, buddy," she said to him, chuckling.

Annabelle went over and patted him on the back. "Do you want go play with some toys? Aunt Katarina can come with us," she told him soothingly, while smiling just like everyone else.

Leroy nodded his head vigorously and wiped away a big tear with his little fist. He reached out his arms to Katarina, who willingly took her small nephew and marched off with Annabelle to the little playroom at the front of the house. As they passed the front door, it opened up and Benedict and Caitlyn walked in.

"Hey! Look–it's Uncle Benedict and Aunt Caitlyn!" Katarina exclaimed in a teasing tone as she saw them.

Leroy squealed a hello as Benedict shook his head, grinning. "Please don't call me an uncle!" He was joking and you could tell.

"But you are Uncle Benny," Annabelle teased back and scrunched her nose up.

Caitlyn giggled and turned to Leroy. "Hello, birthday boy! Where are you guys off to?"

"To pway!" Leroy said, ecstatically clapping his hands.

"Oh, you're going to go play?" Caitlyn asked curiously.

Katarina nodded and replied, "Yup; to play with all his toys."

"Yes!" Leroy grinned happily.

Caitlyn giggled at how cute Leroy was. Benedict noticed the look on his wife's face and grinned. He took her hand and made as if to walk out of the front hall.

"Come on Cait; let's go say hello and then you can find some random baby to glue yourself on."

"Fine. But there aren't any random babies to glue myself on except this adorable guy and his sister," Caitlyn protested as she let her husband drag her to the living room and kitchen to say hello.

"Hey! Where is the little girl!?" Katarina asked, suddenly realizing she hadn't seen her darling baby niece. Annabelle shrugged,

"I think Antoinette said she was sleeping still."

"Oh okay." Katarina looked down at her nephew as they walked into the playroom. "Where's your sister, Leroy? Where's Gina Maria?"

"Sleep!" he said proudly.

"Where?" Annabelle asked.

"Upstairs!" he said, pointing to the ceiling, looking even more proud at knowing something his aunt and her cousin didn't.

Annabelle giggled at him as Katarina set him down so he could play. She turned to her cousin.

"Annabelle, you stay here. I'm going to see if I can snag my niece from her bed."

"Okay," Annabelle replied, kneeling down on the floor next to Leroy as Katarina departed from the room.

"So, Leroy, what do you want to play?" Annabelle asked the little guy in a confiding voice. Leroy smiled a big one that spread across his face.

"Sweeping wady."

"What?"

"Sweeping wady!"

"What type of game is that?"

"You know! The girw goes to sweep! And the boy," he puffed up with pride at having a guy role, "kisses the girw!"

"Oh!" It dawned on Annabelle suddenly that he must mean *Sleeping Beauty*. "All right; let's play it."

"You be the pwincess! And I be the pwince." He said this with lots of pride.

Annabelle grinned and laughed a merry laugh. "All right; sounds like fun!"

Chapter Twenty-Five

"Can I wake Gina Maria?" Katarina burst out when she found Antoinette in the laundry room getting a glass of wine.

Antoinette chuckled and replied to her sister. "She's sleeping," she protested.

Katarina sighed and looked pleadingly at her older sister. "Please!?"

"Fine; she usually wakes up about now anyways."

"Thank you!" Katarina hurtled out of the room and ran upstairs as fast as she could to Antoinette and Peter's room.

Antoinette shook her head and sighed as she walked back to the living room. *That girl is never going to grow up; you'd think after everything we've all been through she would be older, sadder, and different. Though, in a way she is different.*

Peter walked over to her and whispered to his wife, "What's the serious face for, my darling?"

"I'm just thinking," she replied with a small smile at him.

He kissed her on the forehead. "What are you thinking about?" he asked her as she took a sip of the wine.

She shook her head and replied, "Just about Katarina."

"Ah." Peter smiled and nodded. "Is that all?"

"Yeah," she replied. He squeezed her hand gently. Antoinette moved to sit down next to Peter's sister, Ariel. Ariel turned and smiled at her sister-in-law.

"Hey, Nettie."

"Hey." Antoinette smiled. "So how's your job going? I've been meaning ask you how

it was going, but forgot."

"Oh! It's been going pretty well; I got bumped up. I'm not just the clean-up lady slash receptionist; I am now the dude's secretary." Ariel giggled when she saw her mother looking at her with a reprimanding look for calling her boss a dude. She just shook her long, curly, red hair and turned back to Antoinette.

Antoinette just smiled and shook her head at her husband's younger sister. "That's neat. What do you do now?"

"Paperwork." Ariel scrunched her freckled

nose up in disgust. "Even more paperwork than before."

"Oh, lovely," Antoinette agreed in a slightly disgusted voice.

Felix, Peter's younger brother, leaned over to the two girls. "She's always hated paperwork–even school papers. Don't even ask me why she took this job." He smirked and Antoinette chuckled and shook her head.

Ariel rolled her eyes and protested, "I took this job because it was the only one that came my way. Sheesh; Felix doesn't know what he's talking about."

"I hope they aren't overwhelming you, my dear," Mrs. Marchen spoke up with concern from the other couch as shook her head at her two youngest children.

Antoinette just laughed and replied to her mother-in-law, "Oh, no; I rather like it!"

"Oh, good. Because if you didn't I think my brother would have had sense enough not to marry you," Ariel said sarcastically while laughing.

Felix nodded his head and leaned towards Antoinette. "She is right. If you couldn't handle the pair of us you'd be smothered by now," he said jokingly.

Peter stepped forward so he could join in the conversation as well. He chuckled. "You see what I had to live with before you came along and saved me?"

"I think we saved each other because my siblings can be almost as bad sometimes," Antoinette said with a grin and a small giggle. She stopped and looked around. "Where are Em and Therese anyway? I know Katarina is upstairs; she should be down by now."

"I don't really know," Peter responded, doing some of his own looking around the room.

"Oh, I wanted to talk to Emiliana," Ariel said, getting up. "I'll help you find them. Peter you stay and talk."

"To whom?" Peter asked in a joking, surprised voice.

"Your brother," Felix muttered, pretending to be hurt.

"Or Nettie's relatives. They like you," Ariel said, dragging her sister-in-law away. Peter shook his head and sat down next to his younger brother.

"Hey, girlie; you just get cuter every day," Katarina whispered to her niece as she picked up the tiny little girl. "Did you know that I was with Nettie when you were born? I mean right before." Katarina shook her head. "Technically I wasn't with her when you were born because she went to the hospital and I had to sit out in the waiting room."

Gina Maria cooed up at her aunt and waved her little fist in the air.

Katarina hugged the little girl. "Did you know that you'll never ever meet your grandparents, my parents? You'll grow up with your daddy's parents but not your mommy's. They died a long time ago, when I was a little–lots older than you, but still little." Katarina paused for breath and looked down at the baby in her arms. Gina Maria stared up at her aunt with wide eyes. Katarina didn't know if the little girl could understand her because she was so young. She didn't know how little babies' minds worked. But she didn't care; she enjoyed having someone to talk to who didn't respond to whatever she asked. Katarina smiled a sad smile and continued to speak as she went and sat down in the rocking chair Nettie kept in the room.

"They died in a car crash, and I miss them a lot. More than I could even tell you. To tell the truth, it broke my heart, and if you want more truths I don't think it's completely healed yet, because sometimes it aches really badly. Especially when I feel sad or when I'm extremely happy—then obviously I'm not that happy anymore, because my heart hurts." Katarina sighed. "I know I told Abi that I was wrong to blame God for it all these years, but I'm afraid I'm still doubtful. I mean," she paused, thinking. "I guess I don't really know what I mean." She smiled a little. "Honestly, I don't have a clue why I'm telling this to you and not anyone else; I mean, you're a baby!" She laughed softly, breaking the stillness.

Gina Maria gurgled happily. Katarina snuggled her close.

"I guess maybe because it's so comforting to be able to hold you and just talk. I wanna believe in God again, honest I do, but truthfully I'm immensely scared to do it. I mean, what if I start to believe and trust in Him again and then something else happens? I just don't know if I can do it." She sighed again. "Alone. Or with help." Katarina felt a lump rise in her throat and she swallowed. She felt a tear slide down her cheek. Katarina cleared her throat and shook herself.

"Well, I guess I should take you down now. Everyone will want to see you." She stood up and set Gina Maria down gently on the bed so she could wipe her face and her eyes so no one could tell she was crying. After picking up Gina Maria, she left the room and headed towards the stairs. Halfway down, she ran into Ariel.

"Hey girl!" Ariel flashed her a smile. "How are you doing?!"

"I'm doing good." Katarina smiled back as happily as she could make herself. "How are you doing?"

"I'm doing awesome!"

Katarina had to chuckle at that; it always

seemed like Ariel was doing awesome. Katarina had never seen Ariel on a day when she was *not* doing awesome. Ariel giggled with Katarina, not even knowing why Katarina was laughing.

"Can I hold her please?"

"Sure." Katarina smiled and handed Gina Maria over to the little girl's other aunt. Katarina started to walk down the stairs again when Ariel looked up from Gina Maria. "Oh, hey, have you seen Emiliana or Therese?"

"No, not since I talked to them in the kitchen. Why? I thought they were in the living room."

"No, they haven't been around since after they first came in."

"Oh, okay. Well, if you guys need me I'll be in the playroom with Annabelle and Leroy, okay?"

"Yup; sure."

Katarina walked down the stairs and hurried back to the playroom. She walked through the archway and stopped suddenly, feeling the urge to burst out laughing. In front of her, lying across the couch, was Annabelle and Leroy was just leaning down, while standing on his tippy toes, to give her a big smooch on the cheek. Annabelle's eyes flew open and she sat up, a huge, cheesy grin on her face.

"You did it! You woke me up!" Annabelle hugged the ecstatic little boy, who couldn't stop bouncing up and down with excitement.

"Yay!! Mawwy me now!"

"Oh, I have to marry you now?" Annabelle asked, pulling him onto her lap and hugging him tightly.

"Yes! That's how it works!"

"Yeah, didn't you know that?" Katarina smiled slightly as she walked into the room and joined them on the couch.

Annabelle noticed that the smile Katarina gave seemed rather forced and she seemed unhappy—well unhappier than she had been when she had arrived. Leroy crawled over and onto his aunt's lap. She pulled him close and cuddled him, feeling safe with him in her arms. Annabelle touched her cousin's arm gently. "Are you all right?" she asked with a sincere look of care showing in her eyes.

Katarina nodded her head firmly, but her eyes showed that she wasn't. "Yeah, I'm fine." Katarina forced her mouth to form a smile for her cousin.

Annabelle nodded.

Katarina was holding Leroy while he just sat still, talking animatedly to Annabelle, explaining how their wedding would go and how she could only have roses because those were Mommy's favorite flowers. Katarina was only vaguely listening as her eyes drifted to the window that looked out onto the front lawn and sidewalk that ran in front of the house. By the lamppost that stood at the corner of Antoinette and Peter's street and the other one stood a young man. The summer evening light reflected on his face, lighting it up for Katarina to see his facial features well. She sucked in her breath sharply and quickly. It was the young man from the hospital again. He almost seemed familiar to her, but she couldn't quite place it. For a moment, it seemed like they made eye contact; weird. She shook herself and turned her head away from the window and found Annabelle staring quizzically at her. She just shrugged in response and did her best to focus her wandering attention on her nephew.

Annabelle vowed to watch her cousin for the rest of the evening because Katarina seemed preoccupied and upset over something. She couldn't make out what it was, but she figured it had to do something with Granny. Annabelle felt her heart tug when she thought of her grandmother being dead. It was hard to believe that her grandmother was gone. Everything seemed empty and quiet without Granny. Annabelle missed her touching hugs, loving kisses, and musical laughter.

Katarina was oblivious that her cousin was going to watch her the rest of the evening. Truthfully, Annabelle wanted to hug her cousin tight and shield her from all the hurt and pain the world had thrust upon her in the last seven years. But she couldn't shield her; she could hug her, but Annabelle was afraid to hurt Katarina's feelings by trying to shove her way into Katarina's little world. Katarina felt Annabelle's eyes on her and she let her gaze wander until she made eye contact with her cousin. Annabelle just gave her a big smile. Katarina tried to smile back but kind of failed. She wished that she could be just as happy as her cousin was on the outside. She knew that Annabelle hurt on the inside but tried not to show and let it take over her life. Katarina did not have long to think about all of this because just then Emiliana appeared in the doorway.

"We're gonna have dinner now, guys."

"Yay!" Leroy crowed loudly and slid off Katarina's lap and ran to Emiliana and took her hand. "Wet's eat!" he cried, pulling her along. Annabelle chuckled at his antics and got up to follow. She stopped when she realized that Katarina wasn't following them. She was staring out of the window again at the street corner. Annabelle studied the window to see what was so fascinating, but there was nothing there.

"Come on, Kit Kat," Annabelle said quietly, tapping Katarina gently on the elbow.

Katarina jumped slightly and she turned to find Annabelle standing right next to her. She responded, sounding flustered, "Oh, right; coming." She followed her cousin down the hall and into the noisy kitchen filled with happy talking and lots of laughter. Katerina's heart hurt; she wished she could happily join in the merriment, but she couldn't. She really just wanted to go home, but she forced a smile on her face and tried to at least appear merry and happy. After grabbing a cheeseburger and some fruit salad, she grabbed a cup of root beer and headed out to the back patio to sit with her sisters and her cousins Faith and Rosalyn.

"Hey, Kat, where've you been? I didn't even know you were here," Rosalyn said, speaking excitedly. Twenty-five-year-old Rosalyn was always happy and excitable, and she never failed to make you feel loved and wanted. Katarina had worshiped her growing up and she still adored her and liked spending time with her even though the girl was five years older than herself.

"Just around. I was with Annabelle and Leroy for a bit and then I was upstairs getting Gina Maria."

"Oh." Rosalyn was about to say something else, but when she glanced at her younger cousin, Katarina was looking across the yard, her attention completely stuck on something behind Rosalyn.

Katarina's facial expression was weird. Not weird, weird, but just a look of confusion and maybe a tad hurt–and she also looked weirded out. Her face was pale as well, like she had a seen a ghost or something she did not expect. All this Rosalyn observed in a matter of seconds. It intrigued her and confused her.

She turned to see what Katarina was staring at, but there was nothing there, and when she turned back, Katarina was busily eating her fruit salad and looking down at her plate. Rosalyn squinted her eyes, trying to figure out what had just happened. Emiliana must have felt like the weird pause had gone on too long, because she brought up the subject of TV shows, which attracted everyone's attention—even Katarina's.

Chapter Twenty-Six

"Sorrow has changed my life. It has changed my view of things. I am not the same person I once was. The little girl I used to be those seven long years ago is nowhere to be found. I wish I could find her among the dust and rocks of pain and sadness that first surrounded me that night so long ago. The pain has been so intense sometimes it makes it hard for me to breathe, but I keep on breathing somehow. Sometimes I feel like I will stop breathing and never take one more breath again. But that never happens. I guess that is good—that I am still living. There must be a reason that I'm alive and not my parents. I don't know what that reason is, and I wonder if I will ever find it out. It better be worthwhile. I'm trying hard to trust in God again. It's so hard. It's like I'm climbing up the side of an incredibly steep mountain with lots of jutting plateaus and pointing rocks. Sometimes I feel like I will never make it back to where I was in my faith before. Other times I suddenly feel like it's not worth it and I want to give up, but a silent voice tells me to keep going and that I will make it one day. Today the voice is ever persistent. It's strange that when I suddenly feel down and helpless, like I'll never make it, I usually look up and walking by or just standing near, wherever I happen to be, is this young man who has the calmest look, mixed with a bit of sadness, urging me on. When I look again, he's gone..."

Katarina set her pen down and stared out of the window, almost expecting the man to be standing there; he wasn't. He only showed up when she least expected him to—that was the weirdest part. She sighed and turned back to her journal and continued to write thoughtfully, pouring out her feelings into words on the pale sheets of paper.

"...I wish that all my pain would go away.

It makes me feel miserable and I haven't felt peace in a while. I feel like it's been forever since I've felt peaceful. I want to relax and forget about everything, but I can't. I want to move on, but I can't. I don't know what to do. I know I can always talk to Abigail or even my sisters. But I don't know how they can help me because even Nettie wasn't sure how to help me when I gave her back that journal I wrote in seven years ago. I heard her admit to Granny and Em that the situation was even worse than she thought."

A tear slipped down her cheek and plopped onto the page of her journal. Katarina quickly put her hand up to her face and wiped away the tear that followed. She sniffed and laid down her pen. Getting up, she walked over to her bookshelf. Her finger trailed across the row of notebooks that filled half of the top shelf. Each of those notebooks was precious to her because they held her deepest thoughts. Thoughts so deep she had never shared them with Abigail, Therese, or even Granny before she died. With a sigh filled with pain, Katarina reached her hand forward and pulled the first notebook off: the well-used leather journal with the midnight black embroidered butterfly and daffodil. Katarina held the journal in her hands. It seemed heavy to her, like the thoughts and notes in it made it heavier than it really was. The notebook was slightly battered, for Katarina had used it every day and brought it with her everywhere. Katarina turned and walked to her large, queen-sized bed and lay down on her pillows. She leaned over to the nightstand next to her bed, pulled the drawer out, and retrieved the key to the journal. She leaned back into her pillows and unlocked it. Katarina flipped carefully through the pages, skimming each entry until her eyes fell upon a particular one.

"Dear Diary, October 13, 2013

> Today I feel like I'm stuck in a deep, black hole and I can't get out. I want help. But I can't get it and I don't know where to look for it. I wanted to stay in bed this morning, but Nettie made me get up and come with them to Mass. I didn't want to leave the house. I feel the same way every Sunday because I don't want to visit God without Mommy and Daddy. They are my key to God; they taught me to love Him and Jesus. Without them I feel like a door's been slammed between me and God and I don't have a key to unlock it again, and I feel like I have no help from the other side as if God does not care for

me anymore. I feel like my heart is shut off from His love and I'll never get it back. I really don't know how to describe it. I've tried to hide myself from it all but, aside from really nothing, there's not much I can do to hide, so I have to satisfy myself with going under the covers of my bed with my special blanket and you, diary. I'm going to try and sleep now. Goodbye.

~ Katarina Rebecca Anderson"

Katarina looked through the rest of the book, finding more and more journal entries filled with despair and pain and much sadness. She almost couldn't bear to read anymore. She slammed the journal shut and held it in her hands for a few minutes before getting off the bed and going to the bookshelf for more journals. She came back with four more. She opened the first one on the pile; she knew this one was from sometime during 2015 before Gramps had died. Katarina glanced at the date of the first entry: January of 2015. She skipped to the end of the book and checked the last date: May third. Flipping back to the beginning of the book, her eyes fell on an entry toward the middle. She read part of it.

"My life feels empty. You would think by now I would be used to my parents not being alive, but I'm honestly not. Why can't I feel like

I used to feel? I want to be happy and carefree and have parents again. I want to live again. I need to get out of this empty hole where nothing is right."

Katarina stopped herself; she couldn't read anymore. She felt like she was getting more depressed, rather than happier. She knew that the rest of the journals wouldn't get much better overall. It would just get more depressing and painful to read about her little self's pains and sadness. Katarina felt the tears slip down her face again. She wanted to try and brush them away, but it felt like she had no energy at all. She could hardly move her arm. Her shoulders shook with each horrible sob. Katarina pulled her legs up and laid her head face down on her knees and just let the tears run free. She let the sorrow drip down her face in the form of tears. She just let it all out.

Let the pain release me.
Let me go.
I want to be free
From all this pain and sadness.
I want to breathe in a new life.
I cry out,
Let me go.
I want freedom.

My heart yearns for a new life.
One free of pain and sadness,
Hunger and thirst.
I beg,
Let me go.

Arms slowly, with a tad of reluctance, wrapped around Katarina and squeezed her tightly. Katarina lifted her head to see who was next to her. It was Brookelyn.

"Hi. I wanted to stop by and see you, since I don't go to the same college as you, like Monica," she spoke shyly. Brookelyn knew that she and Katarina weren't as good of friends as Katarina was with Abigail and that made her shy around her.

Katarina could tell that Brookelyn was shy with her and she knew the real reason. "Brookie, you don't have to be shy with me; we're friends," Katarina said with a catch in her voice from crying. "Best friends."

Brookelyn just smiled and replied, "Are you sure?"

"Why wouldn't I be? I said it." Katarina's mouth lifted at the corners into a small smile.

"Gosh, thanks," Brookelyn whispered, a little shocked that it was actually true. The room was silent for a few moments before Brookelyn remembered the reason she had actually come to visit Katarina. She scooched Katarina over a bit so she could sit on the bed comfortably as well. Putting her arm around Katarina again, she spoke up, "How're you doing, Kat?"

"Not good," Katarina answered truthfully with a loud sniff.

Brookelyn sighed and, speaking softly, she asked Katarina, "What's bothering you?"

"Everything. Life, death, people."

"Ahh." Brookelyn knew from experience–and Abigail–that she had to just let Katarina talk it out slowly, at her own pace, or she would never talk about her innermost feelings.

"I just can't deal with this pain anymore; it's driving me insane. I've lived with this pain and loss for seven long years. Brookie, why can't it just leave! Or lessen a ton."

"I don't know."

"I want freedom. I want faith again," Katarina said simply and hushed.

Brookelyn did her best to keep the smile off her face at what Katarina had said. "Truthfully?" Brookelyn asked.

"I think so; I think I want to believe and trust in God again. I know, though, that I want to be loved and be faced with an open door, not a closed one. I just don't know how to do it."

"Well, you could talk to Father Vincent at church."

"Yeah, but I feel awkward talking to him."

"He'll put you at ease. And we will help you all we can," Brookelyn assured her, patting her gently on the arm. "Do you still love God, Kat?"

Katarina sat silently, thinking really hard before answering Brookelyn's question. She dug deep to figure out an answer, a true answer, the right answer. Nodding her head slowly, she said, "Yes." She kept nodding. "Yes, I think I still do a little bit," she added, turning to look at Brookelyn with a tiny smile on her face.

Brookelyn smiled back encouragingly.

"A lot," Katarina added softly.

Brookelyn nodded her head. She suddenly had a good idea. "Well, now that you've found out that you still love God–which is fabulous!–" Brookelyn was off the bed by now and was bouncing on her toes, "–I think you need a break, so I am going to take you to the movies and we're going to invite Monica and Abigail."

"Okay. What movie?" Katarina asked her friend.

Brookelyn shrugged and replied, "We'll see when we get there; I think I saw the name of a good movie but I can't remember correctly."

"Okay, let me get my purse and find some money," Katarina said, slowly getting off her bed.

Brookelyn stopped her, protesting, "No, I was gonna pay for it–and you might want to get dressed before we leave." She gestured to the pink and purple, polka dot pajamas that Katarina had put back on after coming home from church.

Katerina blushed to the roots of her hair. "Oops."

"You get dressed, and I'll call my sister and Abigail to make sure they can come as well." Brookelyn scooted out of the bedroom so that Katarina could get dressed to go.

Left alone in her room, Katarina went to her closet and pulled out a pair of jeans and went to her drawer and grabbed a pink t-shirt with white lettering on it. She figured it was appropriate to wear to the movie theater. Katarina quickly threw on the clothing and grabbed her cell phone and ChapStick. Shoving them into her pocket, she left her room to find Brookelyn. She found her sitting outside the bedroom door on the floor.

"Can they come?"

"Yes!" Brookelyn said, excitedly bouncing up from the floor.

The closest thing to a real smile that had been seen in awhile now spread across Katarina's face.

The two girls grabbed hands, dove down the stairs and ran out the front. They flew past Therese, who had just stepped out into the front hallway.

"See ya! We're going to the movies, Therese!" Brookelyn flung over her shoulder as they slammed the door shut.

"Wow. It's already getting pretty warm out," Katarina said, slightly surprised at the rising temperature.

Brookelyn smiled and winked. "It's summer, of course."

"I know." Katarina pouted playfully. Brookelyn giggled as they climbed into her car and drove away.

Brookelyn was glad that Katarina was joking around and not looking as she had only–,she glanced at the clock–fifteen minutes ago. She knew that Abigail and Monica felt the same way as she did about hating to see Katarina like she had been the last seven years.

Katarina turned to Brookelyn and asked, "Did Abi and Monica say they'd meet us at the movie theater?"

"Yes. They did," Brookelyn answered, skillfully turning onto the street that led to the movie theater.

"Okay." Katarina lapsed back into silence again.

Brookelyn glanced swiftly over at her friend and sighed inaudibly. "So have you met anyone interesting at school?"

"Interesting as in what?" Katarina said, smiling a bit while squinting from the sun.

"Interesting as in boys or boyfriend," Brookelyn tactfully drifted off at the same time Katarina gave a small laugh.

"No."

"Why not?" Brookelyn inquired as she turned into the parking lot of the movie theater and started to look for a parking spot.

Katarina shook her head and replied with a small smile, "Because I'm not looking for one right now. I'm not ready for one."

"Well, that makes perfect sense," Brookelyn said as she pulled into a parking spot near the doors of the theater and turned the car off. The girls climbed out and quickly walked through the doors and into the movie theater.

"You're here!"

Katarina and Brookelyn looked to their left and saw Monica and Abigail waiting excitedly for them. Abigail came hurrying over and gave Katarina a huge bear hug.

"Whoa! Hey," Katarina said, slightly surprised.

Abigail just laughed. "Hi, girlie." She turned to Brookelyn and gave her a hug as well, only maybe not quite as large of a one as Katarina got.

Brookelyn smiled and hugged Abigail back.

Monica came up behind Abigail and gave Katarina a squeeze of a hug. Once they finished saying hello, they drifted over to the ticket booth to see what movie they should watch. Katarina pointed to one of the signs that had two young girls on it, looking maybe to be fourteen or thirteen.

"What about that one?"

"Oh, I've seen a preview for it on TV and it looks interesting," Brookelyn commented.

"All right; sound good with you guys?" Abigail asked, looking at Monica and Katarina who both nodded yes.

After buying the tickets, the girls filed into the darkening theater and quickly found seats. Katarina glanced around the theater before the lights were dimmed. She started and gripped the arms on her seat. It was him. He was sitting two rows behind and three seats away from Katarina. *Why is he following me around?* Katarina asked herself the same question she'd asked every time she had seen him.

Abigail glanced over and saw Katarina shifting nervously in her seat. She leaned over to her. "Is something wrong?" she whispered.

Katarina looked at her friend; her eyes held a bit of fear in them. She shook her head. "No, everything's all right."

The lights dimmed and the previews started, so further conversation ceased.

Two and a half hours later, Katarina, Abigail, Monica, and Brookelyn stepped out of the movie theater and into the bright, hot sun beating down upon the parking lot. Katarina glanced around to see if the guy was still there, but he wasn't. They paused off to the side of the doors so that they could discuss the movie they had just seen before they parted ways.

"So, that was an interesting movie," Monica commented casually.

Brookelyn glanced at Abigail, who cracked a grin, causing her and Brookelyn to burst out laughing hysterically.

"What's so funny?" Monica asked, glancing at Katarina who was trying not to smile but didn't succeed and started to laugh quietly.

"It's just the way you said it, that's all," Brookelyn answered, giggling.

Monica giggled as she spoke, "I guess that was kind of weird."

Abigail nodded her head as she continued to laugh. Katarina's phone buzzed and she jumped. She pulled it out and checked it; there was a text message from Therese. Katarina glanced at it and looked up.

"I have to go home now. We're going to go have dinner with Peter and Nettie and then go visit Grandpa. Who wants to take me home?"

"I'll do it," Abigail offered quickly.

Katarina smiled slightly again. "Thanks." Katarina said goodbye to Monica and Brookelyn. "Thanks for thinking of going to the movies!"

"No problem," Brookelyn replied with wide smile.

Monica nodded in agreement. “Yeah; it was fun.”

“Thanks,” Katarina said again as she walked away with Abigail.

Chapter Twenty-Seven

Several days later, she sat on the window seat in the upstairs hallway. The rain was pouring down, breaking the steady heat they had felt for the last two weeks. Katarina felt a little better than she had lately. She had felt like she was being smothered and sometimes it was like she could not breathe. But the rain came almost like a refreshing glass of water. Katarina hadn't worked up the courage yet to go talk to the priest at her church. She felt ready to love someone again, but she wasn't entirely sure about trusting people. Sure, she trusted her siblings and Abigail, Brookelyn, and Monica, but she didn't trust any of them nearly as much as she used to. A tear glistened on the window pane, blending well with the raindrops that ran down the other side of the glass.

Out of the corner of her eye, she noticed a movement. Turning her head, she looked down at her street. Katarina could see a guy standing there in the rain. At a second glance she recognized the guy. It was him. Why was he here again? Katarina was ready and curious enough by now that she wanted to know who he was and what he was doing following her around. She quickly jumped off the window seat and tore down the stairs as fast as she could go. Skidding to a stop, she flung open the front door, letting it bang against the wall; thank goodness her sisters were out of the house so they couldn't scold her. At twenty, she still got scolded for some things. Katarina slipped and ran down the front steps and walk. The guy was still standing across the street, but he started to walk away.

"Wait!" she called. He stopped and turned. She paused for a moment; he looked sort of handsome. Katarina hurried on. She had no time to delay or she was afraid he would leave for good. Katarina slipped as she tried to stop.

"Whoa!" She almost fell backwards but he caught her quickly. He helped her stand up and held her arm so she could steady herself. Once she was fine he let go quickly. He just stood there staring at her. Katarina shifted awkwardly. Why had she come out here? She was already getting soaked.

"Um, hi." She waved a little bit.

His mouth spread into a small smile. Not mocking but gentle. "Hello." His voice was deep and smooth also extremely considerate.

"Wha–wh–wh–" Katarina was becoming flustered and embarrassed. "Why have you been following me!?" she burst out and turned a bright cherry red and quickly looked to the ground.

His smile grew bigger. "Because, I thought you looked miserable that day in the hospital, and I wanted to make sure you were all right," he said, turning a little pink himself. Finding her courage, Katarina looked back up at him and started to smile a little.

"How did you find out where I lived?"

"I followed you home."

"You are such a stalker."

"That's what my family says." He smiled back at her.

"What's your name?"

"Liam Farrell."

"What's my name? If you're such a stalker?"

"Katarina Rebecca Rachel Anderson." He responded promptly with much pride and satisfaction in himself of knowing it.

"What?!" She gasped and stared at him, shocked. "You definitely are a stalker, Mr. Farrell!"

"My name is Liam. My dad was Mr. Farrell," he corrected her politely while chuckling.

"Oh, sorry," Katarina replied getting flustered again.

"No worries."

"So what else do you know about me?" she asked curious as to how he could have found out her full name, confirmation name included.

"Well, I know that you have had a lot of sadness in your life and that you have been having a hard time trusting people and you lately you've felt like giving up on life."

"Where," She paused and spoke again, only softer. "Where did you find that out?"

"Um, I just can tell by what I've seen," he answered, shifting awkwardly from one foot to the other. "Because I've felt the exact same way." He took a deep breath, "Kat–"

"Please don't call me Kat; I don't really know you very well."

"Oh sorry, I've just felt like I've known you forever so I started calling you that."

"Oh, what were you about to say?"

"Kat–Katarina, you can't let sorrow take over your mind, it causes you to be miserable and unhappy and it's not good. It can ruin your life. I barely was able to save my own self. I was letting it take over my mind and heart and I was letting it be the center of my life, which was the wrong choice. It was actually my mother, who was also grieving, who helped me."

"Why? What happened?"

"My father died five years ago and my little sister died when we were little. She was five and I was seven."

"Oh." Katarina spoke softly. "Do you have any other siblings?"

"Yes I have five other siblings. I'm the youngest now that my sister isn't living."

"Oh. I'm the youngest too. My older brother also died a couple days after he was born. That's weird."

"Very," he said quietly. He looked up at the sky; it was still pouring rain. "Do you think we should get out of the rain?" He glanced at her soaked clothing, not even bothering to see that his clothing was just as drenched. Katarina looked up at him again, about to speak, when she paused in shock. Liam looked at her weirdly; her mouth hung open in complete shock.

"What?" he asked.

Katarina stared at him hard. Liam's face and eyes looked strangely familiar. Where had she seen him before? That short, flaming hair; where was it from? She looked at his eyes. They looked familiar too.

"Do I know you, Liam? Have we met before?"

"Um, yeah, a long time ago. Seven years ago to be exact. We were both young then. You're even more beautiful now than you were then."

"Oh." It hit her. She did know him! "You

were Granny and Gramps' next door neighbor! The 'dude' kid!"

"'The 'dude' kid'?" he questioned, trying not to laugh out loud.

Katarina waved him off. "It's just what Abi and I called you."

"Oh, are you still friends with Abigail?"

"Of course." Katarina glared at Liam. "Why wouldn't we be friends still? We've been friends since we were toddlers!"

"Whoa! Sorry there, didn't mean to get on the wrong side."

"It's fine. It's just sometimes people don't get how you can have the same friends all your life."

"Oh, yeah, understandable how that can get a little annoying."

"So, do you want to go inside?" Katarina asked him casually as if they had known each other all their lives. Liam shrugged his shoulders and thrust his hands in his pockets.

"Sure, why not."

"Okay, c'mon on," Katarina said, beckoning him to come with her to her house.

Liam chuckled and followed her across the street and into her house. Katarina shut the door behind them and led him into the kitchen.

"You stay here while I go change."

"All right; sounds good," Liam answered and sat down gingerly on a kitchen stool at the counter.

Katarina headed to the door then paused. "Oh, I don't think I have anything to give you to change into. Benedict doesn't live here anymore."

"Oh, that's fine; it doesn't matter," Liam responded, shooing her away.

"You could throw it into the dryer real quick," Katarina suggested, starting to grin.

"Um, okay?"

"You'll just have to stay in the laundry room until it's dry," Katarina said, giggling.

Liam nodded. "All right, that's fine with me. Just point me to the laundry room," he said, getting up from his chair and looking at her expectantly.

Katarina's eyes sparkled for probably the first time in seven years. She pointed behind him to a short little hallway that led to the garage and the laundry room. "It's right there. The first door you come to. See ya in little while." Katarina ducked quickly out of the room and ran, dripping, upstairs. She grabbed a towel from the bathroom and then slipped and slid into her room, shutting the door behind her. Running to her dresser, she pulled out a pair of shorts and a tank top. After drying herself off she pulled them on. Taking the towel up from the floor she dried her hair as best as she could and then hurried back downstairs to get some coffee ready. The rain had cooled off the air so much, the house felt a tad damp and chilly. She went to the cabinet to get the coffee beans out and then ground them up quickly. Then she added the water.

Liam came out about half an hour later, after his clothes had finally dried. Katarina gestured to the coffee pot on the counter.

"You can have some coffee if you want."

"Oh, thanks." Liam walked over to the counter and poured some coffee into a mug. Katarina took this time to study Liam. Liam had become broader in the shoulders and much, much taller than he had been seven years ago. He had cut his hair; it was now really short. He almost looked better with it short–more mature. It was still the color Abigail had termed "bonfire looking."

Liam turned around and came back to the counter. He sat at one of the stools and blew on his coffee to cool it off a bit. He took a sip and turned to look at Katarina.

"So, how have you been?"

"Not totally good. I thought you already knew that since you've been stalking me these last couple years," she responded a tad tartly. He shook his head at her.

"No, I didn't say that. I've only been *watching* you, not *stalking* you. There is a difference you know."

"Fine." Katarina pouted as she took a sip of her coffee.

Liam smiled tauntingly at her. "You are more

moody than I remember you being. But in looks you have grown more beautiful," he commented.

"Why shouldn't I be? I have a right to be moody," Katarina responded.

Liam shook his head. "But you also have the right to avoid being moody."

"So? Why would anyone choose that?"

"Because being moody or miserable usually disrupts either your life or the people you spend the most time with."

"Why would they care whether I was moody or not?" Katarina asked.

"Because they are your family and they care about and love you," he answered confidently.

Katarina snorted and took a drink of her coffee before she spoke again. "Fine. I agree with you."

"Good. That's a start." Liam grinned at her.

Katarina shook her head. "What are you going to do with me since you seem to be acting like I'm your student?"

"I'm going to make you happy," he replied enthusiastically, after draining his cup of coffee.

Katarina snorted again, raised her eyebrows at him, and shook her head. "Really. I'm plenty happy."

Now it was Liam's turn to snort and shake his head. "Oh, yes you are."

"Told you I was," Katarina said smugly. She stood up and carried her coffee mug to the counter, washed it out, and set it in the dish drainer. Liam walked over to her and handed her his mug to wash as well. Katarina just rolled her eyes and washed the mug quickly. Turning around again, she crossed her arms over her chest.

"Well, what would you like to start with?"

"Oh, I wasn't going to start today. All my notes are at my apartment. Sorry to burst your bubble."

"Your notes? Really, I don't remember you being like this when we first met."

"A lot of people can change in the course of seven years." Liam responded in a suggestive tone that caused Katarina to close up.

"Well, I'm busy, so it's a good thing you can't start today. I'll talk to you later." Katarina pointed to the hallway. "The front door's that way. Make sure you close it good."

"Yes ma'am." Liam headed to the front door, a small smile playing on his lips. As he reached the door, he was about to open it when it opened itself. Emiliana walked in, staring in shock at the guy in her front hall.

"What the heck?! Who are you?"

"I was told to leave," Liam said, winking at Emiliana and walking out the door.

Emiliana turned to her youngest sister and stared, her mouth open.

"I'll be upstairs if you *must* know," Katarina retorted and stalked off to the stairs.

Emiliana raised her eyebrows and shrugged her shoulders in confusion. "Whatever. I don't need a reason for why my sister is acting like a crab and why there was a random guy in the house. I'm perfectly fine with not knowing." She walked into the living room and dropped her purse on a chair. Therese walked in through the front door as Emiliana finished muttering.

"What were you talking about? And who was that guy who walked out of our house?"

"Don't know and I'm assuming we aren't going to get an answer anytime soon."

"Moody?"

"Crabby" was the crisp correction.

Therese nodded and walked to the stairs and headed up to go to Katarina's room. "Knock knock." She smiled playfully.

Katarina shook her head and replied to Therese's unspoken question, "I don't want to talk."

"Oh," Therese replied faintly and came into the room anyway and sat down gently on the edge of Katarina's bed. "Why are you crabby?"

"Why does everyone think I'm always crabby?" Katarina burst out in a fit of emotion.

"Well..." Therese started to answer.

Katarina stood up and shook her head again. "Don't answer that."

"Well, then why was there a random guy in our house?"

"Because I saw him out on the street and thought he looked familiar."

"Oh," Therese spoke quietly knowing that wasn't the real reason; she felt a bit hurt Katarina wouldn't tell her. "Was he familiar?"

"Yes." Katarina glanced up and looked through her hair at her sister and saw the look of hurt and realized that Therese deserved to know the truth even if no one could help her fix it. She walked back to her bed and sat down next to Therese and fiddled with her hands. "Truthfully, I went out because I have been seeing him everywhere I go since the day at the hospital when–" her voice caught, "–Granny died. So I wanted to know who he was–and, well, now I know."

"Who is he?"

"Liam Farrell; he was Granny and Gramps' next door neighbor in Ohio seven years ago, and Abigail and I met him when we were there for that month. He, apparently, is watching me because he wants to help me."

"Help you with what?"

"To stop being the stupid person I am," Katarina spit out tartly.

Therese burst out quickly, "You aren't stupid!"

"Fine," Katarina said, glaring at her rug. "He wants to show me that I can't let all my pain and misery take over my life. I have to keep it at bay. And he *knows* how to do that since *he's* gone through it too." The last sentence was loaded with sarcasm and that was clearly noticed by Therese.

"How has he gone through it?"

"He lost his dad around the same time as we lost Mom and Dad, and he lost his little sister when he was seven and she was five."

"Oh," Therese breathed out softly. "Then he should know how. Don't be so sarcastic."

"Therese! Why would I let a guy who I haven't seen in years waltz up and take charge of my life! I'm not weak, no matter how silly you guys all think I am," Katarina said with indignation.

Therese sighed. "We do *not* think you are silly, and I *don't* expect you to let him take over your life, but maybe you should give him a chance to help you."

"Why?" Katarina asked gruffly.

Therese just shrugged. "Because it hurts me to see you like this all the time, never getting so much as a little break from anything."

"Oh," Katarina whispered. She had never thought she had been hurting anyone other than herself. She knew that her siblings had been just as crushed by everything that had happened, but she never realized how self-centered she had gotten in the last several years and she also had never realized that none of them wanted her to feel like that by herself. Several memories came back of her family trying to help her out, like Antoinette giving her that journal so long ago and then Therese always asking if she wanted to talk about anything, and then Grandma always saying that it sometimes helped to talk or write everything down. Through the mist of her fogged brain came another memory from so long ago.

They sat silently on Katarina's bed for a bit. Katarina fingered the pattern on the comforter.

"Abi?" she spoke softly.

"Hmm?" Abigail lay back on the bed.

"I wanna change the world." Katarina spoke this confidently.

"How?"

"That's the problem; I'm not sure how." She lay down next to Abigail and propped her head up with her arms.

"Well, let's think then," Abigail spoke thoughtfully.

"Kat?" Therese waved her hand in front of her sister's face.

Without realizing it fully, Katarina had zoned out. She shook herself and turned back to Therese. "I know what I'm going to do," she said, speaking confidently–something she hadn't done in what seemed like an extremely long time to Therese. "The only problem is I don't know

Liam's phone number."

"That's a problem," Therese said, already guessing what Katarina had in mind.

Katarina stood up, "I have to go say sorry to Em for responding in such a rude way."

"All right." Therese was smiling again.

Katarina hurried out of the room and downstairs. She found her older sister in the living room. "Sorry for being crabby, Em."

"Oh." Emiliana looked up at her and smiled. "It's all right. I'm used to it by now."

"Okay." Katarina smiled back. She turned quickly away because she suddenly got an idea. Hurrying again, she ran through the kitchen to the laundry room, and–weirdly enough–there sat a piece of paper with Liam's cell phone number on it.

"Sweet." She picked the paper up and read it. Walking back to her room, she picked her phone up and sent him a quick message.

Sorry about b4; meet at park by my house? want to talk again.

She hit send and waited in anticipation, hoping beyond hope that he would respond right away. And he did. Her phone buzzed, making her jump she was so anxious for him to respond.

Sure, see you in five.

With a feeling of warmth that she hadn't felt in a long, long time, Katarina slipped on a pair of flip flops and stepped out of the front door.

Chapter Twenty-Eight

"You found the note." Liam wandered over to her, hands in his pockets. "What's with the sudden change in attitude?"

"It's because of the sudden change of heart," Katarina responded, smiling up at him.

"Oh, really?" His eyes held a questioning look mixed with interest.

"Yes; I just realized I can't do it on my own. I also realized that by shutting myself off and locking myself inside all my pain and agony, I'm not only hurting myself but I'm hurting the people around me too." Katarina smiled faintly and added, "And I wanted to change that."

"That's the spirit!" Liam burst out in excitement, grinning with joy.

"I need your help–well, rather, I want your

help."

"Well, then you've got it; hands down, I'll totally help you," he promised with strong feeling.

"What about your notes?" Katarina inquired.

Liam just chuckled heartily before explaining. "Oh, that. I was just pulling your leg. You were acting grumpy so I couldn't help doing it. Sorry." He smiled ruefully.

"Oh," Katarina spoke, suddenly feeling rather foolish. "So, how and where do we start?"

"Well, technically you already completed the very first step."

"And what was that?"

"By wanting to change for the better and stop hurting other people and yourself as well as being willing to accept help," Liam informed her.

Katarina nodded; she looked extra thoughtful.

Liam noticed it right away. "There's something else, right?"

"Yeah."

"Want to tell me?" he asked patiently.

Katarina glanced up at his face. The look told her that she could trust him and that he would never speak to anyone about it.

"Well, I just thought of something that I used to always want to do."

"Used to?" Liam questioned casually.

"Yeah used to," she confirmed with a nod of her pretty head.

"What did you used to want to do?" he asked.

"Well, Abigail and I used to talk about this sometimes, but I always wanted to try and change the world. I know it sounds kind of stupid."

"No, not really. I used to want to, too." Liam shook his head.

"Well, what I was thinking was that I was close to thinking the right thing when I wanted to change the world I just needed to shrink my horizons a little bit."

"How do you want to shrink your horizons?" Liam prompted her, his voice filled with encouragement.

"Well, by shrinking, I mean focusing on the lives around me and then trying to, not exactly change, but brighten them while changing my own life for the better," Katarina finished speaking, her voice rising to hint of triumph at the end.

Liam nodded his head, grinning. "That's perfect!" he praised her joyfully. "But one more thing."

"What's that?" Katarina asked, confused; she had thought she had gotten everything.

"You're going to leave sorrow and selfishness behind you, all right? This is your chance to change, and I think God wants you to snatch it up and take it–and I think your parents want you to, too." Liam let what he had said sink in and Katarina dwelled on it for a bit.

"I bet Gramps, Granny, and Grandma do

too, right?" Katarina looked up at him, her face pale and drawn.

Liam nodded. "Undoubtedly, yes."

"Okay. I'm going to do it," Katarina said, deciding determinedly. She nodded her head firmly.

Liam grinned happily at her. "Good."

"Gosh," Katarina said after a moment of silence. "I already feel better than I have in a long time."

"That's great! You're already one step closer to your destination!"

"Liam?" Katarina walked over to a picnic table as she spoke. Liam joined her and the two sat down together.

"Yes?"

Katarina picked at a sliver of wood coming off of the table. "Do you think I'll ever be like I was seven years ago? Before everything happened?"

Liam didn't respond right away, but when he did it was in a quiet tone of voice. "No, you won't ever be the same. Because you've tasted pain and sorrow and it's changed you, even more than some people because you've held onto it for so long."

"Oh."

Katarina's phone buzzed loudly, letting her know she had a new message. She pulled her phone out of her pocket to check it. It was a message from Therese asking her to come home. Katarina stood up and looked at Liam across the table from her.

"I have to go; Therese wants me to come home."

"All right, that's fine." Liam stood up as well. He looked Katarina straight in the eyes and asked her a question. "So we're friends for now?"

"Just friends." Katarina smiled and turned and walked off.

If Liam had expected a different wording to her answer, he didn't show it. "Goodbye Katarina."

"Goodbye!" she called back over her shoulder.

Katarina walked into her house again, the setting sun streaming through the front door behind her.

"Therese!" she called out with a cheerful tone to her voice—something that hadn't been heard in a long time.

"Oh, good! You're back!" Therese leaned over the banister; her hair fell over her shoulders. "Come on up to my room." Therese beckoned to her younger sister.

Katarina smiled up at Therese and nodded. She ran up the stairs quickly, skipping every other step. Therese led Katarina into her room.

"What did you want me for?" Katarina asked after they had both climbed onto Therese's bed and sat cross legged, facing each other. Therese smiled at her sister.

"Where did you go to? Did you talk to Liam?"

"Yes. We met at the park and we talked over a few things, and I decided officially: I'm going to change and let my pain and sorrow go. It's gonna be hard and slow; oh, I know it. But I have to take one step at a time, and according to Liam I've already cleared one step–deciding that I was going to do it and try and stick to it."

"Good, I'm glad." Therese spoke in a cheerful tone of voice.

"And, I'm going to do what Abigail and I always talked about. I'm going to change the world of the people around me, family and friends." Katarina grinned; the grin not only appeared on her lips but spread to her eyes as well.

Therese noted that once again it was a true smile, not a forced one. "I'm really, really glad about this. Like, really glad."

"You are?" Katarina asked. "Why?"

"Because it hurt me to see you so upset like that and it made *me* feel miserable. I mean, of course I was or am upset with everything but it hurt me worse to see you so beaten with it all."

"Oh."

The girls sat quietly, just enjoying the silence

together as sisters. There was the sound of something sliding up. Therese turned to look at her sister.

"What was that?" she whispered.

Katarina shrugged and replied, "I don't know."

They went back to thinking quietly when another sound caught their attention again. It sounded like something being taken out and thrown to the ground. They looked to the window and saw that nothing was there. Therese got off her bed, followed by Katarina.

"Where's my screen?" Therese asked, looking at the empty window. Katarina stuck her head out and looked up and down but saw nothing. Nothing at all. She looked at the side of the house and squinted up at the roof but couldn't see anything there either.

Katarina pulled her head back in and looked at Therese. She shook her head. "There's nothing out there."

"That's really weird then," Therese replied.

"Totally." Katarina nodded her head. "I don't have any clue how it happened."

"Oh well. I'm hungry; let's go and start dinner," Therese suggested.

"Okay."

The two sisters turned and headed to the bedroom door. Suddenly there was the sound of something scuffling against the siding on the house. The girls started to turn back. Therese screamed and Katarina jumped two feet off the floor. Therese stared with wide eyes at the floor and Katarina with curious eyes. On the floor in between them lay a rubber chicken.

"What is that?" Therese asked.

"A rubber chicken." Katarina picked it up with the tips of her fingers and held it in front of her.

Therese calmed down and looked closely at it. "That is extremely wild."

"What just happened?!" Emiliana was standing in the doorway with a worried and wild expression on her face. Her younger sisters turned to her; Katarina still held the rubber chicken in her hands.

"A rubber chicken just got thrown into Therese's room," Katarina said with a hint of amazement.

"What?"

"That's what I say," Therese responded.

Katarina walked back to the window and stared out at the street. She looked in both directions but saw no one. Turning back, she shrugged.

"Oh well; let's just bring this downstairs with us and have chicken for dinner! We'll find the screen later." She grinned a bit. Her sisters chuckled and after Therese shut the window they all headed downstairs to get dinner started.

Once downstairs, Katarina took the rubber chicken outside and headed to the garbage can at the end of her driveway. She lifted the lid, wrinkling her nose. As she was about to drop the chicken into the can, she heard a whimper behind her. Katarina turned about, still holding the chicken in her hands. She saw no one, so she turned back towards the garbage can.

"Hey! That's my brother's rubber chicken!"

Katarina swung around to face a young girl with hands clenched into fists and glaring eyes. Behind her stood a little boy who seemed to be about seven years old.

"Oh, I'm sorry." She didn't recognize the girl and her brother. "I didn't know it was his. It got thrown into my sister's room, and because I didn't know whose it was I was going to throw it out," she explained. "But since it's his he can have it back." Katarina held it out to the little boy.

"Thank you!" he whispered shyly up at her.

"You're welcome." Katarina smiled down at him before looking back up at his older sister. "I'm sorry; I don't believe I know you?"

"I'm Brielle Mortan and this is my little brother Elliot," Brielle spoke crisply, still looking a bit mad. Katarina smiled and stuck her hand out to her.

"It's nice to meet you both, Brielle and Elliot. I'm Katarina Anderson."

Brielle shook Katarina's hand stiffly.

"Well, I have to be going now. See y'all later." She turned and headed back to the house. Looking back over her shoulder at the sister and brother, she waved goodbye.

Back inside, the sisters worked together like a machine making dinner, doing every little thing mechanically as if they were half asleep. They didn't talk to each other or to themselves, either. Working together so well got dinner in the oven in no time. Once in, the girls wandered together to the living room and seated themselves down on the couch next to each other. Katarina sat between her sisters, instinctively feeling like they were squashing her, almost as if to protect her. She wanted to tell Emiliana.

"Hey, Em?"

"Yup." Emiliana thoughtfully braided her hair and then rebraided it. She kept doing this, so Katarina kept talking.

"So, I wanna tell you something."

"Yeah?"

"I want to tell you that I'm going to try..." She drifted off, not entirely sure what she was going to say.

Emiliana sat forward and turned to look at her younger sister.

"I want to try and change..." Katarina took a deep breath. "...for the better. Not be so mean and not pity myself. I want to put others before me and I want to be happy again."

"Really?"

"Yes." Katarina spoke in a positive tone, so Emiliana knew she was telling the truth and was actually going to try. Katarina turned to look at her older sister. "I'm serious."

"I know; I can tell and I'm glad for you."

"Is everyone really glad for me?" Katarina asked, curious but slightly miffed as well.

Therese giggled slightly. "Yes we are, truly."

"Gosh." Katarina snorted.

Therese just hugged her sister.

Katarina shut the door behind her and skipped down the front stair. She was on her way to Abigail's house. Hopefully she was home; Katarina wanted to talk to her about everything that had taken place over the last day. Already Katarina felt new and happy–and just different. She couldn't believe the change that had already started coming over her. Overall she was rather glad that this had happened; she had needed it and was finally ready for it. Katarina grinned and hugged herself happily. Quickening her pace, she gave a little skip of joy. Ah, here she was; Katarina hurried up the driveway to the Dunham's house. After ringing the doorbell, she waited for someone to answer. Mrs. Dunham answered the door. In the background Katarina heard the strains of Abigail and her mother's favorite TV show.

"Hello, Katarina! It's a pleasure to see you!" Mrs. Dunham grinned readily.

Katarina smiled back. "It's a pleasure to see you, too, Mrs. Dunham! Is Abigail around?"

"Why, yes! She is. Come on in! We're just watching some TV." Mrs. Dunham held open the door and let Katarina come in. After slipping her shoes off, Katarina walked into the living room. She strolled over to where Abigail sat in the deep green, lounge chair.

"Hey Abi!" Katarina grinned.

Abigail shot up from her seat to her feet. "Hey, Kat!! What are you doing here, grinning like that!?" Abigail smiled back, slightly confused.

Katarina's grin grew. "I want to talk to you about something special."

"Okay! Let's go to my room!" Abigail excitedly grabbed her best friend's hand and yanked her to the hall, up the stairs, and into her bedroom. They sat down on her bed, facing each other. Abigail gave a little jump of excitement—worthy of a six year old, not a twenty year old. Katarina giggled, making Abigail jump up and down. Abigail felt extremely happy; she had not heard Katarina laugh like that in years. It had always been a forced laugh so no one could tell she was faking it.

"What's so special that you want to tell me?" Abigail begged to know.

Katarina smiled before answering. "Well, so you know the guy who's been following me?" she asked.

"Yeah...what about him?" Abigail prompted.

"Well, it's Liam–Granny's next door neighbor back in Ohio."

"Really?! Liam?! Does he still have long, bonfire hair?"

"Sort of. It's darker now and lots shorter." Katarina giggled at the memory.

"Okay, what about him?"

"Well, I talked to him and he told me that his father and his little sister died years ago and he was as upset about it as I was, and he almost let his grief take over his life like I almost did." She paused for breath.

"Almost?" Abigail stared at her closely. "Is there something you aren't telling me, Kat?"

"Well...I've decided not to be upset anymore, and I realized that I want to be happy again. I know it's going to be hard, he warned me it would be, and he also mentioned that I won't be completely the same, because I've tasted pain and sadness and it's changed me. But I want to be happy again, and I know my parents want me to be too." Her voice faltered and she paused again. Abigail scooched closer and put her arms around her best friend.

"I want you to be happy, dearest!"

"Thanks. Can you help me too? He said it would be kind of hard at first." Katarina looked straight into Abigail's eyes.

Abigail stared back at her best friend. "Of course. What are best friends for?" she replied. Katarina smiled happily back at Abigail. She stuck her hand out in between them.

"Friends forever, Abi?"

"Friends forever," Abigail responded, placing her hand on top of Katarina's and smiling. The two girls hugged each other extra tightly.

Abigail was right, of course. She did help Katarina along the way. Liam was right as well; it was tough. Katarina had many breakdowns and many times she insisted she couldn't do it–she missed her parents too much. But slowly she made it closer to the end of her path.

She was becoming noticeably happier and nicer and better company. Before she would be silent and really wouldn't bother making herself enjoyable to be around, but now she was slowly changing that; step by step, day by day. Katarina was letting go of her sadness and slowly turning back to happiness. Soon she would be even closer to that. She was already starting to change her own world and the worlds of the people she loved the most. She was still that girl, and she was ready to take on the rest of the world.

Acknowledgments

First off, I would like to thank Rivershore Books for helping with this book. It's been great working with you; thank you so much! I also want to thank my mom for patiently reading through the book twice and being willing to take the pictures for the cover! For my younger sister not minding when I read her chapters from the first draft, thanks, girl! I love you guys!

Thank you to Genevieve Berman for being my cover model! I had lots of fun getting together to take the pictures.

Thank you also to everyone who offered me support throughout the writing and editing processes; it is very much appreciated. Thanks goes to my sisters for helping me, at different times, and figuring out and fixing the holes in my plot.

Lastly I want to thank God for the grace and blessings He showered on me throughout this journey, because without Him I would not have gotten through it all. I'd still be at the beginning, so thank you!

Thank you to everyone who will read this book. I appreciate it and I hope you enjoy it! Love you all!

Rivershore Books

www.rivershorebooks.com
blog.rivershorebooks.com
forum.rivershorebooks.com
www.facebook.com/rivershore.books
www.twitter.com/rivershorebooks
info@rivershorebooks.com

Made in the USA
San Bernardino, CA
16 June 2016